Nick Walker is a writer and [...] media production company cr[...] projects and radio. His work has been screened on television [...] cinemas, and presented to audiences from Slovakia to Seattle. He lives in Coventry.

Praise for *Helloland*:

'As nifty as his debut *Blackbox*'   *Guardian*

'One of the funniest things I've read for ages. Walker deserves to be huge'   *Time Out*

'Walker's second novel perfectly captures the essence of modern man... well worth reading'   *City Life, Manchester*

'It will intrigue you. Dark and deadly comedy'   *Daily Mirror*

'Another fast-paced, well-structured black comedy'   *The List*

'The dialogue is crisp, strange and compelling'   *Sunday Herald*

'*Helloland* is the dish of the day. Snappy, imaginative, chock full of mega-hip references and post-post-modern irony'   *Venue*

'This morbidly funny brew mades for a memorably idiosyncratic tale'
Big Issue

Also by Nick Walker

Blackbox

HELLOLAND

Nick Walker

review

First published in Great Britain in 2003
by Review

An imprint of Headline Book Publishing

First published in paperback in 2004

10 9 8 7 6 5 4 3 2 1

ISBN 0 7472 6532 1

Typeset in Gillsans Light by
Letterpart Limited, Reigate, Surrey

Printed and bound in Great Britain by
Clays Ltd, St Ives plc

Headline's policy is to use papers that are natural, renewable and recyclable
products and made from wood grown in sustainable forests. The logging and
manufacturing processes are expected to conform to the environmental
regulations of the country of origin.

HEADLINE BOOK PUBLISHING
A division of Hodder Headline
338 Euston Road
LONDON NW1 3BH

www.reviewbooks.co.uk
www.hodderheadline.com

To Anne, Max and Jessie

Acknowledgements

Lucy Walker, Derek Nisbet, Janet Vaughan, Jim North, Dave Lamb, Simon Trewin, Sarah Ballard, Claire Scott, Bill Massey, a very patient Sarah Keen, Zoë Carroll, Lucy Ramsey, my family.

I would also like to thank Talking Birds who have created the following webworks through which you can engage with both the company and myself:

www.helloland.co.uk
www.talkingbirds.co.uk

'Type the URL into your browser and you'll be transported to a series of imaginative interactive artworks, accessed through a telephone exchange. Overall, the effect is akin to taking part in a David Lynch movie. This innovative and unusual site is a breath of fresh air. Great stuff.'   *Independent*

OUTSIDE LINE.

'If you could see this, Chip...'

'You see it for me.'

'My eyes are bloodshot. I had a fare to Bakersfield.'

'You drove all the way to Bakersfield?'

'And back and I'm here on the nose. Twenty tanks of gas and no sleep and Titusville on the Beeline Expressway but I didn't stop there. I didn't stop at all. I did the full sixty hours. US 1 to the Miracle City Mall. There's an arching bridge along the highway which spans the horizon. I see blotches, Chip. The dreams are squeezing out of me but I think I'm awake now. I think what I'm seeing is real.'

'I should have been your co-driver, Jim. I've got to say sorry for that.'

'You can't drive.'

'But your cab is an automatic. I could drive an automatic.'

'Well, good for you.'

'No gear changes.'

'That's the spirit, Chip.'

'I could put it into drive and it'd be plain sailing.'

'We'll work it that way next time.'

'There'll be a next time will there?'

'You betcha. But this is this time and I made it solo, old friend. I've got chicken under my fingernails and I was sick over my maps. The passenger air bag went off in Orlando and it looked like a big pillow. I bought a magic marker and drew your face on it and talked to it. Have you still got your little moustache, Chip?'

'Not any more.'

'Oh, then I guess this air bag doesn't look like you then 'cos I drew a little moustache on it.'

'I had to shave it off, the hotel doesn't like facial hair.'

'That's too bad. Has the beard gone too?'

'I miss it. My chin looks weak now.'

'Well, I tell you what, Chip, I'm wiping off the beard on the air bag right now and for what it's worth it doesn't make its chin look weak. If anything, this air bag has a manly jaw.'

'Well, that's good.'

'And the moustache is looking rakish. You might think about growing one back. Keeping it neat won't be as easy as it is here on the air bag but the result is pure Errol Flynn.'

'I'll grow a new one right now.'

'The bag started talking to me. It's got your sense of humour and it told me a joke about a pig and a call girl. Made me laugh like a drain but you don't want your air bag telling you jokes so I burnt myself with a cigarette. A burn keeps you awake for three hours. I burnt myself in Denton and Monroe and Hattiesburg and Pensacola and now here I am.'

'Are you parked?'

'I'm all parked up and my arm's a mess.'

'Count the cars.'

'To tired to count.'

'Are you in the trees?'

'Yes, but there's a gap, and there's a kid sawing off some branches for a better view.'

'You see enough sky?'

'It's everywhere. The whole thermosphere. Can you see sky?'

'I can see a desk and a bell and a door and a fire notice and an empty lobby and my shoes and a shitty waistcoat and a "Chip" name badge.'

'I'm your eyes and ears on this one, friend. You stay connected.'

'Room 12 has lit up, have you got a minute?'

'Just a minute but be quick.'

'Climb on the roof of your cab and I'll be right back.'

'Sure thing.'

ROOM 12. MRS BAINS.

'Reception.'

'This is Room 12.'

'Can I put you on hold, Mrs Bains?'

'Why?'

'I have another caller on the line.'

'At this time?'

'Yes, ma'am.'

'Insomniac?'

'No, just another caller.'

'Well, OK, if you're quick. I need service.'

'I'll be as quick as I can, Mrs Bains.'

OUTSIDE LINE.

'You on the roof?'

'I'm there.'

'Tell me what you see.'

'I see a strange crowd. She attracts oddballs, God love her. All wide open mouths and hope behind the eyes. There's a big blue car that's got the best spot. It's owned by a guy with a shirt that's got rockets all over it. He's wearing aviator glasses and he's got this drunk wife. She's got a big brown dress on but she's jazzed it up with fabric planets. She sewed on the Jupiters but glued on the Plutos.'

'Plutos are fiddly.'

'They got here in the middle of the night and put the seats back and ate breakfast out of the ashtrays. He brought a Cuban cigar to celebrate, but he smoked it at four in the morning for something to do. He asked his wife to drive into Titusville to get him another one but she said the bug-eyed creep would get their spot.'

'She meant you, I think.'

'I guess so. So he told her to walk to town for his cigar and she told him to screw himself. I think he wants to hit her. He's a big fat guy but he's managed to get on top of his car and he's there looking west with binoculars. She wants to look too but he won't let her up 'cos she's two hundred and twenty pounds and he's worried about the roof. You can see her nightgown under her dress. He said she had to get her fat ass moving 'cos the situation can get pretty sticky close to crunch time.'

'It can.'

'It sure can.'

'Is it clear?'

'It's as clear as ice. I can't see a cloud. And it's cold too. There's breath everywhere. And the sun's coming up fast and it's big and red and we'll be squinting into it because we're the early birds. And everyone's got their watches out. And there's a big Winnebago with a satellite dish and they've got NASA Select Television, Spacenet two, transponder five, channel nine, sixty-nine degrees west, polarisation horizontal.'

'Love that horizontal.'

'The picture pixelates.'

'Are they letting people watch their screen?'

'For fifty dollars an hour. But we're only a couple of minutes away now, Chip, and we're taking our pleasures live.'

'What does the TV say?'

'It's saying she goes upwards and to the right.'

'Up and to the right?'

'Twenty-eight degrees inclination, and I've got my scopes and I've got a bottle of Orbiter... <pop fizz>... and I'm hoisting it west and I'm shouting "Take me to the stars!"... <whoah hooo!>... hear that? Everyone's whooping at me, Chip. Take me to the stars!... <all right!>... you hear them? This is a family. This is our day <this is our day!>... don't they know it.'

'They know it.'

'You got some Orbiter there, Chip?'

'We don't stock it, but I've—'

'No champagne? It's the perfect refreshment.'

'I've got a mini brandy from the mini bar.'

'Pop it to the Space Station, buddy.'

'To the Space Station!'

'To the stars!'

'To the stars and the Space Station. What time now?'

'T minus two minutes, Chip.'

'Another room wants me, just a second.'

'Be quick, you don't want to miss it.'

ROOM 11. MR MOULIN.

'Reception.'

'What the hell's going on?'

'Sorry, sir, we're very busy.'

'Bullshit, it's five o'clock in the morning.'

'I have two calls on hold.'

'Get rid of them and talk to me.'

'I'll be with you as soon as I can.'

'Cut their calls.'

'I can't do that.'

'You can and you will.'

'Bear with me, sir.'

'Don't you put me on hold, you—'

OUTSIDE LINE.

'Is she still there, Jim?'

'T minus one minute. They're removing ground power. Closing LOX and LH2 outboard fill and drain valves, deactivating SRB joint heaters.'

'You've got the system off pat.'

'I'm in a shuttle frenzy. The air's too fresh. Bring on the spent fuel.'

'Is the kid still sawing branches?'

'He's stuck up the tree now. His mom's telling him he's got the best view but he's telling her that he's facing the wrong way and he can't move. He's jammed in backwards. He wants her to come up and fetch him and she's saying she will in just a jiffy but the T minus is disappearing, and he's howling and trying to saw the tree down.'

'What time now?'

'T minus thirty seconds and we're go for auto sequence...'

'No turning back.'

'Let's say a prayer for the drain valves. Let's say a prayer for the helium.'

'Our father, which art in Helium...'

'It's the last milestone here, only cut-off is available and the clock's still counting.'

'T minus twenty-five.'

'You've got it, Chip. You're tuned in to it. We're all standing now. We're looking out and our mouths are open and we've got a ten-mile stare on... <twenty! nineteen! eighteen!...> Can you hear the crowd counting?'

'I hear them.'

'We're counting down for you, Chip.'

'Count down louder.'

'*Hey! Everyone! Count for my friend Chip who can't be here today!*'

'Tell them I'm a limey.'

'*Hey! My friend's a limey...* <boo>... you got a couple of boos there, Chip. Think some guys are still drunk from the fourth of July.'

'Tell them I'm stuck behind a bloody desk.'

'He's stuck behind a bloody desk!'

'A motherfucking desk.'

'I can't say "motherfucking" for you, Chip, there are kids here.'

'The kid still sawing?'

'Sawing for his life.'

'Tell him to get a good job. Tell him that when he grows up he should try to be like Buzz Aldrin.'

'To Buzz Aldrin, kid!... <Buzz!>... He's with you there, Chip... <Twelve! Eleven!... Buzz! Buzz! Buzz!> The kid's almost through the branch.'

'T minus ten seconds.'

'You're on the nose. Free hydrogen burn-off. System ignition. Go for main engine start... <Eight! Seven!...> The big woman's climbed on top of the car and the roof is bending under her.'

<six>

'Main engine three start command.'

'There's five dogs barking here, Chip. Barking at the sun.'

<five>

'Main engine two start command.'

'I'm on my feet, and I'm hearing the roar.'

<four>

'Main engine one start command.'

<three>

'Close your eyes, Chip.'

'They're closed.'

<two>

'Think of weightlessness, Chip.'

'I'm thinking of it.'

'One. Ignition.'

'Light her up.'

'LIFTOFF!'

<Oooooooohhhhhhh!>

<Oooooooohhhhhhh!>

<Oooooooohhhhhhh!>

<Aaaaaaahhhhhhhhhhhhhhhhhhhhhhhhhh!>

'There she goes, Chip. Bright and brighter and brighter. The lens is flaring. She's spitting out the sparks. She's lifting up her skirts. She's being pulled up, old friend, she's going up, curving up, flying up. The haze giving her the soft focus. Her ass is on fire but she's running away from it. She's got plumes, she billows, she's nosing it.'

'Is she turning?'

'She's twisting round, one eighty roll, seventy-eight pitch, she's showing me her belly, she's pirouetting us. There's atomised aluminium in the air, it's in our lungs. Shuttle perfume.'

'Remember that smell.'

'It's in my clothes.'

'Is she a mile high?'

'She's ten miles, she's twenty miles high and climbing.'

'Can you hear her?'

'She's roaring at me. She's throaty.'

'Smoke in her lungs.'

'A ten-million-a-day girl. She's too bright. She's a point in the sky. She looks like a comet. She's on fire and she's flying free.'

'Get a picture.'

'No camera, friend. It's just me and my cab and the phone and whatever I can tell you.'

'Turn the phone to her. Let me speak to her.'

'Hey there! This is my buddy Chip, he's working the shit shift at the E Z Sleep Hotel!'

'Don't tell her that.'

'She's going up fast, friend, you've got to be quick.'

'I can't think of anything to say.'

'Think on your feet, it's now or never.'

'Hey! Chuck down some space junk! Chuck down a bad satellite! Chuck it down and make it land on the E Z Sleep Hotel!'

'I don't think she heard you, Chip.'

'Or let it land on me!'

'Shout louder, buddy.'

'I love you!'

'She's outa here.'

'Whooooo hoooooooo!'

'She's just a smoke trail.'

'Christ alive.'

'Christ is right. She ascended good.'

'My throat's hoarse.'

'There are no voices here either, Chip. The fat lady's crying. The kid's on the ground howling. The TV's breaking up.'

'Amen.'

'What an exit. When you go, you've got to go quickly.'

'And don't look back.'

'Take a look outside, Chip, you might be able to see the smoke trail.'

'I can't. Room 12 is still holding and Room 11 will want a chiropodist, or a hooker, or an omelette.'

'My legs are weak. My breath's frosting and I'm just going to stay here for a while.'

'I wish I was there, Jim.'

'I wish you were here too, Chip.'

'I regret it. I'm regretful.'

'I know.'

'About so many things.'

'Don't be, Chip.'

'Today is a day full of regret.'

'Come on...'

'I'm dizzy with it.'

'She went up safe. You get back to work.'

'I feel nauseous.'

'You'll be fine. You sit tight.'

'I'm woozy, Jim.'

'Deep breaths.'

'I'm fainting.'

'You go ahead and faint.'

'I'm just going to … I feel bad.'

'You'll feel better.'

'I feel anxious.'

'She's in the sky. Safe and sound.'

'I'm going …'

'You faint away, you lose it, Chip.'

Spots appear in front of Chip's eyes. His breath comes short. Sweat breaks out over his face. The lobby turns grey. Then white. His hand shakes. He's clammy. His blood is lead. He puts his head between his knees.

In the E Z Lost Property, the cleaner is tuned to ninety-one point five FM and there's a guy going crazy for Jesus. She has the volume up loud. It filters through to the lobby. The evangelist is saying the countdown is satanic. The lockout, the high point bleed valve and the helium fill are demonic.

He hates the lift-off but he knows the system.

Forgive us, he says, we don't know what we do. He speaks in tongues. He prays for the Lord to look kindly on mankind's hubris, on mankind's overreaching. He curses the space tourist. He says she's the worst. She's just a passenger, an onlooker, a voyeur. The Lord will reach out His hand and throw the shuttle back down on our heads. We pierce the heavens at our peril.

ROOM 12. MRS BAINS.

'One moment, Mrs Bains.'

ROOM 11. MR MOULIN.

'Just a second, sir.'

Dread floods through Chip's body. He gasps and bites his tongue. He grabs the edge of the desk. Bright flashes appear beneath his eyelids and he hears a popping in his ears. His legs weaken. He falls to the floor.

The dread swells and becomes a taste, metallic in his mouth, his tongue is steel, his breath fizzes.

It becomes a colour, dark blue, violet, it spreads through the lobby till it's around him and moving through him.

It becomes a smell, salty, fleshy, then sickly sweet.

It becomes a sound too, a growl, coming from his belly. He hears it bounce off the walls and off the floor.

The *Hey Jesus* evangelist says that if mankind thinks the shuttle's boosters are hot, mankind should consider the fires of Hell which burn with the power of a hundred shuttles, a thousand, a million.

Chip shouts at the cleaner to turn *Hey Jesus* down.

She turns it up.

He hallucinates. He sees the space tourist. He sees her wave at him. He hears her speak to him. She tells him not to panic. She says in a minute the fear will pass. With each pulse it will edge away and he should count the seconds. And so he counts.

1 . . .

2 . . .

3 . . . he tells himself that people move on.

4 . . .

5 . . . he tells himself that today is a day for . . .

6 . . .

7 . . . for embracing the human spirit.

8 . . .

9 . . . for wiping the slate clean.

At ten the sweat stops popping.

He counts slower.

…12 …13 …

At twenty he can open his eyes.

The white lobby bleeds colour round the edges.

The space tourist tells him to hold his head up high.

… 23 … 24 …

At thirty he slumps to the floor.

… 36 … 37 …

At forty his breathing regulates.

The space tourist tells him she's proud of him.

… 42 … 43 …

At fifty he opens his mouth and licks his lips.

… 58 … 59 …

At sixty the lobby throbs like a heart.

In his ears he hears the *Hey Jesus* evangelist say that Heaven isn't on the moon. Heaven isn't in the Space Station. Heaven isn't up, up, up. Heaven is in the heart.

But he's wrong there, says Chip.

He sure is, says the space tourist.

Chip dabs his eyes with an E Z Moist Towelette.

H er heart beats at a rate within acceptable launch parameters. The crew is closed out.

The clock is holding.

She verifies console programmes. She switches to channel 212.

The weather is fine. A good day for picking flowers. A bad day for kites.

Her head prickles and her jaw is clenched.

Do you want to be here? she asks herself.

No.

Do you want to be somewhere else?

Also no.

Do you want to be down looking up, or up looking down?

The first, I think, or the second. I don't know.

Does this matter?

It's the only thing that matters.

She is the ideal temperature.

Flow rate good. Both herself and the machine.

She is Sally. She knows that she is right here in this moment in a perfect state.

There are others around her. They glance at her occasionally. It is possible that there is irritation in those glances. Disapproval. Contempt.

But she is entitled to be here. She's proud to be here.

She puts disapproval and contempt out of her mind and lets her heart flutter. She lets it thrill.

She calls on God. God doesn't answer.

Topping valve closed. Vent valve closed. Bipod heaters off.

She could still scream. She could still let out a great, end-of-the-world scream.

One might slip out anyway. There was one building in her belly. It could burst out like a train whistle.

Then the commander would hate her. The mission specialists would hate her. The pilot would hate her. Perhaps they hated her already.

She closes her visor. She swallows.

She checks the physics. She does sums in her head. Parabolas. Asymptotes. Differentials.

Everything's auto. She doesn't have to do anything except let it happen. It will happen.

She tries God again. Nothing.

She wonders who could be taking up so much of His time.

She distracts herself. Did she pack her toothbrush? Will the water give her the shits? Where can she buy dirty postcards? Seconds pass. As long as hours. As short.

And then she blazes. She flies. She rips herself free.

She feels the sensation of rapid ascension. There is n-n-n-nothing in the w-w-world l-l-like it. Her speech is broken. The shuttle is shaking. The G-force is rising. Her face is flapping. Her lips are stretched back from her teeth, her cheeks rippling. Her head is like plasticine, five times heavier. Her words fall out like stones.

To C-C-Captain C-C-Cook, she shouts. To adventure. To a life full of endeavour, exploration and excess. To seeing Venus cross in front of the sun.

The solid rocket boosters separate from the external fuel tank and fall back to earth. Parachutes open and the tanks land in the ocean off the coast of Florida. The fishermen clear out. There are other boats. They'll wait to recover the boosters and tow them back to shore. A different catch. Her bulging, billiard-ball eye glances out of the window to try and spot them. But it doesn't. The eye sees only blue sky turning bluer and bluer then black.

She thinks Captain Cook would've liked to have set off like this. Even with crowds lining the harbour and the Queen giving him the regal wave, he'd have liked to set off at shuttle speed. A boat crawls away. He'd have seen the crowd losing interest before he was gone from view. He'd have heard the cheers dying out. People going home. People clapping a juggler on the quayside. Cook will have only just started and everyone else is already thinking of the next trip.

But she's in a catapult. People are still squinting into the sun and she's out of sight.

She thinks of the difference between a hundred miles high and a hundred miles as the crow flies.

She thinks of latitudes and longitudes and weightlessness and spacesuits and oxygen and low orbits.

She feels perfect, but though she doesn't know it yet, she is not perfect. She's a tiny, tiny, microscopic bit unperfect.

Too small to notice.

She thinks of alternate lives and she thinks of the here and now.

The E Z Clock chimes in the lobby.

A little figurine emerges from a hatch below the clock face.

He's dressed in a long nightshirt and a hat. Wee Willie Winkie. He's late. He carries a tiny candle with a flickering electric bulb representing the flame. He yawns mechanically and says: 'Five o'clock and all's well.'

The sun rises.

The fluorescents buzz.

The switchboard hums.

Chip stays down. His ear to the floor.

Underneath the town is a river. Built over with roads and buildings but flowing nonetheless.

It approaches from the south. At this end of town there is a hole down which the river flows. At the north end of town there is a hole through which the river emerges to continue its route visibly across the countryside. In the middle of town, off the Spring Street alley, there's a flaw in the concrete and the river can be glimpsed through it.

Oily. Grey. Bubbles at the surface.

It runs under the Treasures o' the Deep Aquarium.

It runs under the Getcha There Cab Company.

It runs under the E Z Sleep Hotel.

It runs under properties without the owners realising. Until the foundations rot and they crumble into it. According to town records, a dentist's practice collapsed in this way, washing the dentist and his family into another state. But he was something of a butcher and the town was glad to see him go. A man who'd had his teeth chipped and his jaw broken called it the Righteous Stream.

It's just the vanished river now and no one pays any attention to it. Except insurance companies.

Chip arrived in this town. Sore. Sad. Suffering.

He slept outside. He slept in the library. He slept through cramp and in his dreams he was paralysed. He walked slowly. He let the sun brown his skin and the moon make him pale again.

He found an old map which charted the vanished river's course. He walked its route along streets and down roads and through shops and out towards the town's boundary. He walked by the river through malls and shops and gardens. He found a little red ball in a gutter. He picked it up and walked to the south hole and dropped the ball into it. He raced across town to the north hole to see if it would emerge.

He ran through the streets, knocking into people, crashing through shops, pushing people out of the way. He sprinted down the Spring Street alley. He glimpsed the ball's progress so he kept his speed, a water-flow speed. A kid chased him, so did the kid's friend. Along the way three more kids joined in, and some more, so that when he arrived at the north hole a dozen of them stood with him panting and gasping for air.

'What are you running for?' they asked.

Chip was out of breath.

'Are you running away from something?'

He wiped the sweat off his brow.

'Is your house on fire?'

He shook his head.

'Did a monster bite off your arm?'

He shrugged. Something like that.

'What are you looking for?' they asked.

'Any second now,' said Chip, 'a red ball is going to come out of this hole.'

They watched. A minute passed. A minute's a long time for a kid and one of them said he was talking hooey. Another one said he was a mad man who probably ate his own arm off. One pulled his arm out of his sweater and flapped the empty sleeve around. He jumped up and down saying 'I'm... I'm the...' but he couldn't think of any famous one-armed people so he said, 'I'm that guy there,' and pointed at Chip.

Then out the ball came. It bobbed up, it twirled. Slimy but still red. It rode the current. It cleaned itself in the swirl. It drifted out of town.

The kids laughed.

Chip laughed. The first for a while.

The tunnel was free flowing. A water subway with no stops and no obstacles. A ball could bypass the town and reappear, blinking into the light.

'Are any more going to come out?' asked the kids.

'On Thursday there'll be a green one,' said Chip. 'At eight o'clock in the morning precisely. On Friday there'll be a blue one. Same time. But on Saturday—'

'Yes?'

'On Saturday there'll be a gold one and it'll have ten dollars taped to it.'

The kids jumped up and down.

Chip went to the Fun Thingz toy shop.

On Thursday at the north hole there were the same witnesses plus a few extras. They got there an hour early and spent the time clearing stones away.

As eight struck, a dozen digital watches bleeped and the green ball came out to whoops and claps.

On Friday there were fifty at least. Word had got around. Kids shoved and pushed for a view. Someone blocked the hole with his hands and got cuffed and slapped.

The hole was clear at eight and Blue popped out on the nose. They pelted Blue with stones and it bounced and jumped and flowed away from them. Some ran after it along the river's edge. One kid stayed with it for seven miles and had to be brought home by the police.

On Saturday there were a hundred witnesses. The bank got muddy and the view was restricted. They had nets and rods and buckets.

Some kids from different schools fought with each other. Some made new friends. Someone sold candy and made a killing.

Eight struck and there was nothing.

Newcomers started chanting and mocking. The faithful shouted them down. Three minutes later most were hollering and a couple were crying. One kid pissed in the river.

At five past someone tried to send a cat down to find out what had happened.

At six past, everyone was comparing watches, some had the gold ball ten minutes late and counting.

At seven past, many kids started to drift off since there was no action at the stupid muddy...

Then it popped out. Gold. Grimy. Ten dollars wrapped in a little plastic bag flapping at its surface. Perhaps the money had held it up.

Everyone screamed. Seventy jumped in. The river bed was sharp and uneven and there were fourteen broken ankles and thirty cuts needing stitches and jabs. The kid who got the ten dollars was beaten up by the original dozen who thought they were entitled to it for having witnessed Red.

One kid got a lung full of water and stopped breathing. The others didn't know what to do with him. A big girl sat on him and he shot out half a pint. He was taken to hospital but the Righteous

Stream was full of crap and something grew on his lungs and one of them became useless. The other one made a little whistle when he breathed.

The mayor put a fence up. And Chip stopped throwing things in.

Chip found the kid with one lung in the Treasures o' the Deep Aquarium. Chip apologised.

The kid took his hand and led him to a dark room at the back. He showed him a flat fish which just lay on the sand at the bottom of its tank.

'Is it dead?' asked Chip.

'No,' said the kid. 'This type of fish is born with an eye on either side of its head. It's normal. But soon after it's fully grown it drifts to the bottom and lies there. One of its eyes points upwards and can see fine. The other is pressed against the sand. It's useless.'

'Why doesn't it swim around?'

'I don't know.'

They watched it. The one eye roved.

The kid said that during the course of its life, the eye that was pressed into the sand travelled over to the other side of its head so both eyes were pointing upwards. It was the migrating eye fish. *Platichthys albigutta*.

Chip thought it must be some strange tropical thing, or made in a lab. But it wasn't. The kid said it lived right there, Florida, right on their doorstep.

'How about that?' said Chip.

'You make the best of things,' whistled the one-lunged kid, looking at Chip's empty sleeve.

So Chip bought newspapers. He circled jobs in red. He went to interviews and said he could work just fine. He was given shrugs and excuses.

He asked if there was anything at the Treasures o' the Deep Aquarium. There wasn't. They told him people would think he was a shark attack victim and that was bad for business.

He tried Getcha There Cabs. They told him their cars were all stick shift.

He went to the E Z Sleep Hotel. Glass doors opened automatically for him. They said, 'Welcome to the E Z.' It was a woman's voice but overuse had made it slow and it sounded more like a man's. A man who'd been hit on the head.

Chip went inside.

The lobby shimmered.

The Fresh and Clear water machine gurgled.

The plants were fakes.

The noticeboard said, 'Hiring now – E Z switchboard operator.'

A cleaner asked him what he wanted.

Chip said he'd come about the post.

The cleaner pointed to the stairs. Room 11, she said.

Static electricity gathered underneath his feet. It crackled. Brass rails were screwed to the walls to assist those guests too old or obese to walk unaided through the E Z corridors. He touched them and they sparked.

He passed rooms:

16 Do Not Disturb.

15 Please Clean Urgently.

14 More Towels.

13, where a superstitious guest had torn off the numbers with his fingers, leaving nail chippings on the floor and little drops of blood on the door. The numbers had then been rearranged so that it had become Room 31.

12 Checked Out <money under the pillow>.

11, Mr Moulin.

Chip knocked.

'Come in.'

An old man sat on a bed leafing through brochures.

Relaxation? We should call ourselves Hotel Relaxation. A drink, a back rub and mm-mm the holiday has begun.

The man threw the brochure on the floor.

Night time snax, we never sleep.

He ripped it up.

Lonely? Call for company, September's recommendation — Wanda.

He pulped it.

Chip said, 'Sir, my name is…'

High drama at the Hotel Pantheon. Meet Clara Bow at the breakfast table. Refreshments are brought to your room by Fatty Arbuckle. Let Johnny Weissmuller put you through your paces in the gym. And to round off the evening, real live murders from history are performed in the Sun Lounge by a cast that changes daily.

'What the hell is that?' said Mr Moulin.

'I don't know, sir.'

'Would you want refreshments brought to your room by Fatty Arbuckle?'

'I don't think so, sir.'

'Course you wouldn't. You wouldn't want that fat asshole anywhere near your food.' The old man kicked paper. 'I should have an office,' he said. 'I should expand. I should extend.'

He took off his shoes and threw them at Chip.

'Shine them good, I like to be dapper.'

'I don't shine shoes, sir, I'm here about the job.'

Moulin looked him up and down.

'Were you in a war, boy?'

'No.'

'Have you been tortured?'

'No, sir.'

'I thought maybe someone had yanked off your arm in order to retrieve some information.'

'I don't know anything that important, sir.'

'No, I guess not. I guess no one is going to yank your arm off in order to find out the best way to shine shoes.'

'No, sir.'

'No matter how dirty they are.'

'Indeed.'

'Have you had any experience shining shoes?'

'Not really.'

'Well, it's easy to pick up. Any asshole can do it. What's your name?'

'Chip, sir.'

'What kind of name's Chip?'

'It's short for Christopher.'

'Chris is short for Christopher.'

'I know. But I'm called Chip.'

'Why?'

'It happened at school.'

'A school here?'

'No.'

'You sound weird. Are you South African?'

'English.'

'Christ, you know what the English did to America?'

'Yes, sir.'

'I should kick you out.'

'I apologise for our past behaviour.'

Moulin found a piece of paper on the floor. He lay back on the pillow and told Chip to take a seat. There were no chairs so Chip stayed standing.

Moulin read: 'What would you do if a person rang up saying he wanted to spend his first night out of jail at the E Z Sleep.'

'I would give him a room.'

Moulin ticked a box.

'What would you do if a person rang up saying he wanted a room but he might die in the night.'

'I would give him a room.'

Moulin ticked a box.

'What would you do if you suspected a person of being a spy from the Cactus Inn.'

'I would say the E Z was fully booked and would be for months.'

Moulin nodded. 'Ever worked a switchboard?' he asked.

Chip shook his head.

Moulin told him of the fear of the disembodied voice. It terrified humanity in the eighteen seventies and it terrified humanity still. Hearing voices when there was no one there. A characteristic of mystical communion, of insanity. It was the preserve of the spirit world. The switchboard was a Ouija board to a sensitive mind and Chip should be aware.

Chip said he would be.

Moulin said on the whole, it wasn't disembodied voices that were the trouble, it was embodied voices he'd have to worry about. Embodied voices that spat in his face, laughed at his arm, and ran off without paying.

Chip said he wasn't afraid of rude guests.

Moulin told him he should never unplug. Never leave his post. It created a land of disconnection. A land filled with the confused murmur of a hundred voices.

Chip said he never would.

Moulin got off the bed. He asked Chip why the hell he wanted a job in a hotel. The hotel would grind him into the floor. The cleaner would hate him, the guests were perverts and the switchboard was a hundred years old.

Chip said he wasn't afraid of hard work.

Moulin had others to see. The other applicants were women and Chip was up against stiff competition.

'The role of the telephone operative is feminine,' said Moulin. 'It's enabling. It's intermediary. Men are too impatient. They put up a fight if the caller speaks roughly or rudely. Every man is a crank on the phone. If someone complains to a male telephone operator about a crossed line or a bad connection he tells the caller to fuck themselves in the eye.'

Chip said really.

The E Z, on the whole, favoured woman operators. Women never told callers to fuck themselves in the eye, even if they deserved it. Women were restrained, conciliatory, sympathetic. 'Unless you feel their titties, then they quit and sue you.'

He looked at Chip's missing arm and asked him how he lost it.

Chip said in a... he tried to think... in a car accident, in a bomb blast.

Moulin got close. He breathed in his ear. He warned Chip that there was an eroticism in the switchboard. There was a delicate suggestiveness there. If Chip did the job properly and was patient, conciliatory and sympathetic, callers might fall in love with him. The operator was a romantic figure, constantly being wooed down the wires. Moulin told him that the standard romance story of early switchboard times was that of a lowly operator attracting a millionaire through the voice alone. He asked Chip if he was lowly.

Chip said yes.

Moulin stared out of the window.

'Why do you want this job?' Moulin asked. 'Why did you come here?'

'I want to be near the... I like... I like the...'

Moulin huffed. 'You won't get out to see it. You won't get the time off.'

Chip said it didn't matter. He could—

'See the trail?'

'Yes,' said Chip.

'You asshole.'

Chip's missing arm tingled.

'All right,' said Moulin. 'Wait in the lobby.'

An hour passed.

There was a pile of E Z Maps on the reception desk. He picked one up. The map took liberties with scale. The hotel was the size of the Pentagon. Pancake Parlour looked like a Vegas casino. Sponsors had marked their properties with bloated arrows. There were comic-strip cabs bowling down the road with smiling fenders. In the distance a submarine periscope popped out of the ocean and winked. Birds sat on top of telephone lines, thrilling at the buzz of emergency calls. Fat green trees were drawn where no trees existed. The E Z's competitor, the Cactus Inn, was boarded up and there were hood-lums on the corner of the street. Cops were in another part of town, eating doughnuts from Mighty Fine Rings without a care in the world. The Sassy Strip Club looked like the Moulin Rouge. The mayor smiled at the doors of the City Hall. The aquarium had a shark's fin sticking out of the roof. The sun in the sky was grinning like an asshole. A shuttle passed overhead. The astronauts waved. It headed towards the Milky Way where, amongst the stars and the auroras, there was an E Z constellation. An E Z satellite span. Beaming TV into a hundred smiling dishes.

A waitress walked into the lobby.

She looked Chip's way and smiled.

'You here for the job?'

Chip nodded.

She said she worked at Pancake Parlour across the street. An E Z company. The E Z gave guests a voucher and they used it on breakfast.

Chip smiled. Good system.

She'd come in to get some complimentary E Z Sleep match-books. 'Don't they have Pancake Parlour matchbooks?' asked Chip.

She shook her head. Pancake Parlour was a non-smoking establishment.

She put a cigarette into her mouth. She looked at his missing arm.

The arm fizzed. It twitched. It wanted to reach into Chip's pocket and produce a lighter and light her cigarette.

'Does the owner want you to have a fake one?' she asked.

He shook his head. 'I don't have one if he does.'

Uh-huh, she said.

She started to leave.

He didn't want her to leave so he told her that some people made themselves new arms. A homemade limb was found in Capri dated 300 BC.

Uh-huh, she said.

He told her about the Alt Rubain. An iron hand which knights in the fifteenth century used if their real ones got hacked off in jousts. He told her about the *A. A. Marks Manual of Artificial Limbs*, a Victorian catalogue where you could order arms by mail. Some models could rotate above the elbow and had a hook.

Uh-huh, she said.

She was beautiful. She made him blab.

He told her that E Z policy probably wouldn't permit hooks. It might frighten the kids like in *Peter Pan*.

Uh-huh, she said.

He bit his tongue to stop himself from saying anything else.

She said, 'Nice to meet you.'

She said, 'Good luck.'

She left.

Chip told himself that if he saw her again, he wouldn't talk about artificial limbs. That would have to be a turn-off in anyone's book.

Mr Moulin came out of the lift. The lift spoke. 'Ground floor, lobby and reception services.' The voice was still fresh. It was a young voice. It had dropped only a fraction and sounded suggestive. It might even have been the same voice as the glass door but from a different time. The glass door was an old hag, in the lift she was in her prime.

Moulin said the woman who recorded the voice for the door and the lift looked just like Vivien Leigh. He couldn't keep his hands off her. She had black hair, big eyelashes and said 'Welcome to the E Z' like she wanted to screw you. She was going to be a big star and she negotiated up and up and up, and he said yes, yes, yes. He was so weak. Every time someone came into the E Z she got an eighth of a cent. She didn't make it big, though. She saw her career slip down the toilet. The E Z's eighth of a cent was the only thing keeping her in booze. His wife. He employed her as a cleaner. She slept in Lost Property. She wore forgotten items. She lived second-hand.

Moulin looked around the lobby for other applicants. The lobby was empty.

'Still just you, huh.'

'Yes, sir.'

'Damn it.'

'Yes, sir.'

'All right, the job's yours.'

'Thank you, sir,' said Chip.

Moulin issued him with the E Z *Manual For Effective Hoteliering*. He said it would fully apprise him of E Z procedures.

Chapter 1: The E Z 'Howdy'. Lobby Greetings.

Chapter 2: Appearing Natural and At E's.

Chapter 3: Offering Subsidiary E Z Products and Services.

Chapter 4: Switchboard Protocol.

Chapter 5: Problem/Violent Guests.

Chapter 6: The E Z Anthem <CD supplied>.

Chapter 7: Emergencies <non-natural>.

Chapter 8: The E Z 'See Ya'. Lobby Farewells.

He said, 'You work nights. You get here on time. You don't make private calls. The management is me. I'm the guy who's bankrolling your paycheck, I'm the guy who chooses the carpets. I'm the guy who'll make you wear the Chip name badge. You keep your registration cards neat. You get a haircut. You keep your teeth clean. You don't steal booze. Use the Manual for reference. I live here. In Room 11. That's such a depressing state of affairs that I don't need to be reminded of it. So never call my room asking for advice or help or assistance. You get paid next month. You'll stand behind the desk and take calls. Angle yourself away from the door so that the first thing people see isn't the damn empty sleeve.'

The hotel was an hour from the launch pad. It was busy on lift-off days. Chip worked the switchboard. He said, 'My name is Chip.' He said, 'How can I help?' He took room reservations. He pushed plugs and wished his switchboard could connect him to an astronaut. Chip to the shuttle pilot. Chip to space. Chip to history.

He ordered mini-bar refills. He clocked in. He clocked out. The cleaner would walk through the lobby at the end of each shift.

'He gave you the job, huh?'

'Why do you keep asking me that?'

She smelt of bleach. She poured water into ice dispensers. She spat on plastic plants and wiped the leaves. She stowed mops in the E Z Cleaner store cupboard. She tried to pull off the E Z Cleaner sign. She didn't think she was E Z at all. She thought she was one tough cookie. The sign never budged.

'Are you really Mr Moulin's wife?' he asked.

She sprayed air freshener.

'You're the voice of the doors too?'

She told him to stop asking personal questions.

He asked her if she ever saw a shuttle trail.

She said the space race left her cold. The E Z left her cold. Chip left her cold. Stop talking to her. Her daughter could've been the switchboard operator but her crazy husband preferred a stupid one-armed English jerk.

'I could've been someone,' she would say.

'Not too late,' Chip would say. 'Just need a lucky break.'

She said she wasn't going to get into a conversation about luck with a one-armed receptionist.

She locked herself in Lost Property. She made it snug. She sprayed herself with forgotten cologne and wrote up her day in lost diaries.

Chip worked the desk. He took calls, reservations, double shifts. He shined shoes. He polished fruit. He shredded E Z Complaint Forms.

He watched the waitress park at Pancake Parlour and wave at him before going inside. He took up smoking so she would help him change the flint on his lighter. Use her nails to prise it open. Share a cigarette so he could put his lips where hers had been. She told him to stop smoking when she noticed it was giving him bronchitis.

Wheeze shmeeze, he said.

She asked where he was from.

England, he said.

What brings you here? she asked.

The quality of the pancakes, he said.

He got anxious about the day when ambition would get the better of her and she would leave. Ambition would screw things up. Ambition was a bastard.

He kept the switchboard clean. He marked time. He tested sprinklers. He filed registration cards. He ordered Fresh and Clear refills. He found constellations and he watched NASA TV.

He occasionally heard a scream drifting through the walls. He kept a record. He logged the time and timbre.

20 December, squeaky and suppressed. A Christmas gift is found.

3 February, quick and sharp. A wax in the beauty salon.

8 April, prolonged. A woman in pain calling for a midwife.

12 June, short and violent. A hand caught in the trouser press.

5 August, high and gasping. A painful orgasm.

9 September, full of longing. A young female groupie thinks she's found a boy band.

28–29 October, wailing, won't stop.

31 December, blood-curdling. Mine. Time to move forward. And so he wrote some letters and posted them. He muttered 'good, good, good'. Then he ran back to the post office and asked for the letters to be returned to him but he was refused. So he wrote more letters saying please ignore the first letter, I don't know what I was thinking. But he missed the post, and the next day he shredded them, and so now he knew it was done. He knew it was dusted. And he waited for today with his heart in his mouth.

And today came. It's right here. Right on him.

Chip gets to his feet. He sways. Blood works its way through him. Colour returns to his face. The desk steadies. The lobby stabilises. Over the road an old man sits in Pancake Parlour and watches him. Chip smiles. Chip splashes himself with Fresh and Clear. It stings his eyes.

He looks at the clock. Eight minutes past five. Still too early for ghosts.

ROOM 12. MRS BAINS.

'Sorry for the delay, Mrs Bains. How can I help?'

'What happened?'

'I had a complicated inquiry and it's just me on the desk.'

'I've been holding for… Goodness, I don't know.'

'Eight minutes.'

'Why aren't there more staff on?'

'It's five in the morning, it's usually a quiet time.'

'Five?'

'Yes, ma'am.'

'I used to be able to sleep all the way through. Eight hours. Dreamless too. I wish I could still do that, but I'm too old.'

'What can I do for you? I have other lines holding.'

'Are you called Chip?'

'Yes, ma'am.'

'Are you a military man?'

'No, I'm a receptionist.'

'Which arm did you lose?'

'My right arm, ma'am. What do you—'

'Like Horatio Nelson?'

'Yes.'

'Nelson lost his arm at sea.'

'So I believe.'

'Tenerife. I could give you an account of the Battle of Trafalgar if you like.'

'No thank you, Mrs Bains.'

'It's a terrible story.'

'I'm sure it is.'

'The sea is such a dangerous place.'

'Uh-huh.'

'More dangerous than space, I would say.'

'You may be right.'

'My son's in the navy. Did you know that?'

'No, Mrs Bains, I didn't.'

'Well, he is, and if anyone should appreciate how dangerous the sea is, then it's him.'

'I'm sure he already knows.'

'I don't think he does at all, Chip.'

'Well…'

'He doesn't know the half of it.'

'What do you want, Mrs Bains?'

'I don't have a room service card. Would you send one up to me? But don't bother knocking, just slip it under the door.'

'Certainly.'

'And those pre-wrapped crackers that you do, would they slip under the door too?'

'I think they may be a bit thick.'

'Do you have any foodstuffs thin enough to slip under the door?'

'I don't think so.'

'OK, just the room service card then.'

'Certainly, Mrs Bains.'

ROOM 11. MR MOULIN.

'You shit. Don't ever put me on hold again.'

'I'm sorry, there's—'

'You get someone else to answer me.'

'It's just me on the desk.'

'I listened to that crappy song four times through.'

'It was an orchestral arrangement of "California Dreaming", sir.'

'I could have been ringing down to ask for assistance with a heart attack and the muzak could've finished me off.'

'I hope you're not unwell, sir.'

'Were you making a private call?'

'No, sir, it was someone inquiring about a room.'

'Don't lie to me, boy.'

'I'm not lying.'

'No one takes ten minutes to inquire about a room.'

'Well, there were a number of complications...'

'You were making private calls, you asshole. Ten minutes for an inquiry is horseshit. Average inquiry time is one minute eighteen seconds. Anyone will tell you that.'

'I'm—'

'In ten minutes after a heart has stopped the brain loses oxygen and the body turns blue.'

'Do you need a doctor?'

'I'm saying my heart could have stopped and by the time you got off the phone I could be blue here. Dead in my bath.'

'I'm sorry, sir.'

' "We endeavour to answer your call within thirty seconds." I got that printed on the room service card. Now I look like a prick.'

'I'll try and be quicker next time.'

'You better.'

'What was it you wanted, sir?'

'Club sandwich. Brown bread, crusts cut off. No tomatoes.'

'It'll be ten minutes, sir.'

'Aim for eight and a half.'

ROOM 15. NANCY CARTER.

'Reception. Sorry to keep you.'

'It's Room 15.'

'I know, miss.'

'Did I just hear screaming?'

'You may have done, people get upset early in the morning.'

'It sounded like it came from the lobby.'

'It was me, as you ask. I was shouting at the shuttle.'

'I thought perhaps you'd had a shock.'

'A shuttle went up this morning. I gave it a shout.'

'I see.'

'If you look out of the window you might see its trail.'

'My curtains are drawn.'

'You could open them.'

'I like it dark. I'll look later.'

'Was there anything else?'

'What time is it?'

'Just gone five.'

'This room has two single beds in it.'

'It's a twin.'

'Did I ask for a twin?'

'You asked for a double.'

'So why am I in a twin?'

'We don't have any doubles available.'

'Do you have any later? I'd like to move if you have.'

'We don't, I'm afraid.'

''Cos I walked past Room 11 and there's just one guy in there and he seems to have a double bed.'

'He's the owner. He lives there.'

'Do you think he might switch with me?'

'I don't think so, miss, he's rather particular.'

'Could you ask him?'

'If you want me to I can try.'

'Thanks.'

'The owner might put a surcharge on the room...'

'That's fine. My husband will pay, he wanted me to get a double. He insisted.'

'I'll see what I can do.'

ROOM 11. MR MOULIN.

'Where the hell's my club sandwich?'

'It's on its way, sir. I was just calling to ask if you would be prepared to switch rooms with 15 who—'

'No.'

'She's got a twin room, sir, and her husband—'

'No, piss off.'

'It would communicate the E Z's willingness to—'

'Get off the phone.'

'I was just—'

'Get me my fucking sandwich.'

'Yes, sir.'

ROOM 15. NANCY CARTER.

'I'm sorry, Miss Carter. Room 11 would prefer not to switch.'

'Why?'

'He didn't say.'

'He's just in there on his own.'

'I know.'

'What does a small old man want with such a big bed?'

'I don't know.'

'Has he ordered hookers?'

'Um…'

'Never mind.'

'So are you OK to stay put?'

'I guess I can always push the beds together to make it seem like a double.'

'The beds are bolted down, Miss Carter, you can't move them.'

'Oh.'

'We'd rather guests didn't rearrange the furniture.'

'I see.'

'Policy.'

'What is it with the old guy? Can I speak to him? I'm sure I could get him to change his mind.'

'I wouldn't advise that.'

'I can call him room to room, can't I? That must be possible.'

'It is, but his mind seemed made up.'

'You can't get two people in one of these single beds.'

'Well…'

'It's too cramped, there's nowhere to put your arms.'

'I don't know, I—'

'Have you ever done that?'

'Um...'

'You ever taken anyone up to one of these E Z Sleep twins and tried to cram yourself and your lover into one of these damn single beds?'

'Well...'

'After the fun and games are over I tell you the Sleep isn't so fucking E Z.'

'Miss, it's—'

'Mind you, it's probably E Z for you with your one... I'm sorry, that's... you don't need to respond to this.'

'All right.'

'I'm... OK, never mind.'

The guests here are strangers. Later, the hotel will fill up with... acquaintances. Chip doesn't know how many. His letters didn't ask for RSVPs. He prepares conversation for today. Some hotel anecdotes. The food poisoning incident at Pancake Parlour. The Righteous Stream. He will talk about his new friends: the waitress, who is as pretty as pie; and Jim who he met in a bar – The Sea Of Tranquillity, astronaut memorabilia on the wall. Buzz's glove. Neil's boot. Shepard's golf club. Jim hopped up to him, drunk, ragged, unshaven and asked Chip if he needed a cab.

Chip said no, he was just having a quiet drink and a quiet think.

Jim said he shouldn't be put off by the missing leg, he could drive just fine, in fact, better than most, he was an expert driver. He even lived in his car.

'Really,' said Chip.

'Buy me a drink,' said Jim.

'I don't earn much.'

'Me neither. The cab business is crooked. I used to work for Getcha There Cabs but got fired for not wearing the corporate uniform or singing the corporate jingle.'

Where do you want to be?
'Cos anywhere's all right with me.
Just give me your destination,
And I'll give you a price estimation.

He sang it loud. The bar laughed.

Chip said the E Z Sleep had one too.

Take a while,
And go that extra mile,
You'll check in with style,
And find that the E Z's prices are very reasonable.

The bar laughed harder.

'You English?' said Jim.

'Yes,' said Chip.

'Buy me a drink.'

'No.'

Jim said he'd rather lose an arm than a leg any day. Chip had it easy.

Chip said he couldn't play pool.

Jim said he couldn't run away.

Chip said he couldn't touch-type.

Jim said he couldn't ice skate.

Chip said he couldn't juggle.

Jim said thank God for that. Juggling sucked.

Chip conceded. He said, 'You win.'

'Buy me a drink,' said Jim.

'No,' said Chip.

'How did you lose your arm?'

'Bomb blast,' said Chip.

'Bullshit.'

'Shark attack.'

'Bullshit.'

'Industrial accident.'

'Forget it,' said Jim. 'If a one-armed man can't tell a one-legged guy, a guy who might understand, then you must be one asshole.'

'Anyone calling a one-armed man an asshole must be an even bigger asshole,' said Chip.

Jim hit him.

Chip fell to the floor.

Jim got kicked out. The barman helped Chip up, let him off the tab, and told him not to come back. The Sea Of Tranquillity had a tranquil reputation to maintain.

Outside, Jim was waiting by a smashed-up cab. He apologised to Chip for hitting him and asked if he could give Chip a complimentary lift anywhere.

Chip said he didn't know where he wanted to go. He was new in town. He rented an apartment but the windows were covered by thin blinds and they let in the light. His houseplants were healthy but he slept badly. He didn't want to go there yet. It was his birthday and he ought to celebrate.

The twenty-seventh of March was a bad day for a birthday. It was the day that Yuri Gagarin's MiG 15 crashed near Kirzhach in 1968. A black day. For a long time Chip lived by the idea that the very second Gagarin died he was reborn again as little boy Chip. This was how the pioneer system worked. The handover. Little boy Chip thought he would be the first man on Mars. He had colic as a child. His parents went nuts from the crying. They would put him in the garden. He would look up. His infant eyes could only see a few metres, then further as he got older. Eventually he could see the stars. Something up there calmed him and his parents left him there longer and longer. One day they left him there so long that someone else collected him from the garden. Someone in authority. He wasn't taken back into the house. He was taken to another place with other children. And there he grew up. He found that the road to an astronaut's life was littered with engineers, scientists, and flyers. It required a brilliant schooling and healthy vision. And as Chip struggled through school, struggled through university, and his eyesight started to fail, Chip wondered if perhaps Gagarin wasn't dead at all but that space had sent him crazy. He'd lost his reason and thrown champagne in Brezhnev's face. He was in a mental institution doing physics on the walls. And if Gagarin was alive then Chip must be someone else's reincarnation. Some no-mark. He certainly hadn't made any progress as a pioneer.

'How about we take a drive?' asked Jim.

Chip got in Jim's cab.

They shook hands. Chip still had a shaking hand.

Jim drove him to the Sassy Strip Club. They had birthday specials. The strippers let you choose the costume and danced for you in a special booth.

Chip asked her if she had a spacesuit.

She didn't. She had a jumpsuit and her boyfriend's crash helmet.

That would do, said Chip.

She danced to Michael Jackson. She moonwalked.

Chip didn't find it erotic. He had trouble keeping back the tears.

Jim took him out of there.

They scanned cab frequencies and heard on the Rides With Style airwaves that a Gladiator and an Incredible Hulk wanted a ride to a fancy dress party.

Jim put his foot down and beat the cab company to the pick up. The Gladiator and the Hulk complained that their Ride didn't have much Style and they didn't tip.

The party was giving prizes. A bottle of something.

Jim and Chip wanted the bottle bad so they followed the Hulk inside as victims of *Jaws*. Underpants. Ketchup over their stumps.

A couple of guys at the party laughed but most got upset and some cried.

Jim asked why everyone was making a fuss. He figured the time for crying at fancy dress parties finished at the age of five. They were told to leave. They refused. 'What's the matter with everyone?'

They were given the bottle. They were kicked out.

They drove around the town.

Chip stuck his head out of the sunroof and looked for meteors. He made up new constellations. He looked for footprints on the moon.

Jim drove up Supply Way and cut through Rainwater Lane. He took a back route round Chalk Pass and drove up a mud path. They hit the reservoir. It was full. They watched the pattern of ripples across its surface. They traced the wind. A bird flopped around in the water, dying.

Jim said his missing leg was twitching. It wanted to pull Jim into the water. It wanted to wrap itself round some twine and hold him under till he stopped breathing. Jim asked if Chip's arm did stuff like that.

Chip said especially when it got drunk. It was drunk now. It was slapping him round the face.

They flung themselves in.

Chip and Jim clung to each other. They swam like shipwrecked men. Jim told Chip his passengers gave him facts, figures, anecdotes. They would talk and talk and talk. They would talk in order to bring him round to the subject of his missing leg. To check it wasn't caused by reckless driving.

'And was it?' asked Chip.

'Yes,' said Jim. 'There you are. You ask a straight question. I give you a straight answer.'

He raised a quid pro quo eyebrow at Chip.

Chip pretended to choke on reservoir water.

OUTSIDE LINE.

'You know, buddy, if I'd have slept, I'd have missed it. Passed out in Tallahassee, three hundred miles short, looking up and wondering if the high-up cloud was the drifting shuttle trail but not knowing.'

'Cutting it fine is good, Jim.'

'You're right there. If you cut it fine, if you're still breathless from the journey, if your hands are cramped from gripping the wheel and there's blood on your tyres from roadkill, if there's sweat on your back and creases on your forehead, if you've spent three thousand miles thinking "I'm going to miss it, I'm going to miss it" ... ah, when you get there just in time and you do see it...'

'Nothing like it.'

'Nothing like it in the world.'

'Got to get close to a big lose, now and then.'

'Damn right, Chip.'

'As long as you don't actually lose.'

'I guess that's the key.'

'Will the shuttle see planets, Jim? Will she see Mars? Venus?'

'Venus has been checked out already. By Captain Cook and by *Pioneer 1*.'

'So where is she now?'

'She's at T plus twelve and counting. So soon her engines will fire again and send her into low orbit. Into the ionosphere. Here ions are created as sunlight hits atoms and tears off electrons. Auroras happen here. Perhaps she'll see a few on her way up.'

'Auroras are marked on the E Z Map.'

'It's a certainty then.'

'Sure.'

'Are you feeling OK now, Chip? Not so dizzy?'

'Phantom arm playing up.'

'Pesky spooks.'

'You said it, Jim.'

'Did you get into trouble?'

'A bit. It's quiet now.'

'Here too. The sky is going to be blue and the trail is becoming clouds, you might see it.'

'I can't. I've got a club sandwich to microwave.'

'Take a peek if you can.'

ROOM 12. MRS BAINS.

'What happened to my room service card?'

'It's on its way, ma'am.'

'I'd like to know what E Z services are available to me.'

'I'll bring one up as soon as I can.'

'I was also wondering about the shuttle launch. Do you think I'll be able to find something on the TV?'

'I'm sure the news will have it, Mrs Bains.'

'Do I have to pay?'

'No, you can watch the TV for free.'

'It's not the same as seeing it live though, is it, Chip?'

'No.'

'Didn't you want to go and see it live?'

'I had to work.'

'I'm sorry about that.'

'Me too.'

'I was going to go and see it live myself, but I decided I'd better stay here. The early morning air can be chilly and this room is very snug.'

'Uh-huh.'

'Almost womblike, you might say.'

'Well, good.'

'So, the room service card's coming?'

'Yes, ma'am.'

ROOM 11. MR MOULIN.

'Has the girl in Room 15 got a tight ass?'

'I... I don't recall, sir.'

'How old is she?'

'I'm not at liberty—'

'Don't fuck around, how old?'

'I don't know for sure.'

'Guess.'

'Well, perhaps twenty-four, or twenty-five.'

'Twenty-four is all right. Nineteen would be better, but twenty-four is acceptable. If this twenty-four-year-old girl in Room 15 has a tight ass I think I could be persuaded to let her have my room.'

'Right.'

'Tell her if she comes in here and lets me touch her ass, she can move straight in. It won't take long, she just has to lift up her nightdress or whatever the hell she's wearing and I'll put a hand on each cheek and I'll keep them there for a minute or so.'

'I think—'

'But I'm not interested if she's saggy. That isn't going to do anything for me at all. So you find out. Unless you've seen it already. Did you catch a look at it when she checked in? Did you watch her ass as she walked up the stairs?'

'She was wearing a long coat, I didn't—'

'Then you'll have to check it out for me. You can ask her outright but she'll tell you she's got a tight one whether she has or not. I mean, a twenty-four-year-old kid's gonna be able to truss herself up in tiny jeans so that just about anything is tight, but once they're off, and that's the deal by the way, it can just flop out all over the place. I've seen it happen, Chip, and it ain't pretty. So you'll have to make the judgement. You tell her the deal, check her ass and if it's tight then send her over.'

'Sir, I—'

'In the meantime, sandwich now, move. Come on.'

ROOM 15. NANCY CARTER.

'Sorry, Chip. I didn't mean to embarrass you about the twin beds and all.'

'You didn't, that's fine.'

'I'm just tired.'

'We all are, Miss Carter.'

'What's the time now?'

'Quarter past five. Um, Miss Carter…'

'So the shuttle went up, did it?'

'Yes.'

'Mission to Mars?'

'It's delivering a robotic arm to the International Space Station.'

'Is it? How interesting.'

'It's a fifty-six foot long arm and it has seven joints on it.'

'Seven, huh.'

'All multi-directional. They can twist right round the bone. They give the arm highly flexible and precise movement. The arm has a hand on each end which are called Latching End Effectors and they're used for grappling. It's a very versatile arm.'

'Sounds it.'

'Seven elbows, you could say.'

'Imagine.'

'I wish I had seven elbows.'

'Bet you wish you were up there yourself, Chip.'

'Yes… Miss Carter, Room 11 is willing to swap with you but—'

'He's reconsidered?'

'He has but he's put a condition on the room which…'

'What kind of condition?'

'A particular condition which you might find…'

'Spit it out.'

'Well, it's rather…'

'What?'

'I don't know how to put it really.'

Pause.

'Oh, I get the picture.'

'Yes.'

'OK, Chip, look don't tell me.'

'No, quite.'

'I can guess.'

'Indeed.'

'I might have known.'

'I'm sorry, I don't know why I even...'

'What an asshole.'

'Yes.'

'Tell him, "in his dreams".'

'Certainly.'

'God, what's happened to the world?'

'I don't know.'

'I'll stay put. Whatever it is, he isn't getting it.'

'Right you are. Is there anything I can get you? Club sandwich?'

'No. I feel sick.'

'I'm sorry.'

'I'll eat when my husband gets here.'

'OK.'

'He should be here by now.'

'Perhaps he got held up.'

'If he comes, you'll send him up, won't you?'

'Of course.'

'If he asks, tell him I requested a double. Don't mention the Room 11 deal.'

'I won't.'

'God, what an asshole.'

Chip tosses the miniature brandy in the bin. He sucks a breath freshener.

He takes off his shoes and imagines they are weighted and by removing them he'll float away from his desk.

He closes his eyes and conjures up the waitress who walks through the glass doors and sees him hovering in the lobby. She tells him that he has a pretty neat trick there.

He sees her hair tied back and her face wiped clean of make-up. Brown eyes, white teeth, clear skin.

He floats over to her, picks her up and flies them both out of the hotel, through the shuttle trail, across the state highway, and up towards the mountains.

She asks him, 'Aren't you throwing a party today?'

He says, 'I can be fashionably late.'

She says to him, 'What a way to travel.'

He says, 'It's all in the breathing.'

As they climb higher, he asks her if she can see her house and she says she doesn't want to look for it. The roof needs repairing.

Her apron is flapping in the wind so he tells her to take it off. And she does. And from her apron pocket the order slips fly free and float to the ground and land in people's gardens. There is a little boy playing in a pool, and he picks up 'Parlour Special' and wonders what makes it so special. He doesn't know that it's special because it's served by a waitress whose smile would melt you like butter over a Pancake Parlour waffle.

Chip tells her their clothes are stopping them from picking up speed so they shed them over the ground below. Her dress falls over a hedge. His jacket lands on a guy reading a paper. Her shoes hit the road and bounce around. His tie drapes over a TV aerial.

And as they fly, she asks Chip how this is possible. She tells him that only astronauts can float and that zero gravity isn't for the likes of check-in clerks and waitresses. Not that she isn't enjoying herself, she's having a ball.

Chip tells her that astronauts are still under the influence of the earth's pull just like everyone else, just like her, just like him, but because astronauts fly round the earth so fast, the centrifugal force pushes them out the same amount as the earth pulls them in. The two forces cancel each other out and so they appear to float.

She calls him a bright penny.

He tells her that their own trip has nothing to do with physics, it's just a little bit of magic that he has up his sleeve.

She tells him that since his jacket landed on a guy reading a paper and his shirt landed on top of a telegraph pole, he hasn't got a sleeve up which to have anything.

Chip says, 'That's true.'

He asks her if she has any idea how to get down again.

She tells him that, as he can see, she hasn't got anything up her sleeve either.

And he looks at her bare arm. It's smooth and brown with tiny blonde hairs pricked up by the wind, with a pale watch mark round the wrist, and fingers which are long and slender.

And he says in the absence of a plan, they'll have to crash land into the side of a mountain.

She says, 'In the absence of a plan or in the absence of a plane?'

He says both.

T PLUS 00HH 16MM

Sally catches her breath. She can almost see a whole globe. The main engine's been shut off and she's flying free. She hears someone say Jesus. She hears someone say the angle is A-OK. She hears her own breath in her ears.

A birth. A rebirth.

She calls God. He says she's looking good. He tells her her heartbeat stayed below one hundred and ten beats per minute during lift-off. He's technical. He's medical.

It's not God, it's Houston.

She says a little prayer to Houston, thanking it for sending signals to an antenna at White Sands in New Mexico. She thanks White Sands for relaying the signals to a pair of satellites in orbit above the earth. She thanks the satellites for relaying the signals to the shuttle. She thanks the commander for replying so well, so appropriately. She tries to see the satellites but they're too high. They're 22,000 miles up in a Clarke orbit. Clarke did the sums. Clever guy. She wishes she'd brought one of his books with her to read in a leisure moment. She knows the schedule inside out and she's got wall-to-wall leisure moments. She is required to exercise, drift, and keep out of the way.

Someone says everyone OK?

She says yes. Even though a little, tiny part of her isn't. She is up, she is light, she is high and she has eleven layers in her spacesuit. She's as warm as toast.

She's so excited, she hopes she doesn't piss herself.

ROOM 15. NANCY CARTER.

'How do I get an outside line on my telephone, Chip?'

'You dial nine, then wait for the tone to change, then enter the number.'

'Thank you.'

'My pleasure.'

Pause.

'Was there anything else, Miss Carter?'

'Just say yes or no, but I can't get this out of my head. Did Room 11 want me to perform oral sex on him?'

'Oh God. No. Not that.'

'OK, I just needed to know.'

'He didn't mention that at all.'

'Fine. Night, Chip.'

'Night, Miss Carter.'

ROOM 11. MR MOULIN.

'You know at the E Z Rest Hotel a club sandwich takes six minutes and twenty seconds.'

'I'm sorry, sir, it's on its way.'

'At the E Z Slumber Hotel it takes five minutes five seconds.'

'They must have a speedy chef.'

'Chef? Chefs don't come into it, the sandwiches are packed in plastic bags and some asshole puts it in the microwave.'

'I was going to fry up the bacon specially, sir, but the phones keep ringing.'

'Fry it up specially?'

'Yes, sir.'

'You jerk. Just microwave the ones the fucking club sandwich company made.'

'OK, sir.'

'Don't try to impress me with specially fried up bacon.'

'Sorry.'

'So what's Room 15's answer? She gonna let me touch her ass?'

'She's, well...'

'Still thinking, huh? Christ, we could've been done already. In and out in less time than it takes you to microwave a damn club sandwich.'

'I'll be up with the sandwich in two minutes, sir.'

'Two and a half, I want the bacteria killed.'

ROOM 15. NANCY CARTER.

'Did Room 11 want me to put something up his ass?'

'Um...'

'Yes or no.'

'No. Although it did have something to do with, well, backsides.'

'OK, I don't want to know.'

'Certainly.'

'Don't tell me.'

'Sure.'

ROOM 12. MRS BAINS.

'Have you got children, Chip?'

'No, Mrs Bains.'

'They kill you with worry.'

'So I believe.'

'You have to hide it from them. Even when they're grown up. And if they're in the navy… well, it's agony.'

'I'm sure.'

'My son's in the navy.'

'So you said.'

'He hates me telling him that I'm worried. He says it's the worst thing I can do.'

'I imagine.'

'He says my letters are too vague and ambiguous and it makes him anxious.'

'I see.'

'I ask him how to write and he tells me to talk about how the town has got a new café or that the model aeroplane shop has been closed down. Make jokes. Avoid rumours. Date the letters so that if he receives more than one at once he can read them in the right order. If I have bad news then I should give it clearly and exactly and not hint at it and make him read between the lines.'

'Uh-huh.'

'Avoid phrases such as "Without you I am falling to pieces". Or "The absence of you around the house makes my life a bleak and empty charade". He says if I write things like that again he won't reply to me.'

'I see.'

'But it's how I feel.'

'Right.'

'It's how I feel, I'm a mother.'

Pause.

Sniffling.

'Can I get you anything, Mrs Bains?'

'You can get me a room service card.'

'Oh yes, sorry, I've been—'

'If you were somewhere. Out at sea. You wouldn't mind your

mother telling you she was worried, would you?'

'My mother's dead, Mrs Bains.'

'Oh my goodness.'

'Yes.'

'Oh Chip that's terrible.'

'Don't worry, it was a long time ago.'

'I shouldn't have asked. I'm sorry.'

'Forget it.'

Pause.

'Did you see her die, Chip?'

'No.'

'Well, that's something.'

'I suppose.'

'It's not much, but it's something.'

'I have to go now, Mrs Bains.'

'I didn't mean to pry into your personal life, Chip.'

'Don't worry.'

'I feel just awful about it.'

'You weren't to know.'

'No.'

Pause.

'Can I just ask?'

'What, ma'am?'

'Can I just ask, if your mother was alive, do you think you'd have minded her worrying about you?'

'No, Mrs Bains.'

'Thank you. You're a comfort.'

'Sure.'

Pause.

'Do you have a father, Chip?'

'No.'

'OK. I'll let you go.'

Five thirty. The kid with the whistling lung appears. Delivering free newspapers. He carries them round on a little cart because the bag makes him wheeze. He drops a pile in the lobby.

'This is you making the best of things?' he says.

Chip says he has assets. A job. Two new friends. He gets to watch the lobby TV. He gets free club sandwiches. He keeps his head down.

The kid doesn't think he's keeping his head down that well. There is talk of him in town. He delivers papers to The Sea Of Tranquillity and they talk of an English guy who's had his arm bitten off by a tiger. He delivers to the mayor's office where the secretaries talk of an English guy who clears mines for the army. He delivers to the rival newspaper where a journalist talks of an English guy who has a space party planned today.

Chip is a little bit famous. The kid wouldn't be surprised if there is something about him in the rag he's delivering. He looks through it. Nothing but NASA news and adverts for sex chat lines. The kid is disappointed. When he fell into the Righteous Stream he got a double-page spread.

Chip wants to know how news of his space party has got out. The kid shrugs. It's a nothing town. Spice is thin on the ground. The woman at the post office opens people's mail. There are no secrets anywhere.

Chip says it's a private matter, a personal matter, he doesn't want...

The kid tells him he should spruce himself up if he's having a party. Comb his hair. Straighten his tie. Have some pride. He leaves, the wheel on his cart squeaking in time with his lung.

OUTSIDE LINE.

'E Z Sleep.'

'Nancy Carter please.'

'Putting you through, sir.'

ROOM 15. OUTSIDE LINE.

'Hello?'

'It's me, sweetheart. You got a nice room?'

'Uh-huh.'

'I spoke to the guy at reception.'

'Yeah.'

'Has his party started yet?'

'Not yet. How far away are you?'

'Wait. I'm going to pull over. I want you to tell me what the room's like.'

'No, keep driving. You can describe landmarks to me as you pass them.'

'There's nothing here.'

'Then make some landmarks up.'

'Well...'

'Tell me you're driving past the Eiffel Tower.'

'You what?'

'Or the Prado, tell me you're on the Paseo del Prado and the streets are quiet because it's early and you can just park up by the botanical gardens. Tell me you're getting out the car and going inside and it smells so fragrant and you've found an orange tree and you've picked an orange off it and you'll peel it and you'll bring it to me in Room 15 and you'll wake me by squeezing a drop of it out so it lands on my lips.'

'This is somewhere in Spain, right?'

'Or tell me you're passing Edinburgh Castle and it's lit up and you can hear bagpipes in the distance. A lone piper on the battlements.'

'What are you talking about?'

'Or the leaning tower of Pisa.'

'Nance.'

'I've just written two thousand words on the geysers in Iceland.'

'I don't need travel pieces, Nancy, I need—'

' "I stand like an Eskimo, camera poised harpoon-like before the steaming, aquamarine soup—" '

'Don't read it, I—'

' "—feet frozen, hands frozen, breath frozen and it seems that time too is frozen. But at that point, the point when I think I should turn away before more minutes, or fingers and toes, are lost forever, the soup starts to swell. I see it rise and expand as if a thick membrane has grown over it. It quivers and bloats, pressured from below by a hot-breathed giant who gulps and then blows, gulps and then blows. Aquamarine turns to turquoise, a great swelling pupa ready to burst. Or a jellyfish forcing itself through a bottle neck. I ask myself if I am standing too close but the thought comes too late because here, suddenly, the membrane bursts and all at once I am not standing on the earth any more but on a giant whale—" '

'Nancy—'

' "—whose breath has been held for a decade, a whale which has swum around the world and come back to this spot in order to break the surface and spurt an immense boiling outbreath. And the hot spray shoots high into the air, a liquid skyscraper, constructed in an instant, one hundred, two hundred storeys high. And the lives inside are lived in an instant too because as soon as it is up it is down again. And the wind blows it onto and over my body. And I hear women squeal with excitement. And men roar with pleasure. And then it is gone. Gone but for the fine mist which drifts over the lava fields. And I hear cameras click, too late. And I know that I will stay and wait for it again." '

'The paper's not going to print that stuff, Nancy. Stick with the human interest story.'

'It's done, honey. I've got the geysers and something on a waterfall and a few hundred words about a hotel in Reykjavik which serves shark but the beds are too hard. What did you think? Were you transported?'

'No.'

'Ah, you're just saying that. Wait till it's in print with a picture by the side of it. I think the whale stuff's good. And it's good to get the word membrane into a travel article. Does the skyscraper jar? I might leave that to the editor, he'll sort that out. Even so, even with the soup and the pupae, I'm thinking I'll be getting a congratulatory call. I'm thinking they may send me somewhere exotic. Asia perhaps.'

'It's not going to happen.'

'It might.'

'Concentrate on our current assignment. Do some background. Pump the one-armed guy. Talk to NASA.'

'I hate our current assignment.'

'You don't. Come on.'

'We should give him some privacy.'

'What?'

'I want out of human interest. I want to move to the travel section.'

'Global travel is dead, Nancy. Only space is the story.'

'Then do it yourself.'

'I will. I'm coming, aren't I? I'm on my way. Why are you so grouchy?'

'Don't shout at me when you hear this but I could only get a twin.'

'Oh come on.'

'I'm sorry.'

'So what do we do? Push the beds together?'

'They're bolted down.'

'Bolted?'

'Sorry.'

'What kind of hotel is it where they bolt down the beds?'

'I don't know. The TV's bolted to the wall.'

'That's normal.'

'And I think, hang on … yeah, the bedside table's bolted down too.'

'Really?'

'And they've made the beds really tightly. The blankets and sheets are really tucked in hard. I had to work my way in. I'm vacuum packed in this bed.'

'We'll have to change.'

'I tried. There's nothing going.'

'Aw shit.'

'I know, I don't know why this happens.'

'You do this on purpose.'

'I don't.'

'You don't like me sleeping with you.'

'I do, it's just—'

'Every time. You're on one side of the room, and I'm on the other.'

'It's not deliberate.'

'Why don't you book rooms with big beds? Big beds we can both get inside, so there's proximity, and no mini fridge between us. You know what I think?'

'Come on, honey.'

'I know what this is about. Fastest gun in the west – come on, say it.'

'I won't. I don't think that.'

'I've seen it in your diary.'

'You shouldn't be—'

'Quick-draw McGraw.'

'It doesn't bother me.'

'Just 'cos it's quick, Nancy, doesn't mean it's low-quality.'

'I know.'

'You should be flattered.'

'I . . . well, I am.'

'You're well put together, there's nothing I can do, it's like a reflex.'

'Let's not—'

'So if anything, it's your fault.'

'Oh, come on.'

'You want me to get someone else to do these assignments? A college kid? Someone from the typing pool? Shirley from features is keen.'

'No, honey.'

'I'm hanging up.'

'Don't be silly.'

'I'm joining another freeway. I don't need distractions and I don't need to be humiliated.'

'Oh, come on, sweetheart, this is—'

Chip puts a bottle of Orbiter in the Fresh and Clear barrel to chill. A big bottle. A magnum. Orbiter's survival depends on the shuttle programme. They wanted to sponsor it but haven't got the money. They can only sponsor a tiny little part of it. A nut. Or a couple of litres of fuel. Nothing they can write Orbiter on. Instead they send the Orbiter Girls to the launch and give out free samples. Everyone drinks Orbiter on launch days. It's the celebration beverage, it says so on the label.

Chip has ordered crystal glasses from Booz 'n' Thingz but they haven't arrived yet. He roots around for alternatives. He finds E Z Toothmugs. He stacks them ready.

He has ordered snacks too but the E Z doesn't do plates. He wonders if he could borrow some from Pancake Parlour. Perhaps use the opportunity to invite the waitress to his space party. Give her a mug of Orbiter and get her tipsy. Chip checks the Orbiter. It isn't cold.

He dips his finger in the Fresh and Clear and finds it's tepid. Despite this it still gives him a pain behind the eye when he drinks it. Fresh and Clear probably put a chemical in it. Menthol was Chip's guess. Menthol induces a stimulating action on peripheral cold receptors.

They'd have to drink Orbiter warm. How embarrassing. Chip considers hiring the Orbiter Girls, as a distraction. To sing a song or two, give everyone lipstick kisses. If he could get them over early he could learn their names and introduce them as his friends.

OUTSIDE LINE.

'You seen the Orbiter Girls there, Jim?'

'Not in action, buddy. The Orbiter bus overtook me on the way down. They were inside. I gave them a honk. They gave me the finger. I think they hate these gigs. They have to wear tiny bikinis even though it's freezing. Their nipples get all teased up by the wind and the marketing men dig that. It makes the shuttle watchers think that the Orbiter Girls are turned on by them and they buy more Orbiter.'

'You think they're available to hire?'

'Not on launch days, Chip. After they knock off they spend the day at the sauna thawing out. Why?'

'Just wondering.'

'We've all wondered that, buddy boy. I wonder it most days. I better hit the road, I feel dazed.'

'Sixty hours in a car, Jim, make anyone dazed. It's the static electricity.'

'I believe you. I should stay up here on top of the car but there are fares out there, I've got pick ups. People need driving.'

'Come here and wind down.'

'I stink too much to come to your hotel.'

'No one stinks that much.'

'My passenger up to Bakersfield said she was going to give me a thousand dollars for the ride, so I squirted myself with windscreen wash and wiped myself down with a chamois leather to keep up appearances. Didn't work. She knocked off a hundred, citing bad hygiene.'

'How petty.'

'I stink to high heaven now.'

'You can come and use the staff shower room.'

'You got any of that E Z Shaving Cream?'

'We stopped doing it, it brought people out in a rash.'

'How about the talcum powder?'

'That's gone too. I'll give you a voucher for breakfast. Pancake Parlour's doing Shuttle Shakes today.'

'Will I get served by your waitress?'

'You'll get served by a waitress.'

'You know who I mean.'

'She . . . her shift's finished.'

'Never let a woman get to you, buddy. Get in, get out then get away.'

'I'm not "in" Jim, let alone—'

'How about those E Z Room Fresheners? I could put one in the car. The car's in a worse way than I am. And a headlight's blown. At night people think I'm a motorbike.'

'Or a car with an eyepatch.'

'I could call it the Ford Nelson.'

'You should buy a new one.'

'No dough, buddy. I rented one once. When this heap broke down. They had a medical checklist at the rental firm. There was a yes/no box for just about everything, heart trouble, major operations, blood pressure, schizophrenia, blindness, asthma attacks, you name it. Nothing for the number of limbs you had. I was standing at the counter and the woman could only see me chest up. I filled out the forms, checked "no" for everything, got the keys then hopped out the office. She started calling me back but then changed her mind.'

'Only need one leg for an automatic.'

'That's what she was thinking. Do you think the Space Station is going to get given a robotic leg?'

'I don't see why not.'

'Perhaps it won't need one. Perhaps the Space Station is mostly automatic too.'

'Will the shuttle be weightless now?'

'I'll say, Chip. The engines have fired again and she's two hundred miles high, in the exosphere. Beyond vertigo. Gas atoms wide apart.'

'Will the crew be sleeping?'

'Soon, Chip. They'll be aiming her towards the Space Station, configuring all onboard systems and then just letting her spin round the earth, fifty-one point six degrees either side of the equator, rocking the crew to sleep, giving them eight hours of shut-eye.'

'I can go to sleep too then. So can you, friend.'

'Everyone's split here. Most people are going home, or going to their hotels. The trail's disappeared and no one wants to make a day of it. The caravans have moved on, the fat couple have gone looking for food, and the kid sawing the branch has gone to hospital. I think he broke something. Another casualty of space travel.'

'Explorations are full of these little tragedies.'

'You said it, Chip.'

'Yes.'

'You'd know more than most.'

'I suppose.'

'Now would be a good time to tell me—'

'Jim...'

'Now is the perfect opportunity to tell your best buddy how you came to—'

'Now isn't a good time.'

'Start at the beginning and don't miss anything out.'

Chip cuts the call. He doodles on E Z stationery. He draws solar arrays. A habitation compartment. He adds a laboratory, a cupola, a logistics carrier and a centrifuge unit. He makes the Space Station look a little bit human, a little bit like himself.

He draws the robotic arm and goes to town on the detail of the hand. He gives it ten mechanical fingers and three mechanical thumbs. Double-, treble-jointed. A hand that senses forces and movements. A hand that compensates and reacts. A hand that swats space junk.

The TV shows a flashy graphic. Chip compares it unfavourably with his own drawing. Clumsy. Naive.

Can't let the space party see that. He puts it in his pocket. He closes his eyes. He breathes in through his nose. He sucks in the smell of lemon disinfectant, stale deodorant, processed air, plastic plants, spilt coffee, and hot syrup from Pancake Parlour. He reaches the top of his breath and breathes out carbon dioxide mixed with odours of digested food, tooth plaque and indigestion tablets.

He repeats the process, taking deeper and deeper breaths until his head feels light and colours start to burst and morph under his eyelids. And in that state he feels a phantom arm reach up and take off his headset. A phantom hand scratches away the ridge in his hairline. He feels a tingling in his phantom fingers and loose skin collects under phantom fingernails. He takes another breath and his phantom hand picks up a pencil and twirls it and makes it spin. It balances the tip of it on the end of its phantom thumb. The point digs in, sharp and light. It flicks it up and catches it and slips it between its fingers and writes phantom poetry on a memo pad. In beautiful copperplate, quickly, and as fast as spoken words.

It writes sick notes:

Chip is sorry that he will not be able to attend his space party. He has lost an arm and cannot pull party poppers.

It folds the paper into a delicate origami bird and makes the wings flap and Chip feels the tiny movement of air on his cheek and lips. Then it releases the bird and it flies out of the window and the hand waves it goodbye, waggling its phantom fingers.

Chip gets woozy and sits down. The phantom arm gets pins and needles. No blood is reaching it. It cramps. Chip tries shaking it and flexing it but it doesn't clear. He tries slamming it on the table top. Whacking it down, trying to make the phantom bones crack. His phantom fingers twitch. They poke him in the eye. They slap him round the face. They try to pick him up by the scruff of his neck and shove him out of the E Z doors and into the world and away.

Chip disciplines the arm. He hits air.

The phantom hand writes that today is not the day for embracing the human spirit, or for putting the past behind you, or for looking up and moving on.

Chip opens his eyes and stares at nothing. Nothing stares at him back. Nothing hangs off his shoulder, burning. Fucking ghost, says Chip. He tries to ram it in the shredder. It ducks and weaves and disappears.

Sally sits in her NASA ejector seat, looking at stars. She's too high to eject so the system's disabled.

They hit the angles. The timing is all. It's about the split second. It's about cutting it fine.

She thinks cutting it fine is part of the life full of endeavour, exploration, and excess. She thinks her countryman Captain Cook would tell her the same. He'd tell her when he left Plymouth in September and got to Madeira in October and Rio de Janeiro in November, he'd say he was making good progress. He's standing aboard the *Endeavour* and thinking he should be in Tahiti by February with good weather, March with bad. Either way he's thinking he'll see Venus from the beach in June and cutting it fine didn't come into it.

But then in Rio some Brazilians start thinking Cook's a pirate and they're thinking they'll take offence at him. So now Cook has to convince them he isn't a pirate. He's an explorer, he has astronomers on board, and geographers, and a goat which gives them all milk. Pirates don't keep goats. The Brazilians say how is that proof?

Cook says well, it isn't exactly proof, he was just saying that goat-keeping wasn't very pirately behaviour, plundering was pirately behaviour.

The Brazilians say plundering is exactly what they're afraid of.

After two months, when Cook must have been running out of arguments, someone gets it, or gets bored, and Cook is allowed through.

So now he's late and he's only rounding Cape Horn by February and getting to Tahiti by April.

Then some Tahitians steal his observatory.

Cook runs round the island trying to get his kit back. No one has seen anything. He looks everywhere. He gets rough. He makes threats. He fires off guns. He finds his observatory in pieces. Spread over the island. He tries to fix it but it's sensitive equipment, it has to be millimetre accurate, so he can't rush it.

And Venus is getting closer and closer, and instead of months to prepare he's got no time at all, and what Sally wants to think is this: eight months twenty-one days and fourteen hours after setting out from Plymouth, Cook tightens the last screw on his observatory the second before Venus passes before the sun. One second. If the wind had been blowing a fraction slower, or the sails secured a fraction too tight, or too loose, on any day, or a Tahitian had swallowed a bolt or a screw, he'd have missed it. And because he's cut it fine, Venus is the most beautiful thing in the universe.

She looks out of the window. Venus is the other side of Earth. She'll have to wait for the orbit.

She doesn't mind. She's well strapped in due to the excellent harness developed during pioneering work carried out by Mr Stapp, the rocket man, who went through the mill for her safety, lashing himself to a rocket and giving his body thirty-five Gs, crushing his body and haemorrhaging his retinas and fracturing his ribs so she can sit pretty. And she does.

She'd like to give a nod of thanks, too, to Mr Kittinger, who has reassured her about high-altitude bailout, who exceeded the speed of sound by jumping out of a balloon 102,800 feet above earth, and landing with a smile on his face.

She's higher than that now. Much higher.

She thanks gravity for the orbit and she thanks Einstein for the calculations. She's free to move. The crew is told again that they're looking good. And they are. She's full of admiration for them. So well-trained. So calm. They're told to stand by for post-insertion. They stand by. They have two hours of work. She'll watch them. They won't speak to her unless she gets in the way. They might not speak to her then either.

Then she'll be pre-sleep, then scheduled sleep, but she won't care if sleep comes or not. She'll be content to just drift.

She'd like to thank her father for not crying and her mother for running away and letting a new mother come and encourage her from school to launchpad.

She'd like to thank the crew of the *Challenger* for making her own flight so much safer.

She'd like to thank Fresh and Clear because they've put a lot of money into her visit, they've put a little logo on her excellent spacesuit and she won't break a contract.

She'd like to thank her lucky stars.

But most of all she'd like to thank Chip.

Thank you, Chip.

5.31 a.m.

Hey Jesus blares from Lost Property. The evangelist says that the world is crashing down. Matter is falling from the sky. Don't be afraid to look up, though. This could be our lucky day. This could be our Second Coming arriving like a blazing comet. The evangelist has seen patterns in the sky and heard voices in the air. Cover your heads and pray. He curses the shuttle for trying to get itself a sneak preview. He hopes the shuttle gets whacked for impudence. He wants people to ring in and tell him if their houses have been hit by divine rocks from the trail. He wants to know who's being targeted. Who's been chosen. Red hot metal is landing in the ocean and making it steam and bubble. He says the lines are open.

Chip bangs on Lost Property. The *Hey Jesus* vibes are too strong. It makes the reception bell buzz and creates ripples on the surface of Fresh and Clear. Chip doesn't want it overpowering his party tapes.

ROOM 11. MR MOULIN. OUTGOING CALL.

'Thank you for calling the E Z Slumber Hotel and Conference Facility for the discerning business or leisure guest. The E Z Slumber is part of the E Z Hotel chain, my name is Dennis, how may I—'

'Stop right there.'

'Sorry, sir?'

'That is far too long for a telephone introduction. Who gives a shit if you're part of the E Z chain, or that your name's Dennis. People want a room, they don't want to know how many times you jerk off in reception. Christ, I thought the Chip prick we had here was bad enough.'

'Do you want a room, sir?'

'No, I have the misfortune of already having a room. I live in the E Z Sleep downstate. Just put me through to your manager.'

'Um, Mr Jackson I believe is—'

'Come on, you asshole. You've got to be quick, this could be an emergency.'

'Is it, sir?'

'It is for you, sunshine. Do you know who I am? Don't you recognise the gruff voice so badly and misguidedly mimicked by jackass junior staff such as yourself?'

'Oh, sir, yes, of course, one minute.'

'Get a grip, for Pete's sake.'

'Sorry, hang on, transferring you now.'

Click click click.

'Jackson here.'

'What moron is on the front desk?'

'Who is this?'

'It's me, you prick.'

'Oh, hello, sir, sorry, I—'

'You sound half asleep.'

'I was, well, I was asleep.'

'You got a chambermaid with you?'

'No, sir, of course I haven't.'

'Don't give me that. That's why you hire them.'

'I—'

'You hire young blonde kids with slim legs and big tits. Then you ask them to clean under the bed to test their aptitude and when they bend down to vacuum you yank up that tiny black dress you make them wear and slip it to them.'

'I assure you, sir—'

NICK WALKER

'You tell 'em it'll all be over in a matter of minutes.'

'That's not true.'

'You make them wear garters for easy access, you tell them if they keep quiet and hoover a few more rooms in that position you'll give them a free holiday at the E Z chain's showpiece hotel, Honolulu's E Z Carumba.'

'Sir, I—'

'I'm only pulling your cord, don't sound so guilty.'

'Oh, I see. Very amusing.'

'That's why I hire them, but then I'm the boss.'

'Yes, you are, sir. How are things? You've living at the ...?'

'E Z Sleep. We should call it the Shitty Sleep. I shouldn't have hired a cripple for the desk.'

'Chip, sir? I wouldn't have said he was—'

'Twenty minutes ago he starts screaming in the lobby.'

'Screaming?'

'Maybe someone was yanking off his other arm. Maybe that's why my club sandwich is taking such a long time.'

'Is he all right?'

'Course he's all right. He's a shuttle nut. Some fucking lump of metal hauls itself into the sky and the kid can't keep his mind on the job. I hired him 'cos he's English, I figured he'd have a sense of reserve, he'd keep himself to himself, bottle things up, and here he is screaming all over the place. Why have I got a one-armed screamer fronting my hotel?'

'I didn't know it was a shuttle day, sir.'

'You're senior management, Jackson. I thought you were all supposed to be smart pennies? The cream of the crop.'

'We are.'

'If you're the cream of the crop then you should have your finger on the pulse.'

'I'll keep an eye on the papers, sir.'

'Damn it, the E Z Sleep Hotel has a one-armed cripple on the desk and the E Z Slumber Hotel has a senior manager who hasn't got his finger on the pulse.'

'It's very early, sir. I'm much better once I've had breakfast...'

ROOM 15. NANCY CARTER.

'Chip, does Room 11 want to suck my tits like a child?'

'Miss Carter...'

'Yes or no.'

'No.'

'Does he want to piss on me?'

'No.'

'Does he want me to piss on him?'

'No.'

'Does he want to bite me or hurt me?'

'No.'

'OK, go on then, tell me. I've gone through the worst I can think of. What does Room 11 want for this double bed?'

'He wants to put his hands on your backside for one minute.'

'What?'

'Or maybe a few seconds over the minute.'

'And that's it?'

'Yes.'

'Well, that isn't so bad.'

'Well...'

'That's not such a big deal. That happens in bars most days.'

'Does it?'

'Sure.'

'Do you want to go ahead then, Miss Carter?'

'Would you be in the room too, Chip?'

'No, absolutely not.'

''Cos I'd find it reassuring if you were. Just to arbitrate that ass-touching was all that was happening. You could perhaps time it. Call out when the minute's up.'

'Um...'

'It would make me feel a lot better.'

'Right.'

'So after it's all done, he'll let me have the room?'

'That's what he said.'

'That's good 'cos it's really gonna help me to have a double bed. My husband thinks I don't want to sleep with him and, you know, he may be right but I don't need the aggravation today.'

'Well, if you're sure you want to go ahead.'

'You call up Room 11 and say it's a deal. Say I'll knock on his door in ten minutes.'

'OK.'

'What's his name?'

'Mr Moulin.'

'Mr what? Is he French?'

'I don't think so.'

'Maybe he's got French blood.'

'Perhaps.'

'I don't know if that makes me feel better or worse.'

'I couldn't say.'

'Does he want me to wear anything in particular?'

'He mentioned something about a nightdress.'

'OK, I've got one of those.'

'And he specified that... oh no, forget it.'

'What?'

'No, really, it's not an issue.'

'Spill it, Chip, I don't want you keeping secrets from me before I let an old man touch my ass. I'm vulnerable here.'

'Well, he wanted confirmation that your backside was... I don't know how to put it really.'

'Oh, I see. I get the picture. He likes them firm, I'm guessing.'

'Well, yes. I'm sorry, look this is a bad idea, why don't we just forget the whole thing?'

'Did you tell him I had a fat ass?'

'No, God, not at all.'

"Cos I don't, Chip.'

'I'm sure you don't.'

'Let me tell you I don't anticipate any complaints from Room 11.'

'I'm sure there won't be.'

'You could bounce a tennis ball off my ass and it'd ping back and hit you in the nuts before you had time to blink.'

'I'll … I'll pass that on.'

'You do that, Chip. Jeez, the nerve of some people.'

'I'm sorry I had to ask, Miss Carter.'

'Tell him ten minutes.'

ROOM 11. MR MOULIN. OUTSIDE LINE.

'…so all in all, Jackson, after staying up half the night staring at these peach coloured walls and at the scary art above the beds—'

'They're painted by a well-respected artist, sir.'

'What the hell are they supposed to be? I'm looking at two green horses leaping through a giant vagina.'

'It's a flower, sir, not a vagina. I think that one's called "Aspiration".'

'Well, they've got to go. In fact the whole damn chain needs a shake-up and I tell you I'm going to start now.'

'I'm not sure if this is the right time.'

'Don't tell me when is the right time or when isn't the right time. I make the decisions in this outfit.'

'I know, sir, but—'

'I'm telling you straight I am plainly depressed about the standard of service in my chain of hotels. I hate our room service menus, I hate our room décor, I hate the staff's uniforms, I hate the trouser press, I hate just about fucking everything. You know our hold music is "California Dreaming" played on some oboe or something?'

'They're pan pipes, sir. Henry Hawkins and his Winds of the Earth Orchestra, they do covers of light rock tunes. It's from *The World's Music* album.'

'I wouldn't call it music, Jackson.'

'We use it because Mr Hawkins hasn't got a business head on him and he signed away all rights. We don't have to pay him.'

'He should pay us. You know sometimes I wake up in the morning and think why are you so hard on yourself? Give yourself a break once in a while, the E Z's not so crappy, and then I try and wash and the soap smells like shit, I go to Pancake Parlour and the food tastes shit, I order a club sandwich and it takes a shit long time to arrive and I start to think that the time has come to transform the E Z chain into a more prestige concern. The sort of place which might attract a captain of industry or a high-ranking Mormon. I'm thinking the name should go. We get ourselves a classier branding, something French, Le Dormier Facile, something like that. We get Juliet Binoche to record the doors, "Bienvenue a Le Dormier Facile". Hang the cost. First up though, we get some prestige reception staff. Ones with brains and two arms.'

'Le Dormier Facile?'

'Wait, I've got another call. Hang on, I haven't finished discussing this . . .'

Click.

'Yes? What do you want?'

'Sir, it's Chip here on Reception.'

'Be quick, I've got someone on the line.'

'Sir, Room 15 is willing to let you touch her backside for one minute in exchange for your double room.'

'Is she? About time. Did you check the firmness?'

'Apparently you could bounce a tennis ball off it and it'd ping back and hit you in the nuts before you had time to blink.'

'She say that?'

'Yes.'

'Normally I wouldn't take a girl's word for it but the tennis ball thing's pretty good. Send her over.'

Click click.

'Jackson? You still there?'

'Yes, sir.'

'I'll call you back in a couple of minutes. Something's come up.'

'Can't our discussion wait till later?'

'No. This is the future, Jackson. I see it clearly, prestige hotels, Le Dormier Facile. I'm on a roll, we deal with it tonight. Stay alert. Keep thinking.'

ROOM 15. NANCY CARTER.

'OK, Miss Carter. Whenever you're ready.'

'Oh God, Chip.'

'He's just down the hall, the second door—'

'I know where it is.'

'OK then.'

'Are you coming up, Chip?'

'I'll be there in two ticks.'

'I'll go in and introduce myself but I'm going to wait till you get there before any ass-touching takes place.'

'I'll be as quick as I can.'

'Have you got a watch with a second hand? Or even better a stopwatch?'

'I won't let it drag, Miss Carter.'

'I've got to say I'm having second thoughts here.'

'You can still back out if you want to.'

'I know but I need the double so fuck it. See you in there.'

'I'm on my way.'

Chip looks under the desk for a sign which says 'Back In Five Minutes'. He finds 'Vacancies'. He finds 'No Vacancies'. He finds 'Ask Me About Vacancies'. He puts them all on the desk.

He walks through the lobby and sees his reflection in the screen of the television set mounted on the wall.

The TV is showing shuttle news. A reporter has put together a launch package. She's vox popped and recorded the commentary and cut it down to three minutes. The sound mutes. Chip hits the TV. The sound buzzes. A childhood photo of the space tourist pops onto the screen. Shot of a building. A school perhaps.

The launch is replayed. Chip sees the shuttle climb up his face. The fuel burn making a smoke beard.

Not looking so bad. Not looking so pitiful. He smiles a welcome smile. Glad you all could come. How wonderful to see you.

The screen fizzes. It crackles and jumps.

He thinks it must be atmospheric interference.

He tries to retune. The picture blurs, breaks up, then disintegrates. A TV satellite tired of its orbital slot, wanting to see more of the world, looking around, shifting longitude and latitude, aping the shuttle, taking a cruise round the world, thinking there's more to the universe than bouncing bad TV into bad hotels, thinking it could go to Mars, or Venus, or spray the pictures over fields and streets, or beam them onto the moon so that everyone could see them.

The picture splutters to life briefly, the lift-off jammed.

The film edges on a frame. A little wince. Then freezes again.

Someone at the broadcast company must have put the tape in the machine and dozed off, or gone for coffee. Now it's stuck and no one knows it.

Chip thinks of a low-paid guy walking down a corridor carrying a

Styrofoam cup of coffee. Someone's buffing the floor and says to him, 'We doing shuttle coverage?'

'Yeah,' says the guy.

'That space tourist...' says the floor buffer.

'Yeah,' says the guy.

'She's one lucky gal.'

'She sure is.'

'Enjoy your coffee.'

'Yeah.'

The guy turns down another corridor. A woman holds open some double doors for him. She says, 'Late one?'

He says, 'Yeah.'

She says, 'Has the taxpayer subsidised that tourist?'

He says, 'Yeah.'

She says, 'I want my money back.'

He blows on his coffee. He reaches the VT door. He punches a code and enters a room with monitors and buttons. He sips his coffee and winces. He's put ten sugars in but it still tastes like burnt soil. He glances at the screen and sees the shuttle stuttering in the sky.

The guy jumps. He spills coffee on his hands. He shouts out and lunges for a button.

And the picture leaps into life. And the world unfreezes. The shuttle flies free.

Chip watches it blaze up the screen. He whoops again. He's dizzy again.

The picture cuts to a shot of a shuttle spectator, someone in the crowd, eyes squinting into the glare. Not roadside Jim. This is an A-list watcher. Her mouth gapes open. She has tears on her face. The mouth expresses joy, desolation, hard to tell.

Her face pixelates.

Chip fiddles with the tuning. She twitches and blurs.

The shuttle spectator perplexed. The spectator in a quandary. She looks as if she's in pain. An exquisite pain. A suspended pain.

The picture steadies. She clarifies.

Chip touches the screen.

She watches the sky. She cries and wails.

Chip knows her.

He hopes she cheers up by the time she gets to the E Z. He doesn't want the space party to be a crying and wailing occasion. That wasn't the idea at all. He thinks he should've specified that on the invitations.

The camera moves onto someone else. Someone happier.

ROOM 11. MR MOULIN.

'Reception.'

'What the hell's going on?'

'Ah, sir, I told Room 15 to—'

'She's here. She's just showed up. She won't let me touch anything till you get here.'

'I'm on my way, sir. I was just—'

'Why do you have to be here? What kind of sick deal have you two struck?'

'No deal, sir, she just wanted me in the room when it happened.'

'You get your kicks by watching folks touch asses?'

'No, she—'

'I assume you still have your jerking off arm.'

'Sir, Miss Carter wanted me—'

'Miss Carter? Is that her name?'

'Yes, sir. She wanted me to time it.'

'Time it?'

'I told her you wanted a minute of... contact. She wanted me to say when the minute was up.'

'What's the matter with this woman? Wait a minute... *Hey you, what's your first name... Nancy? Look Nancy, what's wrong with you just counting to sixty? Huh? You stand there, count out loud if you want to, then at sixty you say "That's your lot" and I pack up and get the hell out of here. What's wrong with that as a plan?'*

<muffled reply>

'Oh for Christ's sake. OK, Chip?'

'Yes, sir?'

'She still wants you here.'

'I'm on my way.'

'You know, boy, I've got to say that you standing in the corner of my room with your empty jacket arm all neatly pinned up, calling out the seconds, is going to take the gloss off this enterprise.'

'I'm sorry, sir.'

'I don't mind telling you it prevents the experience from being the erotic one I'd had in mind.'

'I don't know what to do about that, sir.'

'Nice though the ass is, I'm going to need a lot more off Nancy here to distract my mind from your one-armed watchkeeping.'

'Sir, we agreed—'

'I'm saying if you're going to be in the room then I'm going to need a minute of ass plus extra.'

'What do you mean by "extra"?'

'By extra I mean I want licence to roam.'

'Roam?'

'You got it.'

'Sir, Miss Carter doesn't sound keen.'

'Chip, she's… you could say that's gone down badly, Chip, but that's the deal. Either it's just ass and you're nowhere to be seen or it's you in the room and I get to roam. Take it or leave it.'

'I guess that's down to Miss Carter.'

'She's thinking.'

Pause.

'Come on, Nancy, for Christ's sake. Hey…'

Pause.

'Chip, it's Nancy. I don't like the sound of this "roaming" at all so I'm going for just ass, OK? Which means you don't come up. But this is how it's got to be done. When I put the phone down, you start your watch. A minute later, and I mean one minute, you ring the room. Then the ass-touching stops. If I don't answer the phone then you rush up here as quick as you can and save me.'

'That's a good plan.'

'I mean it, if I don't answer, you sound the alarm.'

'I will.'

'OK then. I'm putting the phone down now and yanking up the nightdress. Don't let me down, Chip.'

'I won't.'

'Start counting now.'

'I will.'

Chip watches the clock. Time passes and his phantom arm spasms. It pulls Chip's hair. It tells him that it would be better if Chip walked through the doors and found a cab on Freedom Avenue, and spent the day engaged in other activities. Parties were for ten-year-olds with clean blood, clean livers, clean consciences. It reminds Chip of the Persian soldier, Hegesistratus, imprisoned in stocks, who hacked off his own foot to escape. Hegesistratus who, like the lizard grabbed by a predator that removes its own tail to save its skin, wrote off the loss and didn't spend his time recreating the event.

Your guests weep, it points out. You saw the TV. It will be a wet occasion.

OUTSIDE LINE.

'E Z Sleep.'

'Can you put me through to Nancy Carter, please?'

'Ah, I think—'

'She's in Room 15. It's a room with twin beds.'

'Actually, sir—'

'Tell me straight, did Nancy ask for twin beds?'

'She asked for a double.'

'Really? Did she specifically request a double bed?'

'Yes, sir. We couldn't accommodate her at that time, however, we think we may have found her a new room. If you just hold for a moment I'll see how that's working out.'

ROOM 11. MR MOULIN.

'Chip, you asshole, that wasn't a minute.'

'I'm sure it was at least—'

'Bullshit.'

'I have a call for Miss Carter on the line, sir.'

'I've still got at least fifteen seconds left.'

'I'm not sure about fifteen.'

'At least. This is outrageous. There's premium ass here and I'd barely started.'

'Well, do you want to just quickly finish off and then put Nancy on?'

'No, that doesn't work for me, boy. The deal was one full minute, uninterrupted, and this is an interruption. I'm going to put the phone down and we're going to start again from scratch, from zero seconds... *don't get whiny, Nancy, your accomplice Chip was too quick off the mark, he's fucked the deal so we start again.*'

'Is that what's happening then, sir?'

'Nancy here is unhappy about the starting from scratch situation but that's what's happening.'

'What does she want me to do with her call?'

'Tell him to call back in a minute...'

\<muffled response\>

'*Oh for Christ's sake, I don't want you on the phone while I touch your ass…*'

<muffled response>

'*…it's obvious why…*'

<muffled response>

'*Well then I'm going to want another thirty seconds to compensate… take it or leave it.*'

<muffled response>

'OK then. Chip?'

'Yes, sir.'

'You can put the call through to Nancy, she'll take the call while we start over. But we're going for a minute and a half so if that FUCKING club sandwich is anywhere near ready, don't barge in for ninety seconds. Jesus, why is this so difficult?'

'I don't know, sir.'

ROOM 11. OUTSIDE LINE.

'Hello?'

'Nancy?'

'Hi, sweetheart.'

'Look, our guy on reception told me you'd specifically asked for a double bed, I'm sorry I got all… you know.'

'That's OK. Are you wearing a watch?'

'No, all I know is it's pretty early. We've got time. There's a clock on the dash here in the car.'

'Does it do the seconds?'

'Only minutes. It's saying five thirty-eight.'

'Tell me when it clicks over to five thirty-nine.'

'Don't worry about the cost, Nancy, we can put it on expenses.'

'It's not that, honey, it's… I'm wearing a face pack, you can't leave it on too long else your skin starts to… I don't know, fall off or something.'

'Well we wouldn't want that.'

'No, so just keep an eye on the time.'

'I will.'

'How's the drive going?'

'I'm on a good road here, there's nothing on it so I can go fast without worrying. The white lines are just slipping under me now. I can drive down the middle if I want. You know what? I nearly got busted about an hour ago. Seriously, I stopped in a wood and picked some magic mushrooms. Don't give me a hard time about it, I thought I was going to fall fast asleep over this wheel. Anyhow, I took some and I was just whizzing down this road, Nancy. I mean it, the lights were flashing past me and the trees were speeding past and the lines in the middle of the road were going so quickly under me that it was like it was one big solid line. I must have been doing over a hundred. Then what happened? I saw a cop bike coming after me. I tried to go faster but everything was a blur and I didn't want to end up in a ditch. So the cop caught me. I think those bikes go pretty fast. So I stopped and he got off and came over to my window. And I rolled it down thinking if he got heavy I could flash my press card and say I was rushing to cover an emergency story, a fire or something. Anyhow, he asked me how fast I thought I'd been going. And I said, all innocent, oh, I don't know, officer, sixty, maybe sixty-five. 'Cos I was going to hold my hand up to a little bit of speeding. You know what he said, Nancy?'

'Mm-mm.'

'He said, "Ten miles an hour, sir. You were doing ten." How about that? It must have been strong fungi, huh, Nancy? Anyhow, he told me to get some rest and then set off again. So now I've got the window open which is why it's a bit noisy but there's this fantastic smell in the air. I must be passing a field of flowers or something. It's been coming on for a couple of miles, getting stronger and stronger, and now it's so fragrant. I wish I knew what kind of flower it is that's making this smell. I'll take some pictures. You would know. If you were in the car with me right now you'd be telling me exactly what kind of flower it was. In fact I think I might just stop and pick you some, then you could tell me what they are. Perhaps I could get a whole bunch of them and we could put them in a vase for our hotel room. Make it smell good. Our one-armed guy said you might have got us a new room. You having any luck with that yet, honey?'

'Uh-huh.'

'You OK?'

'Uh-huh, keep talking.'

'So perhaps this is a meadow here. Perhaps it's wild flowers I'm smelling. Whatever it is I'm going to pull over and grab a handful. It's not illegal, is it, Nancy? I guess they might be endangered, or rare. Oh, what the hell. What's a couple of minutes on my journey if it means I arrive with fresh flowers?'

'Mm.'

'It's heady, Nance, I tell you. Blue. They must be blue irises or something. Is that possible? Are these flowers native to these parts? Or would it be something else? The sun's starting to come up and they're covered in dew. Perhaps they're not blue, perhaps they're violet in colour but the sun's making them look blue. It's really beautiful. We should do a story about America's wild flowers.'

'Uh-huh.'

'I've stopped now and the car's gone quiet. The silence you get after shutting down the engine is so sweet, isn't it, Nance? And now the smell from outside is hitting me like a drug, it's enough to make you dizzy, like those poppy fields in *The Wizard of Oz*. I guess now I'd be the fattest one, wouldn't I? The Lion. Mmm, deep breaths. Deep breaths here, Nancy.'

'Yeah.'

'You sound breathy too, like you're trying to smell them as well.'

'Uh-huh.'

'The clock's ticked over a couple of minutes actually, we're on five forty-two. I forgot to say. Perhaps you should take off your face pack.'

'Keep going.'

'You sure?'

'Yeah.'

'So what do you think these flowers could be? I wish I could remember, I'm sure I was taught this in school. Do they teach that kind of thing? Flowers and stuff? Perhaps they don't. Perhaps I never knew anything about it. Could these flowers be Western Dog Violet, huh, Nance? You used to call me that, the Western Dog. Roving California, full of nectar. You don't call me that any more, but I kind of liked it. Is it because it's a bit of a mouthful?'

'Mmm.'

'Perhaps you could just call me "The Dog", how about that? Start a newsdesk nickname. God, it's such a big meadow, seems to stretch for miles. And here I am standing in the middle of it, looking out over the flowers. And I'm wading into it. And the dew is just coming off and making my clothes wet. It's knee high, Nancy, it's filling my shoes. I wish you could be here.'

'Uh-huh.'

'I'm picking some of the biggest ones now, the ones with tall stalks and big flowers. The ones that the bees love. I'm snapping the stems low, they're thick with water. Got to be two feet high.'

'Yeah.'

'The heads are dry and the pollen puffs off them as I pick them out, and they just break off with a pop between my fingers.'

'Ohh.'

'Nancy?'

'...'

'Nance?'

'Uh-huh.'

'Are you all right, Nancy?'

'Uh ... huh.'

'Nancy?'

'God.'

Pause.

'Oh God.'

'Nancy?'

Pause.

'Nance?'

Pause.

'Yeah.'

Pause.

'You OK?'

'Yep, I'm fine. I'm good.'

'What happened? Are you doing exercises?'

'Nothing, sorry, honey, what were you saying?'

'I'm in the middle of a meadow picking you flowers.'

'That's great, sweetheart. Could you ring back in a couple of minutes?'

'Um. Sure.'

Chip flicks through the channels twice but his crying guest has disappeared. The crowds have gone and there's nothing but shuttle hats and foam gloves on the ground. She's on route perhaps. Drying her eyes in a cab. Reapplying mascara. Putting on a how-nice-to-see-you smile. Wrapping a gift.

A parcel is dropped outside the E Z doors. Chip opens it. Nine party hats. Nine party poppers. Nine crackers filled with novelty space gifts.

He brings them inside and arranges them on the desk. The cracker design is childish, so are the hats. He throws them away, but it makes the place look gloomy so he takes them out of the bin. He tries on a hat. He looks like an idiot. He throws the lot away. He has one or two apologies to make before the fun starts, that should be done with dignity, not with party hats. The party hats could come out later, when the ice has broken and water has flowed under the bridge. He takes the hats out. They're creased. He flattens them with the E Z Register.

Be natural. Be...

The E Z Clock chimes. Far too early. Wee Willie Winkie emerges. His wooden jaw flips open and he says: 'Six o'clock, welcome to a new day.' He snuffs out the electric candle. It's an unreliable manoeuvre and the little wooden snuffer breaks off the candle bulb and scatters fragments of glass in the mechanism. The metal filament twists and sparks. Wee Willie Winkie rotates and goes back inside the clock, his wheels crunching as he disappears.

From Lost Property, the *Hey Jesus* evangelist tells him all his promises to live a good life mean nothing now unless he learns how to repent. The sky is burning, filled with freak weather patterns, angry sun streaks, tumbling aeroplanes, malfunctioning satellites, dying stars, a disappearing moon and flashes of light.

Time to get your house in order.

ROOM 11. MR MOULIN.

'Uh-huh?'

'Mr Moulin? Chip at Reception. I... well, that's your time up, sir. Nearly five, well, almost six minutes.'

'Six, huh?'

'Yes, sir. I would've rung earlier but your phone was engaged.'

'Nancy was on it.'

'So, did everything...?'

'Six minutes, you say? Well, that's not bad. Not bad at all for an old guy. Is the water from the taps OK to drink?'

'Yes, sir, but there's a barrel of Fresh and Clear in the corner, you can—'

'That stuff makes me gag. I need good liquid. I need champagne. Why is there no champagne in the mini fridge?'

'We don't stock it, sir.'

'We're an hour from the launch pad and we don't have any champagne?'

'The guests never ask for it.'

'Not even that Orbiter crap?'

'Not even that, sir.'

'They have it at the E Z Slumber.'

'Perhaps there's more cause for celebration there.'

'I doubt it, have you ever been there?'

'No.'

'Anyone ordering champagne wants to kill themselves with it.'

'I see.'

'Still, at least they've got it. You order some Orbiter for here, Chip, for the future.'

'You could try putting a gin in a beer. The kick's quite similar.'

'Sounds disgusting. Must be a Pancake Parlour tip.'

'Yes.'

'Jeez, that place. You ever eaten in there?'

'Yes.'

'I notice today's special is Shuttle Shake. Whose idea was that?'

'I don't know, sir.'

'Perhaps we'll get a couple of them sent up. Is there any booze in them?'

'It's mostly milk.'

'Milk and what? Hydrogen?'

'I shouldn't think so, sir.'

'What do they cost? Three billion dollars?'

'One fifty.'

''Cos unless they're full of hydrogen and cost three billion dollars

I don't see the point of calling them Shuttle Shakes.'

'No, sir.'

'This is the kind of lazy branding that gets my goat.'

'I see that.'

'Nancy wants a word.'

Pause.

'Chip?'

'Yes, Miss Carter.'

'If my husband calls, could you put him off for a couple of minutes? He's in a field.'

'Certainly. Did it ... did everything work out OK?'

'Yes, thank you. I think there may be some French blood in Mr Moulin after all. We'll be switching rooms in a while, I should think. In the meantime, he really wants his club sandwich. Says he gets hungry after ... so could you bring it up right away?'

'It's on its way.'

'Bring me one too, will you?'

'All right.'

'Mr Moulin says you'll fry the bacon up specially.'

'If you want, Miss Carter.'

'I do want. Knock before you enter.'

'Of course.'

OUTSIDE LINE.

'E Z Sleep.'

'Nancy Carter please.'

'She asked me to take a message.'

'She asleep?'

'I don't know, sir.'

'Do you have a gym at the E Z?'

'No.'

'Not even little exercise bikes in the room?'

'No.'

'I thought I heard Nancy working out.'

'Um…'

'She told you to take a message?'

'Yes.'

'I guess she's asleep. Most people are asleep aren't they?'

'I imagine so, yes.'

'Especially if they've been working out. I'll let her sleep for a while. I'll call later.'

'All right then.'

'I might take a nap myself. I'm in a pretty great meadow here.'

'Uh-huh.'

'I mean really great. You lie down and you're invisible to the world. And the smell just knocks you out.'

Chip enters the E Z Store Room. It's full of cardboard boxes containing E Z Shoe Shine, E Z Shower Caps, E Z Coasters. There's a box with E Z Club Sandwiches written on the side, but it's empty aside from a note which says, 'Remember to order more club sandwiches.'

There's a dummy's arm propped up in the corner. Left from the day a newly married couple came into the lobby. Giggling, burping. The groom's eyes were swimming from booze and the pockets of his morning suit were full of confetti. The bride, lipstick gone, clinging, unsteady, told him he was … so … funny.

'Can I help you?' said Chip.

The groom's wayward eyes swivelled round the lobby as if trying to work out where he was and what he was doing. He caught a blurred sight of Chip. He saw Chip's empty sleeve and he doubled up again.

He reached out his piss-stinking hand and grabbed Chip's sleeve and shook it.

The groom said, 'Good morning. We are a newly married couple, but don't worry, we'll be armless.' He laughed like a drain.

The groom said, 'Do you need a hand with our luggage?' He creased up.

He said, 'Do that guy, not tonight, Josephine.'

The groom was wheezing with laughter, tears dribbled down his fat cheeks.

The bride looked at the groom with new eyes. She flicked Chip a look and smiled at him apologetically.

'What the hell are you doing?' asked the groom.

'Nothing,' said his wife.

The groom shouted at Chip, 'Take your eyes off my goddamned wife!'

'Steady, darling,' said the bride.

'I'll cut off your other arm. And your dick!'

He told her that he couldn't stay in this freak hotel even if they paid him to.

Chip said the hotel was full.

The groom said, 'You're lying, you're fucking lying.'

The wife said there must be some mistake.

Chip asked them to leave.

The groom told Chip he'd ruined everything. He said America had become a sicko circus.

The wife said sorry to Chip and got slapped for it.

Chip told them to leave immediately.

The groom tried to piss in the lobby. He said, 'How do you like this, you one-armed freak?'

But the groom's bladder was shy and nothing came out. 'How do you like this?' he repeated. Nothing came. He stood in the lobby holding his shrivelled little penis. He shouted 'Come on!' to it but nothing came. 'Come on you little fucking bastard,' but still nothing came out.

He called Chip a little shit. He called his penis a little shit.

The groom ran outside and found a shop dummy dumped by the High Fashion trash. He ripped off its arm and ran back to the E Z. He used the arm to bang on the glass doors. Trying to smash them. He hammered till his face turned red.

The bride tried to pull him away, he gave her a black eye.

The doors stayed unbroken. They weren't cracking. Despite the old voice the door still had strength. Like the old lady in town who occasionally grabbed Chip and asked him if he was a veteran.

The groom's strength gave out. He threw the arm down and collapsed on the floor. Moaning and gasping.

His bride helped her new husband into the passenger seat and got behind the wheel.

The truck started up and drove away, dragging the dummy behind it. The foot caught in the bumper alongside the trailing cans and Just Married balloons.

Chip collected the dummy arm and put it in the store cupboard.

He uses it to hang his coat on.

He thinks again of first impressions. He thinks of awkwardness. He thinks of the freak hotel. He thinks perhaps his party will go with more of a swing if he has something cosmetic to put his guests at their ease. He stuffs the dummy's arm in his empty sleeve. The arm is thinner, longer and doesn't bend. His slender new fingers have chipped nail paint. It's a fashion model arm and it seems to point at something. A film star or a exciting piece of tailoring.

Chip rests the arm on his hip, he lets it hang by his side, he props it on the desk. The fingers still point. Over there, they seem to say, how about that? A much better party.

Everyone will spend their time trying to see what's so interesting.

A car pulls up outside. Low slung. Expensive.

Chip's first guest peers out of the driver's window towards the E Z Sleep. Light reflects off the glass and his face is obscured by the neon Pancake Parlour sign.

Today is the day to be natural. Chip takes a deep breath and puts the dummy arm away.

S ally is told all systems are go. She asks for confirmation. She gets it. She says she was unsure of the reading. A blip, she's told, nothing to worry about. Don't ask too many questions. Enjoy the ride.

I am, she says.

She's told to stand by for another burn.

She says how much this experience means to her...

She's told not to distract anyone.

The shuttle re-ignites. She feels it in her blood. Monomethyl hydrazine and nitrogen tetroxide oxidiser meet inside the orbital manoeuvring system engines. There's no oxygen but nonetheless they ignite and burn automatically, no spark required.

One minute. Two minutes. Three...

They place her in her orbital slot. She's on track. She's pinpointed. She's inch perfect. She'll use gravity now. She'll use the earth, the moon, the sun.

She's chasing the Space Station. Covering the distance at the rate of one hundred and seventy miles every orbit of the earth. Moving fast. Once round the world every three hours. Time is moving fast too. It'll be day then night then day again then night again every two hours.

Round and round and round.

The post-insertion time line starts. Action stations.

Everyone around her moves.

They stow their spacesuits and ejector seats and they install computers and cameras. They configure. The shuttle stops being a rocket and becomes a little space station.

It's a busy time. She watches them plug and wire and boot-up. She watches them open hatches and install air ducts. She feels a sensation in her stomach. A tiny thing. A little awareness. Her imperfection.

She floats and smiles and co-operates.

And as she watches them work, her mind goes round and round too. She revisits her own time line.

She was the concentrate of a much larger group. She didn't know how big the group was. It may have been over two hundred thousand but it may have been many more.

Near the top of the Fresh and Clear skyscraper there was an office, and inside that there were personnel who made some effort to read all the applications but as the office filled with paper they applied less stringent criteria and the paper started to fly.

In the first cull they got rid of anyone under twenty, anyone over fifty, anyone who was an employee or relation of an employee of Fresh and Clear, anyone with a history of heart trouble, anyone with glasses, anyone with breathing difficulties, anyone who wasn't born in the UK, anyone obese, anyone with a disability, anyone with high blood pressure, or low blood pressure, anyone with a criminal record, anyone too tall or too short, anyone who had spent any time in a psychiatric institution.

Even this wasn't getting rid of them fast enough so they rejected anyone ugly, anyone with dyed hair, anyone who sounded too strange, too keen, too pretentious, too stupid, anyone with piercings, face tattoos, bad teeth, or a squint.

They discarded application forms that came in colourful envelopes, or recycled envelopes, or by FedEx, or had been sealed with too much tape. They eliminated anyone who wrote outside the box, or in green ink, or made circles over the i's, or whose writing was slanted to the left, or was capitalised, or who rang up to check on progress, or who sent covering letters, or bribes, or who knew any of the selection staff and were calling in favours.

Paper spilled into the office next door and extra staff were hired. The new staff binned anyone they wouldn't screw, or who sounded like they were lying, or were called Kenneth, or Cindy, or who were lookalikes, or who made a spelling mistake, or who sent a tape, or who wrote 'ever since I was a child I wanted to go into space'. They got rid of sex changers and name droppers and those who said they ate astronaut food just for fun, or who called the shuttle 'the ultimate fairground ride', or who called their kids Buzz or Neil, or who gave themselves a funny middle name, Spock, Kirk, Uhura.

They shredded dozens without even looking at them because the day was getting late, they were tired and had dinner plans and paper cuts.

But out of this they got fifty people and they put them in a box marked 'Stage One'.

And she was in this box.

And Chip was in this box.

She got one of fifty letters saying 'congratulations'.

The selectors needed her to send a video of herself, a piece to camera, no more than three minutes long, no nudity. The selectors bought ten VCRs and let the temps go.

A week passed and in the London office the tapes arrived at each post. The VCRs worked overtime and out of the fifty tapes viewed, nine got rejected unanimously, two tapes were eaten up by a faulty VCR, nineteen were fifty-fifties, twenty got a cautious thumbs up. The arguments lasted all night, the loudest voices won out.

In the box marked 'Stage Two' they put thirty names. They wrote to the thirty saying 'double congratulations' and invited them to attend a series of interviews. Twenty-nine showed up. The thirtieth was pregnant; her priorities had changed.

Sally was one of these twenty-nine.

So was Chip.

She took a slow train to London in a trouser suit which she'd borrowed from a friend. It had confetti in the breast pocket and a boiled sweet caught in the lining.

The selectors spilled into the floor above in order to use a large conference room. It overlooked the Thames and candidates could watch the London Eye revolve.

She was given a handshake and a coffee and an hour in front of a panel who asked her if she thought the London Eye was moving.

She said she found it very moving; she'd always loved London.

They said no, was it physically moving round?

Oh, she said.

She watched.

She saw a man wearing a blue coat inside one of the pods. He was banging the glass. Thumping it with his fists. Condensation circles appearing as he shouted. Other passengers had bunched away from him. The pod was at three o'clock and rising. He wanted the ride to stop. He was only a quarter of the way through and had lost his nerve. He threw himself at the glass. The cluster of onlookers broke up and the man was jumped. He was subdued. He was sat upon. People in other pods looked over. The disturbance unnerved them. They stopped looking at the view and started making calls. The Eye speeded up.

She told the panel that in confined spaces it was important to keep a lid on one's panic.

The panel asked her to deliver a short presentation about what outer space meant to her. She said galactic archaeology and illustrated her talk with slides.

They asked her about the future of space travel.

She said wormholes and wrote memorised formulas on a blackboard.

They asked her about a perfect society.

She said ancient Greece and quoted Plato.

They nodded and said they'd be asking each candidate the same questions.

On the panel there were good cops and bad cops and questions came from all sides. Candidates who lost eye contact or lost their cool, those who stammered or got their sums wrong, those who swore or sweated or whose clothes didn't fit or who didn't fake it well enough or who repeated somebody else's story, or whose hands shook or whose laugh was hollow, or who couldn't finish a glass of Fresh and Clear, were out of the door and twenty-nine became twenty in a box marked 'Stage Three'.

She got through.

Chip got through.

She travelled to London again. On a faster train but in the same suit. She'd decided it was lucky. It still contained the confetti and the sweet but there was also an Order of Service in the pocket. The cremation of a man who wanted 'Abide With Me' played at the burning.

A new panel quizzed her face to face and quizzed her with the other nineteen.

She got sessions with psychologists, scientists, fitness instructors, Fresh and Clear executives, and representatives from the European Space Agency and NASA. She had medicals and profiling. She had to co-operate with her competitors to make a bridge over a river and get across it without anyone falling in. She had to make a clock, using matchsticks and elastic bands, which kept time to within five minutes over an hour. She had to race round a track in wet clothes. She had to say what made her happy, sad, mad.

After six hours she was put into a room and told to wait. The others waited with her. They didn't know if they were awaiting a decision or doing another test. After two hours one guy cracked. He said nothing was worth this shit. Someone said they were all in the same boat.

The guy said he had a computer business going to ruin while they pricked about. He left.

The selectors came back with champagne and asked where the computer guy had gone. Someone said he flipped and went home. The selectors were taken aback. They were going to tell everyone who'd made it to the final ten and the computer guy was top of the list. They went away again to rethink.

When they came back they brought Fresh and Clear but less champagne. They seemed woozy.

They said everyone was a winner for having got this far. They said it had been a very difficult decision. They read out the names of ten people. Everyone clapped, some louder than others. Those who hadn't made the list drank the most. No one touched the Fresh and Clear.

She was one of seven women.

Chip was one of three men.

The ten were to report to an address in Hertfordshire a week later and they weren't to speak to any newspapers.

She spent the week taking vitamins. Eating fruit and getting her silver fillings replaced with white ones.

OUTSIDE LINE.

'EZ Sleep.'

'I know it is, Chip. I'm sitting in my car outside your door.'

'I see you.'

'I'm waving.'

'Yes. Welcome. How are you?'

'Am I the first to arrive?'

'Yes.'

'Not surprised. This car flies. Pretty nifty, huh?'

'It's very nice. Can I ask you to park it in one of the designated parking areas? Where you are now blocks the front entrance.'

'I was hoping to leave it here. I wouldn't mind some of the others seeing it.'

'Well...'

'It's a rental car. I picked it up at the airport. I asked them for the smallest car they had and by that I meant to communicate to them that I wanted the most economical car, the cheapest car, but the woman at the counter had a literal bent and gave me the smallest car dimensionally. The smallest volume wise. Hence this sports car. Which is tiny. I can barely move my legs. It's finished me off financially but it turns heads.'

'Would you mind moving it? Where it is now constitutes a fire hazard.'

'I will, I just didn't want you to think I was a pimp for having such a flashy car. Or that I was driving it to compensate for any inadequacies in the bedroom department.'

'Of course not. Come in. Freshen up. It's ... it's good to see you.'

'You've got me a room?'

'Yes.'

'Do I have to pay for it?'

'Of course not.'

'That's good, my credit card's maxed out 'cos of this damn car.'

'Everything's taken care of. I've got you a room and a voucher for breakfast at Pancake Parlour across the street.'

'The place with the pink sign?'

'That's it.'

'What do they do there?'

'They do pancakes.'

'Pancakes, eh? Do they have savoury? I don't like sweet things in the morning. I'm rather particular with my food.'

'They have a variety, I believe.'

'Do they have an authentic espresso machine? Italian made? Because if I'm going to have pancakes I'm going to need something bitter to set them off. It's important to stimulate the entire tongue.'

'They have coffee but I don't know ...'

'I'm going to go over there and take a look at a menu.'

'Oh, OK then.'

He drives away.

Chip smoothes down his hair and makes like a host. He lines up E Z Toothmugs and takes the foil off the neck of the Orbiter. He wonders what has happened to his snacks. He wanted to have little bowls of olives and nuts in case his party guests were hungry after their long trip. All he can find are E Z Mintz which he arranges in ashtrays on the desk.

He has some party music but *Hey Jesus* is still blaring from Lost

Property. Hymns now sung in the evangelical style. He slips the tape under the door with a note. Could you play this instead?

Hymns cut out and the first five seconds of 'Up, Up and Away' come through the lobby speakers. Then it stops and *Hey Jesus* returns with increased intensity. His tape is passed back in two halves.

Chip's hand is steady but his phantom hand is shaking like a leaf. It tries to drag him out of the doors and away. I'm shy, it says. I'm embarrassed. I'm ill-prepared. We don't have snacks. We don't have music. Let's run.

Chip stands his ground. His phantom fingers jam themselves down Chip's throat and Chip is sick on the floor. He heaves. He retches.

The party poppers swim in front of his eyes. Spit and tears drop onto the crackers.

He curses his arm for jeopardising things.

His arm tries to grab him by the scruff of the neck and throw him down the fire escape.

Chip resists and opens the E Z Cleaner cupboard for a mop.

What kind of first impression will a pile of puke give?

OUTSIDE LINE.

'That's fine. Pancake Parlour does bacon and it does eggs and the waitress is kind of pretty. I'll get her to bring breakfast over to me in the car. I'll ask her if she's ever been to Miami because this car could get her there in less than two hours.'

'The tall waitress with the black hair?'

'You got it, kind of busting out of her—'

'That particular waitress won't be on shift by the time you take breakfast.'

'Really?'

'She finishes at six. Then some others come in.'

'How do you know so much about it?'

'I... you get to know these things.'

'Have you got your eye on her for yourself, Mr Check-In?'

'No...'

'I think you have.'

'It's our business to know these things.'

'You dirty dog.'

'I'm not a dirty dog. I just happen to know the shifts.'

'I'm sure you do. Well, let me tell you she's worth knowing about. Those buttons are straining on their threads. If there's any reason for an early breakfast she's it.'

'Knowing the shifts is part of my job.'

'That's the Chip I know. That's the Chip I remember.'

'Are you coming in or not?'

'Sure. Looking forward to it.'

'Then park your car in the car park and come right in and we'll get this thing started.'

'Don't you do valet parking?'

'No.'

'I was hoping that...'

'Park it yourself. I mean, would you mind parking it yourself?'

'All right. Fine. It's probably better actually, you seem a bit pissed. You might bump it. These rental car companies are pretty ferocious.'

'Yes.'

'It's been a while, Chip. Let's not get off on the wrong foot, shall we?'

'No.'

'I'll park up and I'll be in in a minute.'

'Sure.'

Chip cleans up. He masks the puke smell with deodorant. He takes some tinsel from his pockets and drapes it over the switchboard. He's made a desk sign: 'Welcome'. He puts it next to the bell. He checks the bell works. Ting, ting.

He gets a pen and puts an exclamation mark after 'Welcome'. He adds 'Friends'. He puts an exclamation mark after 'Friends'. He underlines it. He adds 'All'.

Welcome! Friends! All.

He isn't sure about All. He turns it into three more exclamation marks. It smudges. It's a mess. He throws the sign away. Should've started preparations earlier, he mutters. Should've...

ROOM 12. MRS BAINS.

'There's an awful lot of noise coming from Room 11, Chip.'

'I'm sorry, Mrs Bains. I'll tell them to keep it down.'

'It's upsetting.'

'Yes.'

'I'm a broad-minded lady. A little old, I know, but this? No one wants to listen to this.'

'No.'

'I don't want to sound like a fuddy duddy. Or spoil anyone's fun, but there might be children here.'

'There are no children in the hotel.'

'There might be, Chip.'

'I'll see what I can do, Mrs Bains.'

'Quick as you can, please. It's turning my stomach.'

Chip handles the champagne with care. Orbiter's a popular brand for launching ships because more prestigious brands have thick glass which clunks against the hull and doesn't smash. Orbiter's glass is thin and substandard. It breaks as soon as you look at it. Delivery companies hate delivering it because Orbiter often explodes in the van. Tension in the bottle is high. Chip feels ready to burst himself.

OUTSIDE LINE.

'Listen Chip?'

'Yes.'

'I'm just outside the door. On foot now.'

'I can see.'

'The battery on my phone is about to go so I'll keep this brief.'

'Please come in.'

'I just wanted to apologise for offending you.'

'You didn't.'

'I get a bit, you know, with waitresses.'

'You can come in, it's fine.'

'I thought what with—'

'What?'

'Well, you know you can't have had it easy what with—'

'What?'

'I mean, your arm. You only have one arm. I didn't visit you in … I'm just saying you can't have had it easy …'

'I manage fine.'

'Sure. You have an old-style switchboard system there I notice. And a little headset type arrangement.'

'Yes.'

'I suppose you just plug in the plugs and talk away.'

'Yes.'

'Very clever. Ingenious.'

'Yes.'

'You've decorated the desk I see.'

'Yes.'

'Nice. That's a nice touch.'

'Thank you.'

'I know I'm early. Perhaps you want to go and get changed or something.'

'I have to stay in this uniform.'

'Sure, of course. I just thought you might want to … well, anyway.'

'Just come in. It's fine.'

'OK. Looking forward to it.'

The man was a chef when Chip knew him. He may be a chef still. He stands outside the doors. He wipes his face with a handkerchief. He breathes hard. He's out of shape. He's let himself go. He shifts his weight from foot to foot. He pats his guts. He gives Chip a weak smile.

'Come in, it's fine.'

'I will.'

The chef doesn't move.

Chip clenches the Orbiter between his knees and untwists the metal cage. The cork shoots out like a bullet and hits a light and breaks it. The emergency light flicks on automatically. It swathes the lobby in green light. Orbiter froths over his phantom hand. The hand wipes itself on Chip's hair. It pokes Chip in the eye. It pulls Chip's hair. It slaps him in the face. Chip slurps the froth. It makes him burp. It gives him the bends. The glass clinks against his teeth. Bubbles fizz over his face.

He pours Orbiter into the E Z Toothmugs. The bottle is large and hard to handle. Orbiter sloshes over the desk. It knocks down a couple of the mugs.

'Come in. Have some fizz.'

'I will.'

Chip mops up the mess. He grabs a crushed hat from underneath the E Z Register and puts it on his head. The elastic is tight under his chin. He tries to smile at the chef but his face turns red. He pulls the elastic away from his windpipe. The elastic snaps. It hits him in the eye. His eye streams. The hat pings into the air.

'Please come in.'

'I think I'll take a little walk first, Chip. Get some fresh air into my lungs.'

Chip throws the hat away. He throws all the hats away. They were off-putting. They were liabilities. One thing guaranteed to create an uncomfortable atmosphere is tight elastic. He wonders if he should check the crackers. And the poppers. He didn't want them to strain the atmosphere, or cause weak laughter, or take out someone's eye. Should've checked the novelties, he mutters. Should've...

ROOM 12. MRS BAINS.

'Did the switchboard explode?'

'No, Mrs Bains.'

'I heard a pop.'

'It was Orbiter.'

'I jumped out of my skin.'

'Sorry.'

'Old ladies scare easily, Chip. Warn me in future, will you?'

'Yes. I'm sorry.'

'The noise from Room 11 has stopped now.'

'Good.'

'What did you say to them? I hope you were discreet.'

'Actually—'

'You didn't mention that I'd complained, did you? I wouldn't want them to think I was an interfering old lady.'

'No.'

'Or a prude.'

'I didn't say anything.'

'I'm glad. I'm as open-minded as the next person, but it was turning my stomach.'

ROOM 11. MR MOULIN AND NANCY CARTER.

'Did I just hear a pop, boy?'

'No.'

'Sounded like a cork to me.'

'It was a car backfiring.'

'If there's any fizz in this hotel I need it upstairs.'

'Yes, sir.'

'Any fizz appears, put my name on it.'

'I will.'

'All fizz is hereby requisitioned by the owner. The owner and his tight-assed companion.'

<giggle>

Chip watches the chef pace the car park. Smoking. Glancing over at the E Z from time to time. Chip gives him an encouraging smile.

The chef walks into Pancake Parlour. The old man who has been sitting in the window seat since Chip started his shift is still there. He watches the chef buy coffee. The chef emerges a few minutes later with his drink in a plastic cup. He sits on the bonnet of his expensive rental car and blows the steam away and sips. The car is uncomfortable with the weight. The suspension is challenged. It may cost the chef his deposit, so he gets inside the car. He switches on the engine to power up the heater. He looks like a man who is thinking that all he needs to do is put the car into drive, let out the handbrake, and he could be back on the road in two minutes. At the airport in one hour. On a plane in two. Ordering duty-free in three. Thousands of miles away from the E Z in ten.

It looks to Chip as though these thoughts are attractive to him.

OUTSIDE LINE.

'I need you to come and help me, Jim.'

'I'm doing a hundred to the airport, Chip. I'm picking up a fifty-dollar fare.'

'I'm having a little ... gathering and it's started badly. I need you to come and oil the wheels.'

'You're having a what?'

'A party. A get-together, here at the hotel. I think it might be a little awkward.'

'Why wasn't I invited?'

'I said you could come over.'

'To have a shower. You didn't invite me to any party.'

'Well, you are invited. I'm inviting you now.'

'Oh, I see. I get an invite when it goes badly.'

'Jim, it was for people you don't know…'

'Suddenly I'm a must-have guest.'

'Don't be like that.'

'Suddenly ol' Jim is Mr Popular.'

'Will you come or not?'

'Like I said, I'm on my way to the airport.'

'Will you come afterwards?'

'I thought I was your friend.'

'You are.'

'I thought if there were parties to be thrown, gatherings, get-togethers, we'd be top of each other's lists.'

'We are, but…'

'But not today. I get the picture.'

'Jim, please…'

'So what's this new list you've got?'

'Like I said, you don't know them…'

'Since when did you get a whole bunch of friends?'

One hour in. One hour high.

Sally has a little camera. She asks the crew if it's OK to take a couple of pictures.

Sure, they say. No flash please.

She snaps the living compartment.

She snaps the instruments.

She snaps the mission specialist. He smiles. He's the one who's going to fix the arm on the Space Station. She'll send that picture to Chip.

She looks through a window. Up. Down. Three sixty.

She looks at the world shrinking.

Black sky, stars.

She checks for space junk. *Mir* had been hit by objects large enough to dent the inner walls of the crew compartment. The Space Station dwarfed *Mir* and was floating around with a big bullseye on its ass. The more it got built, the bigger a target it became. It might be completed on schedule, with a great fanfare, and then get hit by a lump of old satellite and smashed to pieces.

Or get hit by something else; there was a ton of crap up there. Leftovers from thousands of launches, used up rockets, bits of equipment from scientific experiments. Nuts, bolts, lens caps, cloths. You might not think a cloth could do much damage but a cloth travelling at six miles a second could knock your space helmet off.

In 1963 the American Air Force released four hundred million tiny antennas into orbit to see if radio waves would bounce off them. They were still up there too, needles zipping through space. A handful of them could St Sebastian-ise her. Pin her to the Space Station.

There were nuclear-powered satellites leaking coolant. The coolant had been congealing into hard little balls. Bullets to shoot her down. And those golf balls that Alan Shepard sent flying from the moon with his nine iron. They'd give her a nasty lump on the head.

The post-insertion time line ticks over.

The crew stows chairs and helmets and personal belongings. Items that were heavy are now light. They make the place shipshape.

She smiles at them. They nod at her.

She feels a nagging in her stomach. Not a pain. A tiny tug. A little nudge. Adrenalin kills it.

She remembers the address was a large country house in expansive grounds. She wasn't told who owned it, and she didn't try to find out afterwards. It had stuffed heads and suits of armour and oak inside, and lawns and sundials and oaks outside. A high wall topped with a thick loop of barbed wire kept out ramblers and drunkards and sacked temps.

There was a gravel drive leading from a security gate to the front door. It was three hundred metres long and up this drive the ten arrived.

Some came alone. Some with their families, partners. One came in a coach with her friends dressed in fancy dress spacesuits.

She came by cab. She wore the lucky suit, still with the sweet and confetti and Order of Service, now with a pawn shop receipt for a watch – the suit owner had had to buy another suit because Sally was hogging the lucky one.

Men with cameras picked each one up at the gate and followed them up the drive. They filmed the goodbyes. They filmed the just-do-your-bests. They filmed each one greet a man who the ten came to know as the Captain.

Chip was the last to arrive. He made an entrance. He got the taxi to drop him half a mile away and he walked up the drive solo, sweating in the heat.

He had two old brown suitcases, junk shop finds, with faded stickers commemorating trips on ships to Jamaica and on planes to Mexico.

He wore a hat to keep off the sun. A kind of Homburg. She thought he was trying hard to look like a pioneer.

A man with a steady cam strapped to his body met him a hundred metres from the front door. The cameraman walked backwards, filming him looking like the young Dr Livingstone. Chip didn't know if he was expected to speak into the camera or pretend it wasn't there. He said, 'Good afternoon.' He said, 'Beautiful day for...' but couldn't think for what. 'For it,' he said.

He complimented the cameraman on his backwards walking. The cameraman tripped over at the end.

'Don't worry about that,' said the Captain, 'we'll edit that out. Unless you want to do it again?'

Chip said no.

The Captain said he wasn't asking Chip, he was asking the cameraman. The cameraman said no, he'd hurt his elbow.

The house had many, many rooms. Enough for a bedroom each, two bedrooms each. But the ten were all put in one. Communal living, said the Captain, confined space, proximity, you must learn to accept it, embrace it, and love it.

The ten chose beds.

She asked a cameraman why there were so many cameramen.

He wasn't allowed to speak. He whispered that they'd all been allocated a candidate each. He was hers. They were making a fly-on-the-wall and she should just try to ignore him.

The cameras recorded the unfolding scene. They picked out the dominant ones, picked out the team players, picked out the negotiators.

She made snap judgements.

Someone was making suggestive comments about sleeping on top, a big man, cheerful. He sniffed the air and said they were having chicken that night, chicken with rosemary, and it was overcooked. The Chef.

Someone had her fists stuffed in her mouth and couldn't keep still, she didn't care where she slept she just wanted the game to start. The Holiday Rep.

Someone was folding his clothes neatly, and pointing out that it wasn't a game, it was very serious. The Radar Operator.

Someone was asking why most people preferred the top bunk as opposed to the bottom. The Pollster.

Someone cracked gags. The Comedienne.

Someone had brought four types of floss. The Model.

Someone was taking it all in her stride. The Stenographer.

Someone was doing push ups. The Probable Winner.

Chip didn't say much. He looked out of the window and at the clouds. The Quiet One.

She wondered how she was coming across. She had a St Christopher round her neck and checked her blasphemies. Perhaps she was the Believer.

The candidates figured that how they chose their bed would determine whether they would make the grade as a spaceman. They thought it had already started.

In the shower she looked in the showerhead for a camera. She looked in the soap dish for a microphone. She stared hard in the mirror for a two-way. If there was technology there, it was beyond her. Or perhaps she was looking in the wrong places. She decided not to check her appearance too much so as not to appear vain. She noticed a nose hair. She plucked it out and her eyes watered. She peed.

She found Chip waiting outside the door. He asked her if it was private in there. She said possibly. Probably.

He said he had a little tattoo on his groin. Microchip, it said. It was written beside a small scar. He didn't know where the scar came from, a forgotten childhood injury, but he had the tattoo done because he used to like pretending he was a robot.

She told him to keep Microchip covered. No one wanted a tattooed astronaut.

The ten were welcomed in a room which had large double windows that opened out onto the grounds. Natural light helped the cameramen who moved around them getting angles. The Captain put his hands behind his back and told them how only one of them would be in the training programme for the duration.

The ten already knew this.

Each of the others would be eliminated one by one, as the situation dictated. It was survival of the fittest.

The ten already knew this. The cameramen knew this too. They would also leave as the numbers dwindled. They looked jealously at the cameraman who'd been allocated the Probable Winner. He would earn the most, and a bonus, and would do the follow-ups.

The Captain said it would be tough mentally and tough physically. There would be times when they would look on him as a father and times when they would look on him as the devil himself.

The ten already knew this.

He looked them all in the eye and he saw them trying to win by meeting his gaze.

The Captain came across well. He had good bones, good diction, a good tan, and a simple vocabulary. He paced the room as he spoke. He talked about a time to discover what the ten were made of. He talked about a time of self-exploration, a time of boldly going et cetera et cetera. He asked if the group had any questions.

No one spoke.

He smiled and said, 'I've thrown a lot at you, you probably want to let it sink in.'

Chip asked – a camera zipped his way – he asked, 'Have you ever been into space, Captain?'

The Captain looked Chip in the eye and hated the question. He cleared his throat and said, 'I have been part of the NASA space programme for many years.'

'But have you actually been into space?' asked Chip.

The camera stayed on Chip. The ten thought he was digging his own grave.

The Captain thought, we'll cut this out, we'll make Chip seem like the asshole. He said, 'No, I haven't.' He said, 'Next question.'

Someone, the Comedienne, asked, 'When's lunch?'

The Captain laughed, he liked that. He saw a good edit.

The Comedienne thought, I'm ahead, and everyone else was jealous. They thought, perhaps we can't win unless we're comic.

Around a big table with chicken on their plates and Fresh and Clear in their glasses, the Probable Winner told Sally that between her skin and the great unknown there would be a layer of nylon acetate, a layer of Spandex, a layer of polyurethane-coated nylon, a layer of woven Dacron, a layer of neoprene-coated nylon, five layers of Mylar coated with aluminium, then a layer of Goretex and Nomex backed with Kevlar. She said those eleven layers were the only thing between her and outer space.

Sally said there were nine other people between her and outer space.

The Probable Winner looked around the table. The others were prodding their chicken. They didn't think it was cooked properly and were wondering if this was a test. The Captain told them to relax. He said the ordeal started in earnest the next day and so today was a holiday. They tucked in. The Probable Winner thought it was a double bluff and left her chicken alone. See how smart I am? she said to Sally. Champagne was brought in.

The Captain raised his glass and said the road was long et cetera et cetera. The ten clapped and drank a bottle apiece and everyone said it would be hard to see anyone leave as everyone was such a tremendous, likeable person.

Sally was sick into her pillowcase that night. She could've easily made it to the toilet but she thought an astronaut should be able to hold her liquor and she didn't want to be caught by the airvent camera.

Above her was Chip. He heard her puke and offered her his spare pillow. She said he was very kind but she was fine. He said just as well, he'd been sick into his too. Perhaps there really was something wrong with the chicken. They listened out. Everyone else snored.

Chip thought that the two of them would be the first two to go. She agreed.

That night she dreamt of a rough sea.

ROOM 16. THE CHEF.

'Don't feel you have to stay in your room.'

'It's a nice room, Chip, thank you.'

'They're all the same.'

'Even so, you could've put me in the one that had stains on the carpet, or the one where the hot tap drips, or the one where someone got shot or something.'

'No one has been shot at the E Z Sleep Hotel.'

'Or something as bad.'

'What could be as bad as shooting?'

'Oh God, where do I start? I went to a hotel once where—'

'I'm glad you decided to stay. I'm glad you like the room. Why don't you come down? It's easier to talk and I've got snacks coming.'

'Yes, of course. Snacks, you say?'

'Yes.'

'Look, I didn't mean to go on at you in the lobby about your arm, your... you know.'

'I'm used to it.'

'Staring and that.'

'As I said.'

'I didn't really know how to... perhaps we need something to break the ice? Perhaps I should call up a stripper. Just to get things going. There are some numbers here in the book. What do you think?'

'Well...'

'I think that's just the thing to ease the tension. Not that there is tension, it's just that...'

'It's been a few years.'

'Exactly, Chip. Couldn't have put it better myself. It's been a few years. It'll make us laugh and once we laugh... I'll get on to this stripper. We'll be back into our groove before we know it.'

'I don't think...'

'We'll be laughing like drains. Just you wait.'

Chip had tried to meet the chef's eye. Tried to make him feel as if coming here was a good thing, a positive thing. But the chef's eye was everywhere. The plants, the floor, Chip's missing arm, the clock, the desk, Chip's missing arm, the map, Chip's missing arm...

Chip tells himself that the others probably wouldn't be as...

His missing arm lunges for the panic button underneath the desk. Chip yelps. The panic button is for hostage situations. It shuts down the hotel. It alerts armed guards who pump tear gas into the building.

Chip waits for flashing lights or inflatable rafts but nothing happens. There are no alarms, no tear gas, no SWAT teams.

He hears a little voice. He can't place it. He follows the sound. It's elusive. Perhaps it's outside.

It's not outside. It's the doors. They mutter. They chant.

Stay calm, don't panic.

Exit immediately.

Vacate the building.

This is not a drill, please leave now.

Do not stay to collect your belongings.

There's nothing to worry about.

Please exit in an orderly fashion. Don't scream as this will upset other guests.

The doors won't open. Chip pushes them. They won't give.

See to it that you are wearing warm clothes and comfortable shoes.

Do not try to rescue pets.

Do not be a hero.

Breathe deeply.

Think clearly and with purpose.

Deflect panic.

Be selfless.

Chip puts his shoulder to the doors. They resist. He hurls himself at them. They repel him.

Try to put personal problems to the back of your mind.

Try to forget your history.

Try to get a smile in your voice.

OUTSIDE LINE.

'Entrancing Entrances.'

'This is the E Z Sleep, our doors are jammed shut.'

'What kind of door is it?'

'A glass door, automatic. It's muttering too. Can you send someone out?'

'Muttering?'

'Part of the security system. It's malfunctioning.'

'We don't do speaking doors.'

'Well, this one's speaking.'

'Then it's not one of ours.'

'It's got your logo on the hinges.'

'You must have customised it.'

'Well, that's possible but—'

'If you've customised it then your warranty is invalidated.'

'No one can get in.'

'We are quite clear in the terms and conditions.'

'I'm expecting people.'

'They'll have to climb through the window.'

★ ★ ★

A car slews across the car park with one tyre flat and flapping, and with steam coming out of the bonnet. The car squeals. The driver fights with the wheel and the brakes. The rear wheels lock and the front spins round and hits an E Z bollard. The car judders to a stop.

A woman gets out, shaking. She wears sunglasses. She wears a hat. She no longer looks like the probable winner of anything.

Chip tingles. Time to get off on the right foot. Greet her with open arms. An open arm. Put her at her ease. Offer her a hot, sweet E Z beverage for shock.

She catches her breath and steadies herself. She looks at the wretched wheels. She examines the dented chassis. She leans against the bonnet and lights a cigarette. She pulls hard, takes the smoke deep and blows it high. Smoke mixes with steam. The car's in a cloud. Like it's gone to heaven. She looks into the sky. She looks hard. She sees nothing. The sky is empty.

Chip tries to prise the doors open but they're not giving an inch.

Stay back.

Stay calm.

Stay one step ahead.

He wrestles with them. He looks around for a crowbar, or a fire axe.

Don't fight.

Don't run.

Don't think.

He calls out to her. Tells her that perhaps between the two of them, they might be able to...

She doesn't hear him. She takes out Chip's invitation and reads it. She rereads it.

Chip strains and pulls. He shouts a welcome through the crack in the doors. He tells her this is the right place. He tells her that she might have to climb in through the window.

She stuffs the invitation in her pocket and walks away. One leg shakes. The other is damaged. She limps to Pancake Parlour but doesn't go in. She walks to the refuse area and, with difficulty, climbs on a bin. Then she grabs a drainpipe and heaves herself up onto a flat roof. She loses a shoe. She limps across the roof. She climbs onto a higher ledge. It's narrow and she puts her arms out to keep her balance. She walks to the end and looks down. She takes a firework rocket from her bag and puts it inside an empty bottle. She lights the taper and steps back. She leans against one of the big neon 'P's in the Pancake Parlour sign.

She looks spacewards. The fuse burns.

The bottle tips over and the rocket fires horizontally over the Freedom Avenue Expressway. Cars swerve. The rocket hits a tree and kills a bird.

ROOM 11. MR MOULIN AND NANCY CARTER.

'There's a crazy on top of Pancake Parlour.'

'I know, sir.'

'Is that a new kind of advertising? She promoting the Shuttle Shake?'

'No, sir.'

''Cos if she is then no one's watching, except me, and I don't like fireworks. They're a health and safety hazard. Someone might sue me. Nancy thinks the same.'

'Yes, sir.'

'If she's going to make the point at all, she needs to dress up like a Shuttle Shake.'

'Yes.'

'Shuttle Shakes are white, are they?'

'Yellow. It's mostly banana.'

'Then she should wear yellow. Get a yellow wig. Do something funny with bananas.'

'Yes, sir.'

'Juggle them or whatever. But keep the fireworks out of it. Tell her will you, Chip?'

The Probable Winner is anxious about the bird. It looks as if the nest is on fire too. Perhaps the firework is killing its young. She jumps off the Pancake Parlour roof.

It's not very high but she lands awkwardly and doesn't move. The wind knocked out of her. The old man looks out of the window. Loaded fork paused.

The Pancake Parlour waitress rushes out.

She rolls the woman onto her side. She feels for injuries. She feels her legs. She feels her arms. She feels her head. She shouts for help. Someone comes out with a glass of water.

The woman is helped to her feet and carried inside Pancake Parlour.

OUTSIDE LINE.

'Pancake Parlour.'

'This is the E Z Sleep.'

'Hello, Check-In.'

'The woman who just fell off your roof.'

'Yeah. Pretty strange, huh? What the hell was she doing?'

'Is she all right?'

'Just cuts and bruises.'

'OK, then.'

'We've put some Pancake Parlour Plasters on her.'

'Good.'

'I don't know what else to do with her.'

'Give her something sweet?'

'I offered her a Shuttle Shake but she won't touch it. She said it would make her throw up. She's muttering about a bird on fire.'

'Perhaps she should take a lie down. I have a room for her here. Perhaps you could send her over?'

'Do you know her, Chip?'

'Yes. She's . . . I'm having a little gathering here and she's one of my—'

'A gathering?'

'Yes.'

'And you didn't invite me?'

'I . . . well, I would love to invite you. Of course. Come over, you're welcome.'

'You're just saying that. You don't want me there.'

'I do. I really do.'

'If you'd have wanted me there you'd have asked me already.'

'I . . . I'm asking you now. Please come. I can introduce you to everyone.'

'Well, I've already met this one and she's pretty odd. Are they all like that?'

'I'm not sure, it's been a while.'

'I'll stay put, Check-In, if it's all the same to you.'

'Perhaps after your shift then?'

'I'll see.'

'I was meaning to ask you if you had any take-out food which might do as party snacks.'

'You want me to bring some over?'

'That would be great.'

'You want me to be a waitress at your party?'

'No, I—'

'You want me to tiptoe around grinning at your buddies while they drop vol au vents on the floor and watch my backside as I pick them up?'

'God, no.'

'You want me to be suggestive with breadsticks?'

'I didn't mean to sound—'

'You're such an E Z target, Chip.'

'Oh, yes ... very good ...'

'Uh-oh. Your crazy's out of here.'

The Probable Winner leaves Pancake Parlour. Her coat is torn and her elbows are bleeding. She walks towards the highway, towards Freedom Avenue. She steps over barriers and runs across the road, dodging traffic.

She finds the tree and shakes its branches. A burning nest falls to the ground. She puts her coat over it. She smothers it.

Chip sees her look into the smoking remains and put her hands up to her face.

She picks up a discarded cardboard box.

She rips up the box and writes CAPE CANAVERAL on a piece of it.

She stands by the side of the road and puts out her thumb. A car drives past but doesn't stop. And another.

She holds the sign up in front of her. She wipes tears away from her face.

ROOM 16. THE CHEF. OUTSIDE LINE.

<Music>

<Recorded Voice>

'Hi, and thank you for choosing us. I can tell from your breathing that you're a hot guy. My, what—'

Bleep.

'Thank you. If you prefer to—'

Bleep.

'You have elected not to use the credit card option. You will be billed in the normal manner. You will be transferred shortly. In order to match you up with your most suitable hot, hot girl please select from the following options. Press 1 for Ripening Peach, press 2 for Experience Shows, press 3 for Been Around.'

Bleep.

'You have chosen, Ripening Peach. Press 1 for All American Girl, 2 for Hot Latin, 3 for A Taste of the Orient—'

Bleep.

'You have chosen All American Girl. Now please choose from the following options. Press 1 for Young Wife. Press 2 for Office Secretary. Press 3 for Fitness Fanatic. Press 4 for Resting Actress. Press 5 for New Nurse. Press 6 for Nature Lover. Press 7 for Prom Queen Hopeful. Press 8 for—'

Bleep.

'You have chosen Nature Lover. The following are your service options. Press 1 for Friendly Conversation. Press 2 for Light Flirtation. Press 3 for Candid Suggestion. Press 4 for Standard Aroused. Press 5 for Wet and Wanting.'

Bleep.

'You have selected Wet and Wanting. You will be charged at <voice 2> three-oh-four-oh dollars per minute. <voice 1> If during the course of the conversation you wish to speak to a different girl, press 6 to return to main menu. You will shortly be transferred to … <voice 2> Suzy who is a nature lover living in the Los Angeles area <voice 1> and who is looking forward to speaking to you. Thank you for calling us.'

<Music. Elton John>

'You will be connected to <voice 2> Suzy <voice 1> shortly. This call has been <voice 2> zero hours one minute long.'

<Elton John.>

Click click click.

'Hi, I'm Suzy.'

'Hi.'

'Thanks for calling. What's your name?'

'I'd rather not say.'

'That's OK, what do you do?'

'Chef. Actually spaceman.'

'Spaceman?'

'No chef. Well … yes, chef.'

'My father's a chef.'

'Oh, really?'

'Sure, it's a dignified profession, in fact—'

Bleep.

<Recorded Voice>

'You have returned to the main menu. Press 1 on your keypad for Young Wife. Press 2 for Office Secretary. Press 3 for Fitness Fanatic. Press 4 for Resting Actress. Press 5 for—'

Bleep.

'You have chosen Resting Actress. You will shortly be transferred to … <voice 2> Portia who is a resting actress living in the Chicago area <voice 1> and who is looking forward to speaking to you. Thank you for calling us.'

<Music. Elton John.>

'You will be connected to <voice 2> Portia <voice 1> shortly. This call has been <voice 2> zero hours two minutes long.'

<Elton John>

Click click click.

'Hello, I'm Portia.'

'Hi, Portia.'

'Thank you for calling. What's your name?'

'Is your father a chef?'

'Does that matter to you?'

'I don't want to talk to you if your father's a chef.'

'Then he isn't.'

'You can call me, Chef.'

'Hi, Chef.'

Pause.

'What do you want to talk about, Chef?'

'Well, let's see now, why don't we start with what you're wearing.'

'I'm sorry?'

'What are you wearing?'

'I'm wearing jeans.'

'Jeans?'

'Yes.'

Pause.

'OK, what else?'

'A sweater. Trainers.'

Pause.

'I think I may have pressed the wrong button, I was kind of expecting something a little more...'

'What?'

'Is this Friendly Conversation?'

'Well, it's fairly friendly so far.'

'Because I thought I'd pressed Wet... I thought I'd gone for a harder option.'

'Harder? Something more intellectual? That's fine by me but then you'd started talking about clothes so...'

'No, I didn't mean—'

'We can get more challenging if you want, that's fine. It's a bit of a relief to tell you the truth. What do you want to talk about? Contemporary literature or movements in art.'

'I was hoping—'

'How about current affairs? As long as it's American affairs. I'm not so hot on European politics but I'm quite up to date on domestic matters. That might be fun.'

'No, I... OK, look, I'm going to go back to the main menu, no offence but I think I've been given the wrong girl.'

'Oh.'

'Sorry, I wanted—'

'I've let myself down, haven't I? I shouldn't have said I was hazy on European politics. I bet you're a big Europe guy.'

'No, it's not that.'

'I'm not saying I'm completely ignorant about it, in fact, I think of myself as cosmopolitan. I've travelled. I've been to France. I've been to Spain. I've been to Greece. But sunbathing on their beaches hasn't given me an insight into their governments. I'm not going to be able to give you a real run for your money there.'

'Portia, honestly, it's not you, you sound great. In fact, if it wasn't for this little confusion I could really get off on your voice. It's just that for the price of the call, I need to cut to the chase pretty quick, you know what I mean?'

'Just try me. Give me a starting point, see how we do. How about Spain? Let's kick off with Spanish politics post Franco.'

'Really, Portia, another time.'

'Do you think that a post-fascist Spain is more or less prosperous but—'

'I'm sorry, this isn't working.'

'Yes it is—'

'I'm going to try New Nurse. I'm going back to the main menu.'

'You're leaving?'

'I'm sorry.'

'Oh, well, then I guess I'm sorry too.'

Bleep.

<Recorded Voice>

'Press 1 on your keypad for Young Wife. Press 2 for Office Secretary. Press 3 for Fitness Fanatic. Press 4 for Resting Actress. Press 5 for New Nurse. Press 6—'

Bleep.

'You have chosen New Nurse. You will shortly be transferred to... <voice 2> Eloise who is a newly qualified nurse living in the Las

Vegas area <voice 1> and who is looking forward to speaking to you. Thank you for calling us.'

'<Music. Elton John.>

'You will be connected to <voice 2> Eloise <voice 1> shortly. This call has been <voice 2> zero hours three minutes long.'

<Elton John>

Click click click.

'Hello, I'm Eloise.'

'Oh come on, it's Portia, isn't it?'

'Chef?'

'Why has this happened? I'm supposed to be getting Eloise.'

'Well, I just get a name flashed across my screen here. I just answer to that.'

'Eloise is supposed to be a newly qualified nurse living in the Las Vegas area who, I don't know, is going to tell me about giving me a bed bath or something.'

'Well, I can talk about that if you want.'

'Well... isn't the real Eloise there?'

'There is no real Eloise, there's just me and a couple of others who call themselves whatever it says on the screen.'

'Oh.'

'I don't have to be Eloise. It says here that if you want me to be called something else then I can be something else.'

'Well...'

'Do you still want to keep calling me Eloise? Or do you prefer Portia?'

'I don't know. It doesn't matter.'

'You say a name and I'll be it. It's your call.'

'I don't care about the name, I just want—'

'Because if it's all the same to you I'm quite taken with Portia.'

'Fine. Let's go with Portia.'

'Do you still want me to call you Chef?'

'Yes.'

'Portia is a character in *Measure for Measure*. Do you know *Measure for Measure*?'

'No.'

'It's a Shakespeare. She's a lawyer. I thought I might be a lawyer once but things didn't work out.'

'Portia, look, I've pressed New Nurse here. I need—'

'You want to talk about hospital procedures?'

'Well, sort of.'

'I must say, you're an esoteric man. If it's not European politics, it's medicine. That's great. I'm glad you've gone for the nurse actually. I feel much more at home with the hospital theme. I've just been in hospital as it happens. My dad's sick. He's got something wrong with his prostate. Is your prostate up to scratch, Chef?'

'Yes, but—'

'Sounds like it's an awkward organ. Can get clogged up. My dad, who is a chef as it happens—'

'Oh.'

'—is having a terrible time with it. What does it do exactly?'

'Portia, did you say there were a couple of others there with you?'

'That's right.'

'Do me a favour will you? Listen in to one of their conversations.'

'I'm not sure that's allowed.'

'Just for a second.'

'I don't want to get sacked, this is my first day.'

'Call it research.'

'Just for a second then.'

Pause.

'This call has been <voice 2> zero hours four minutes and thirty seconds long.'

Pause.

'Oh.'

'OK, Portia?'

'Yeah, I see what's happened here.'

'Good.'

'The others are kind of moaning down the phone.'

'That's right. That's what this is.'

'I didn't really click that . . . Well, I guess that explains a lot.'

'Portia, that's fine.'

'In a way I'm relieved. I was wondering why I was getting more than my fair share of presumptuous people.'

'Right, so now you know what the deal is—'

'In fact I was starting to lose faith in human nature till you came on, Chef.'

'Really?'

'With your European politics and medicine and everything.'

'Well, that was a misunderstanding.'

'I realise that now.'

'I mean I'm not saying I am averse to a bit of European politics but there's a time and a place.'

'Well, how about now? It'd be great.'

'No, I—'

'Or something lighter maybe, Russian cinema, Italian cooking?'

'Portia, I want to get turned on here, I'm sorry but I need . . .'

'Right.'

'Perhaps we can talk about Russian cinema afterwards, after the moaning part.'

Pause.

'So, do you want to give this other thing a go then?'

'Yes, please, Portia.'

'And, so I'm . . .'

'You're a nurse. A newly qualified nurse.'

'Uh-huh.'

'And you're sort of… well the option was Wet and Wanting.'

'Right.'

Pause.

'I'll start then shall I, Portia?'

'OK.'

'Good.'

Pause.

'So, Portia the New Nurse, it's getting kind of late in the hospital. Most people are asleep but I'm not.'

'No. I suppose, neither am I.'

'It's pretty hot too. I'm just under a light sheet.'

'Shall I open a window?'

'No, that's OK.'

'Do you want a fan?'

'No thank you.'

Pause.

'What are you wearing, Portia?'

'I'm wearing a nurse's uniform.'

'Good. That's fine. Is it short?'

'I don't know how short nurse's uniforms are.'

'It's not a standard uniform, OK? It's a short one.'

'All right.'

'Do you have sexy underwear underneath it?'

'I suppose.'

'Well, do you or don't you?'

'I do.'

'And I guess a couple of buttons are loose on your blouse?'

'Will that help?'

'Oh, yes.'

'Yes, then.'

'And you've got high heels?'

'Yes.'

'And I imagine you're Wet and Wanting.'

'I guess I am.'

'Are you going to give me a bed bath?'

'Do you want one?'

'Yes, I'm pretty dirty.'

'OK then.'

Pause.

'Are you doing it? Are you giving me a bed bath?'

'Yes.'

Pause.

'Would you describe what you're doing?'

'I'm giving you a bed bath.'

Pause.

'You know, Portia, this isn't really working for me.'

'You don't say.'

'There was a girl earlier, she called herself Suzy, she was a Nature Lover, I cut her off but I think she might be a better bet.'

'That was me too.'

'Was it?'

'Yes.'

'Right.'

Pause.

'This call has been <voice 2> zero hours six minutes and forty seconds long.'

Pause.

'This is costing me a fortune. I'm going to ring off.'

'Thank God.'

'Don't be like that, this isn't my fault.'

'What a shitty job.'

'Well…'

'You sure you don't want to talk about Italian cooking? Or anything else?'

'Not at this price, Portia.'

'This is so shitty. I'm going home.'

Cars race past her. Trucks, sedans, commuters, surfers. The displaced wind makes her hair wisp around her face.

No one stops.

She sways.

She rips up CAPE CANAVERAL and writes TITUSVILLE.

Sports cars go by, couples, teens, NASA vehicles.

She tears up TITUSVILLE and writes THE MOON. She tries to stop crying. It's putting people off.

Pick-ups go by, buses, street cleaners, the Jesus Army.

She tears up THE MOON and writes HEAVEN.

A car slows down, the driver tries to read what she's written. He wonders if the hitcher shares his destination and could give him some company.

She's written HEAVEN too small and the driver nearly knocks her over before he gets it. He swerves past and drives on, he's not going to heaven, his car tax has expired and that's a sin.

ROOM 16. THE CHEF. OUTSIDE LINE.

\<Music>

  \<Recorded Voice>

'Hi, and thank you for choosing us. I can tell from your breathing that you're—'

Bleep.

'Thank you. If you prefer to—'

Bleep.

'You have elected not to use the credit—'

Bleep.

'You have chosen, Been Around. Press—'

Bleep.

'You have chosen Hot Latin. Now please—'

Bleep.

'You have chosen Office Secretary. The following—'

Bleep.

'You have selected Candid Suggestion. You will be charged at <voice 2> two dollars fifty cents per minute. <voice 1> If during the course of the conversation you wish to speak to a different girl, press 6 to return to main menu. You will shortly be transferred to ... <voice 2> Daisy who is an office secretary living in the San Francisco area <voice 1> and who is looking forward to speaking to you. Thank you for calling us.'

<Music. Elton John.>

'You will be connected to <voice 2> Daisy <voice 1> shortly. This call has been <voice 2> zero hour one minute long.'

<Elton John>

Click click click.

'Hi, I'm Daisy.'

'For God's sake.'

'What?'

'This is ridiculous.'

'Chef?'

'I press All American Girl and I get you. I press Hot Latin and I get you. I press Ripening Peach and I get you. I press Been Around and I get you. You're Candid Suggestion and you're Wet and Wanting. You live in Los Angeles, you live in San Francisco, you live in Chicago. You're a resting actress, you're a nature lover, you're a new nurse, you're an office secretary. You're Suzy, you're Portia, you're Eloise, you're Daisy. How can you be all these things?'

'Chequered career.'

'And I thought you said you were going home? Going home to bed? Why are you still here?'

'I have to finish my shift. If I don't finish my shift I don't get paid.

But this is the last time this outfit enjoys my services. An hour and I'm outa here for good. This is where this career choice comes to an end.'

'I don't believe it's that bad.'

'It's horrible. Don't bother asking. Let's just get it over with. What do you want?'

'Don't be like that.'

'We all race to pick up anything that's not Wet and Wanting here. I had to be quick just to collar this Candid Suggestion of yours, but even that's no guarantee that it isn't some sick freak. Even the Friendly Conversations. I've had one Friendly Conversation since you last called. It was a guy who wanted me to describe the room I was in, the chair I was sitting on, tell him what colour my underwear was and how I was doing a shit in my pants.'

'Oh.'

'I've just got off the phone to someone who wanted me to pretend I had a cock as well as a vagina and that I was screwing myself.'

'Look, I'm sorry it's been like this for you.'

'I've just got to get through this hour and that's it. That's me out of here. So what's it to be?'

'I don't want it to be you, OK? I've got to believe you're into it otherwise it's meaningless for me. Put me through to someone else.'

'No one here is "into it".'

'Someone must be enjoying themselves.'

'Everyone here is having a shitty time.'

'Don't any of you get off on this at all?'

'No. So, I guess that's you done. Thanks for calling.'

'Look wait. How about this for a deal. Because you've had such a terrible night, you do me a couple of minutes of moaning and then we can do some Italian cooking chat. How about it?'

'Forget it. I've had something of a rude awakening since you last called, OK? You pay your money and you get your fake panting. I understand that now. The time for Italian cooking or Russian cinema is past. You don't have to sugar the pill. If I'm going to talk about Italian cooking, I'd rather talk about Italian cooking properly with my proper friends.'

'What do you mean "properly"?'

'You muttering about pizza toppings with the spunk drying on your belly isn't going to make me feel better about this call, even if it does fill up a couple of minutes.'

'I'm a chef, not some *ignorante* who thinks Italian cooking is just pizza toppings.'

'Whatever. What do you want? "Oh, God yes" type stuff? You want me to pretend I'm in the shower?'

'No wait a minute. Portia is it?'

'Whatever you want.'

'Wait a minute, Portia. I resent the implication that just because I've rung a gentlemen's phone line—'

'Gentlemen's?'

'Just because of that, I'm not going to know anything about Italian cooking.'

'I really don't care.'

'Because I damn well do know a thing or two about it.'

'Sure.'

'I have sophisticated tastes. Italy happens to be a special area of expertise. You ask me anything. Go on, ask me how *prosciutto* is prepared.'

'No.'

'Because I know.'

'Who cares?'

'Salt is massaged into the hind leg of a pig every day for a month then hung in a well-ventilated room for a year to sixteen months. Ask me the best way to cook a wood pigeon.'

'I don't give a shit, I'm—'

'Roasted with olives. Ask me what is the best type of pasta flour.'

'No.'

'Or how a Parmigiano is made.'

'I'm not interested.'

'Or where are the best places to find *porcini*.'

Pause.

'Ah, you see, you do want to know that.'

'I don't.'

'Yes, you do. You want to know about the *funghi*.'

'I couldn't care less about—'

'Oh, yes, you do. I knew it. Well, the best areas are in the valleys of Piedmont in Lombardy and in Liguria, Borgotaro and Emilia-Romagna. You can pick them yourself if you like but, if you go to the market in Trento, you'll find fifty, or sixty different types. The best types are *cantarello* and *spugnola* and once you have a good handful, you should just lightly sauté them in butter with a little garlic and parsley.'

Pause.

'And if you're in Lombardy in the Lange area you might be lucky and find a white truffle. And you could clean it off and shave it thinly and sprinkle it over some *taglierini* tossed in garlic, Parmesan and butter.'

Pause.

'Or make *uova al tartufo*. Eggs and double cream. Baked in a ramekin till the whites have set, truffle on top.'

Pause.

'Have you ever found a truffle, Portia?'

'No.'

'Me neither. I'd like to look for one. I'd take a hound with me. Truffle hunters used to use pigs, but the tubers are so potent the smell sent the pigs delirious and they just gobbled them up as soon as they found one.'

'This call has been <voice 2> zero hours four minutes and thirty seconds long.'

'Truffle is excellent grated over pheasant too. You roast the pheasant, make a sauce with wine and butter and serve it with *polenta*. I had it once in Siena. You ever been there? The town centre is pink and shaped like a scallop. They have a good story about being besieged by Florence and having diseased donkeys catapulted at them in order to give them the plague. This isn't recently. This is a long time ago.'

'This call has been <voice 2> zero hours five minutes long.'

'OK, anyway, I didn't ring to talk about this.'

'No.'

'You've had a bad night.'

'Yes.'

'I just wanted to clear up the thing about Italian food.'

Pause.

'Are you still there, Portia?'

'Yes.'

'So, what do you want to do? Do you want to carry on this Italian thing after a little ... you know?'

'You got a good recipe for rabbit?'

'Portia, I'm on a two-dollar-fifty rate here.'

'I never know how to make them tender.'

'It's a common problem, can we—'

'They always seem to lose their moisture.'

'As I said, I don't want to talk about this, but if it's a moisture problem then try cooking the rabbit slowly in a stew.'

'Yeah? What with?'

'If I tell you do I get some action afterwards?'

'Sure.'

'Right, quickly then, dust the rabbit pieces with flour and brown them. This seals in the flavour. Add onions and garlic, stir in some white wine—'

'How much?'

'Couple of glasses. Add some pulped up tomatoes, stock if necessary, herbs—'

'Which ones?'

'Rosemary or thyme, sage is good too. Perhaps all three. In a casserole dish, you need a good pan. Something sturdy. Lid on. Cook for an hour and a half.'

'In the oven?'

'In the oven, over the hob, either.'

'Because I'm on electric and sometimes it's difficult to control.'

'Whichever is easier.'

'Well, that sounds great. What are we calling this dish?'

'Rabbit stew.'

'Oh come on, Chef, you must have something better than that up your sleeve.'

'Portia.'

'Give me a name.'

'Well, I don't know, it's a Ligurian dish, you could call it *Coniglio Affogato Alla Ligure*.'

'Oh, that's good.'

'OK, then.'

'Chef, that's poetry.'

'Fine. Now—'

'I am going to knock someone dead with that one.'

'I'm sure…'

'Low lighting, wine, heady perfume, strappy dress, announcing that tonight we shall be having *Coniglio Affogato Alla Ligure*. That's classy. That's going to wash away today.'

'Wait, are you—'

'This call has been <voice 2> zero hours six minutes long.'

'—are you, do you have dinner plans, Portia?'

'Dinner doesn't express the half of it. I have *Coniglio Affogato Alla*

Ligure plans. What should I serve with it, Chef?'

'You've got a friend coming over?'

'A friend today, who knows what I'll be calling him tomorrow.'

'Him?'

'He's a him all right.'

'I see.'

'And what a him. You know what he does?'

'No.'

'He smells things for NASA.'

'Really.'

'He's part of a team who has to smell everything that goes into space. He doesn't think it's glamorous, but I think it's very glamorous. And important. He's on an odour panel. Things smell different in space. Did you know that?'

'I did actually.'

'Bullshit. You didn't know that at all.'

'I was nearly an astronaut.'

'Crap. You don't know the half of it. He's pretty shy, though. I think I might need some good wine with our *Coniglio Affogato Alla Ligure*. What do you suggest? Nothing too expensive.'

'I don't know.'

'White or red?'

'I imagined you being single, Portia. The voice on this phone line implies you're single.'

'Yeah?'

'Single and frustrated.'

'It also implies I'm a New Nurse, or a Prom Queen Hopeful, or a Nature Lover.'

'Yes it does.'

'This call has been <voice 2> zero hours seven minutes long.'

'The time's racking up here, Chef. What do you want to do?'

'I don't know.'

'I think you've earned your moaning with that rabbit recipe.'

'I suppose.'

Pause.

'So, a deal's a deal, Chef, do you want me to start?'

'Whatever.'

'All right then. I'll begin.'

'Sure.'

'OK, here goes.'

Pause.

'Oh. Ohh.'

Pause.

'Oh, yes. Mmm. Oh, that's so good.'

Pause.

'Oh, yes. Ohh.'

'Wait. Stop a minute, Portia.'

'What? Wasn't that what you wanted?'

'You're thinking of him, aren't you? You're thinking of the sniffing man.'

'Well...'

'You were, weren't you?'

'Maybe.'

'You were thinking of the two of you blindfolding each other and sniffing each other's body parts.'

'In space.'

'For God's sake.'

'Feeding each other *Coniglio Affogato Alla Ligure*.'

'Right, stop. Just stop right there. I don't want that image in my head.'

'What difference does it make?'

'It makes all the difference. Start again, but don't think about the sniffing man, think about me.'

'How do you know what I'm thinking?'

'I can tell.'

'This call has been <voice 2> zero hours eight minutes long.'

'You want me to start again?'

'Yes.'

'OK, it's your dime.'

'Yes it is.'

Pause.

'Ohh.'

'Right, that's better, carry on.'

'Ohh.'

'Good.'

'Ohh, yes.'

'Say my name.'

'You haven't told me your name.'

'Chef then.'

'Ohh, God, Chef.'

Pause.

'Ohh, yes. Mmm.'

'OK, stop.'

'What was wrong with that?'

'You're just mocking me.'

'I wasn't.'

'Yes, you were. You were with the sniffing man. I can hear it in your voice, it drops down a tone. It sounds more…'

'Convincing?'

'I don't want you to think about someone else.'

'Do you want me to moan or not?'

'It's got to be about me.'

'What's the difference?'

'I can tell.'

'But I don't know anything about you. I don't know what you look like, how old you are, anything. How can I think about you?'

'What do you think I look like?'

'How the hell should I know.'

'You must have formed some impression.'

'I guess you're a middle-aged man. Hair greying, bit of a belly with all that rich food, crooked teeth, hairy, sweaty maybe, I don't know.'

'Jesus.'

'Well, I don't know, do I?'

'I happen to be very good-looking.'

'OK, then.'

'With a trim figure, good cologne and well-tailored clothes. I'm considered something of a catch as it happens.'

'Well, all right then.'

'And I have a good solid penis. Which is very clean.'

'I'm glad to hear it.'

'So, that's what I am. You think about that. Start again.'

Pause.

'Ohhhh.'

'Stop. God I wish you hadn't told me about this NASA guy, I can't get him out of my head.'

'Me neither.'

'This is stupid. It's advertised as a fantasy about me. I expect you to fantasise about my big dick, all right? Not some greasy big-nosed, sniffing freak.'

'He's not a freak.'

'Some oily, rabbit-eating Cyrano.'

'He's none of those things.'

'I nearly got into space, you stupid woman. I nearly got there myself. And not as a bloody sniffing man, as a bloody astronaut.'

'Right.'

'I did.'

'OK.'

'I was almost a spaceman. I was that close.'

'Sure.'

'That should make you bloody Wet and Wanting.'

'Well...'

'I'm going elsewhere, there must be other phones lines which aren't half so much trouble.'

'I'm sure there are.'

'This call has been <voice 2> zero hours ten minutes long.'

'It's been a twenty-five dollar call and I'm not even... Jesus, what's the use?'

She takes her HEAVEN sign and limps out into the middle of the road. Cars take evasive measures, their horns Doppler as they swerve around her.

She tears up HEAVEN and writes ANYWHERE. She spends time over the letters. She makes them large and three-dimensional and she shades the areas not hit by an imaginary light source.

Cars zoom round her. Shouts from angry drivers filter over on the breeze.

She pats her hair. Applies lipstick. Straightens her dress, and dabs at her bleeding elbows with a tissue. She shifts weight off her damaged knee.

She holds the sign out in front of her and tries a brave smile.

A Triple Three cab approaches. She waves frantically. She jumps up and down.

The cab stops and winds down her windows.

She gets in. The car doesn't move off. Trucks drive past honking their horns. The cab pulls into a lay-by.

Chip sees the cab's window wind down. Smoke curls out from inside. Driver and hitcher sharing a cigarette.

Perhaps they're deciding where ANYWHERE should be.

Freedom Avenue swims a little. The early mist has gone. The sun heats the air. Chip sees the road shimmer. The cab shimmers.

Or it could be the Orbiter swilling around his blood.

The cab pulls away. It heads out of town. Traffic is getting heavy. Early morning rush. The cab lane-hops and disappears over a hill.

Chip pops her popper and pulls her cracker. There's no bang and no gift. Perhaps they were all duds.

T PLUS 1HH 25MM

Sally asks a colleague with medical experience if he thinks it's possible to perform an operation in space.

He says he's a bit busy for a chat.

She says hypothetically, though, does he think it's possible.

He says it would be difficult and messy and there are no scalpels aboard. Why?

She says she has a twinge in her abdomen.

He says really?

The commander says really?

Houston says really?

She says just a twinge.

Houston says they'll keep an eye on her temperature.

Thank you, she says.

The commander tells her to go to her room and rest.

She wants to keep watching. She doesn't want to miss a second. She says she's fine.

The crew continue to work. They look over at her from time to time.

She smiles at them reassuringly.

The first day with the ten brought a message from the *Mir* space station. The *Mir* boys were radio hams and the Captain had the voice downlink. It broke up but they caught 'good luck'.

The Captain asked if anyone knew what *Mir* meant. Everyone said 'Peace' and 'World' and 'both Peace and World'.

The Captain said, 'Good.' He was hoping they'd fluff it so it wouldn't seem like such an easy question. He said things were going to get much harder. He showed the ten library footage: men flying prototypes; men writing formulas on blackboards; men running in tracksuits.

Picture of an aircraft. A KC 135. Following a programmed parabolic path in order to create a zero gravity environment inside the cabin. A group of people in jumpsuits had twenty-second bursts of weightlessness. Caption: The Vomit Comet.

The Captain switched tapes. An old astronaut was being interviewed about life on *Mir*. He was saying weightlessness made his fluids flow upwards. It made his blood plasma volume reduce because his body stopped producing red blood cells. He'd become anaemic. He'd grown five centimetres. He'd lost bone mass and excess calcium deposits had given him kidney stones. His piss had been constantly recycled, he'd had to drink it again and again and again. He said he was a mess.

So no illusions, said the Captain.

The ten put their hands on a sensor and a series of pictures flashed in front of them. The sea, a skull, a mushroom cloud, a baby crying, a breast, a needle, Neptune, a firing squad.

The Captain looked at a readout. He said the breast created the most panic, followed by the firing squad.

Lucky there wasn't a naked firing squad, said the Comedienne.

They were put in front of a series of covered bulbs. As soon as one lit up they had to hit it with a hammer. If they were too slow they got a little electric shock.

'Bash the rat!' said the Probable Winner, and she whacked them ferociously. She bashed the most. She never fried.

The Captain made two teams of five and the ten raced each other passing beachballs. The Captain made five teams of two and they blindfolded each other and led each other round the grounds.

They took it in turns jumping off a ledge into the laced hands of the other nine. It was about trust, said the Captain.

He said if you were weightless you could do backflips. The Probable Winner could already do backflips and she did one in the garden. Everyone clapped.

The Stenographer said that women were much better in space because they had lower blood pressure and weighed less. The men sucked in their stomachs and cut out salt.

The Model said that there were good opportunities for successful people with good physiques. She was being sponsored by a toothpaste company on the condition that, if she got to space, she should at some point tell Houston that 'the stars shone as bright as teeth brushed with Whizz Toothpaste'. She opened her mouth wide and showed her teeth. They gleamed.

Chip congratulated her and asked if she fancied her chances.

Not that highly, she said. The Probable Winner had physical stamina, good balance, a low heart rate, firm breasts, and a doctorate in biological science.

Chip said he didn't have any of those things.

The Model said he also didn't have a contract with a multinational corporation and he ought to think about that. She smiled a gleaming smile.

What about Fresh and Clear? asked Chip.

They could swing, said the Model. Off camera.

The Captain did an experiment designed to judge the effects of sleep deprivation on reaction time. The ten were denied sleep that night and put in a fixed-base driving simulator. A computer-generated image projected a twenty-mile loop of a road and they had to drive down it.

Nine of them careered into digital ditches or veered into oncoming vehicles, but the Probable Winner drove down it all night with no accidents. She kept a clean sheet mile after mile.

The Captain stuck polysomnographic monitoring electrodes to her body.

She looked desperate, nodding at the wheel, slapping her face, biting her knuckles, singing at the top of her voice. You'd never want to get in the car with her. But she kept her speed and she kept dead straight and the computer didn't spot any deterioration.

The Captain wanted to keep her going, eighty, a hundred hours but he was told it was inhumane.

She was asked how she did it.

The Probable Winner said she'd been asleep all her life. She didn't need any more.

The ten worked hard. They lost fat and gained tone. Their lung capacity improved. Their tongues were pink. Their eyes were clear and bright. They tried not to look in the mirror but they were all liking the change.

The next morning brought a boot camp reveille. So did the next morning. And the next. Out of sleep and running round the ground in five minutes dead.

Selectors marshalled the track, and men with cameras waited by benches, waited in trees, waited by puddles of sick. But the coverage wasn't perfect and the ten talked unrecorded on these runs. Prison exercise-yard talk.

Sally overheard conversations.

With sweat pouring down him and his face flushed a violent red the Chef told Chip he thought all his Christmases had come at once what with seven women on the programme and only three men, but all this running was draining his sap.

Chip said sap aside, would he be prepared to screw on camera? The Chef said sure, said he'd done it before. Skin flick when he was younger.

Chip told him he ought to keep that quiet if he wanted to progress. No one wanted porn stars in space.

The Chef said he knew that, although Porn Stars In Space sounded like it could be a good film.

The Chef spat phlegm. He was the least fit. As most chefs are.

They came to an area that looked like a children's playground. They were required to climb over logs, step between tyres, scramble under netting, pull themselves up on bars, swing on ropes and wade through mud.

Sally was mid-field. She thought she'd have to work on her chin-ups.

Out of the blue the Probable Winner fell and cut her knee. Badly. Nastily. Thumpingly. Chip was near. He looked shocked.

She lost yards. Chip tried to help her up. She pushed him away, gritted her teeth and pretended it didn't hurt. But it did.

The Captain admired her pluck. She still looked like a winner. She made up the distance and hit the front. She crossed the line first. She laughed it off. She still had a glint in her eye.

But the cut shook her. She let it get dirty and hid it.

Another morning came with another morning run. Then another and her cut wasn't healing. Her performance dropped off but she didn't rest.

A medic saw her and said, 'Oooh, painful,' and strapped her up and told her to take it easy.

The Captain told her that only she knew her limits.

She didn't ease off. She still won races but now she puked on the finish line. She crawled through tunnels crying out. She muttered to herself as she did press-ups. She fainted.

The Captain told her she risked permanent damage. She was given painkillers and antibiotics and advised to rest. But she didn't. She pushed herself harder. She thought she was stepping up the pace but her times were slipping. She would grab the Captain's stopwatch and say 'No!', say it must be faulty.

They gave her injections. They wouldn't let her swim. She had to change her dressing every hour. She shouted out in her sleep. She squeezed her leg and stuff came out. She cried in the toilets. She was X-rayed and a medic told her that there was something badly wrong with her kneecap.

She was summoned to a room where the Captain waited with a grave face. Grave for the cameras. He hid how much he'd been looking forward to this moment. He told her she was the first to be eliminated.

The Probable Winner's jaw bunched up. She tried to nod her head.

The Captain told her that she should be very proud of herself. He watched her swallow. He wondered if she was going to be able to speak.

She breathed hard. She asked the Captain if it wasn't for the knee, would she still be there, still be in the running?

The Captain said if it wasn't for the knee, she'd be in space. Off the record, he said.

A cameraman followed her down the gravel drive. She got in a car and told the driver to take it fast, but the driver wouldn't. She told him she was going to cry and she didn't want anyone to see that.

The driver slowed. The driver let down the electric windows and cameras poked into the car. She tried to get out and run away. The driver put the child lock on.

She covered her face. Her shoulders shook.

The Captain thought of soundtracks.

ROOM 16. THE CHEF.

'I just glanced out of the window, Chip.'

'Yes.'

'Where's she going?'

'I don't know.'

'Why didn't she come in?'

'I don't know.'

'I knocked on my window at her. I waved.'

'Perhaps she didn't see you.'

'She saw me all right, Chip.'

'Perhaps she doesn't want to get into this.'

'She's got no reason to be embarrassed.'

'She might not see it that way.'

'Seems a shame, I mean to come all this way and then just go without saying hello.'

'Yes.'

'Where do you think she's going, Chip?'

'I don't know. Anywhere.'

'Perhaps it's for the best. I don't think she'd have been much fun anyway.'

'No.'

'She seemed a bit... I don't know.'

'Yes.'

'A bit sour. From a distance anyway.'

'Yes. Listen, about this stripper...'

'I haven't got hold of one yet. I dialled a wrong number.'

'Good, because I don't think...'

'Speaking of which, does the specific number that I called appear on my bill?'

'Yes it does.'

'Oh.'

'I think a stripper might not be appropriate.'

'Who sees those bills?'

'It depends who's on the desk when you check out.'

'If it was you, would you look?'

'I usually don't bother.'

'OK. What about your colleagues?'

'I'm sure they couldn't care less either.'

'They don't like to check up on these things and have a bit of a snigger?'

'We're usually too busy.'

'No one's too busy for a snigger.'

'What do you want me to say, Brian?'

'Nothing. I guess I want you to say nothing.'

The E Z doors talk of keeping it together.

Take deep breaths.

Take stock.

Take your life into your hands.

Chip kicks them.

Stay calm.

Stay relaxed.

Violence never solved anything.

Chip tries to prise out the panic button. It's wedged in. He knocks on Lost Property to ask if the cleaner knows of any way to open the doors. Perhaps she could talk to them.

Perhaps voice recognition will loosen them.

She tells him that once the panic button is pushed the doors clam up till the emergency services arrive.

Chip looks at the E Z Map. There isn't a fire service marked.

The cleaner wants to know if the counter is clicking over.

The doors are juddering like chattering teeth and registering one customer a second.

She whoops. That's seven and a half cents a minute. Four dollars fifty an hour. More than she gets cleaning. She could take the day off.

Chip glugs Orbiter. It's getting flat. It leaves his head spinning and a nasty taste in his mouth. Should've kept the cork, he mutters, Should've...

OUTSIDE LINE.

'This is the E Z Sleep.'

'...'

'Hello? This is the E Z, can I help?'

'...'

'Are you in a call box, caller?'

'...'

'Put your coins in now.'

'You know I'm not in a call box.'

Pause.

'Is that you then?'

'Yes it is, Chip. In a Triple Three cab going anywhere.'

Pause.

'Sorry to see you go, I was hoping that—'

'The way in which someone answers the telephone represents their opinion of themselves, did you know that?'

'No.'

'The sound of one's voice communicates whether the person is attractive or not because the voice reflects back, as self-confidence, natural ease, or self-attention, all the desirous and admiring glances they have ever received.'

'I see.'

'This is supposed to apply mainly to women's voices but in my view it also applies to men's.'

'Right.'

'I'd guess from your hello that you haven't had many admiring glances, at least not recently. But then that's probably to do with your arm, isn't it?'

'Yes.'

'I notice you didn't come out when I fell off the Pancake Parlour roof.'

'The doors are jammed shut. I was trying to.'

'I could've been seriously injured.'

'What were you doing?'

'Sending up my own rocket, Chip. A little launch of my own. But accidents happen. I killed a bird, I had a bad fall.'

'Why don't you come back? I've got Orbiter.'

'I nearly didn't come at all. I was the first to get kicked out, I didn't last a week. I figured everyone would be laughing at me.'

'Not at all.'

'But then ... I don't know, as it got closer to today ... anyway I got on a plane.'

'Good for you.'

'I've got a plastic kneecap.'

'Really?'

'Get yourself a plastic arm, Chip. It's a wonderful material. The new knee's flexible, it bends, I've got a scar but normally I feel like a new woman.'

'I'm glad.'

'But not today.'

'No.'

'I saw that chef prick at a window on the first floor.'

'Yes, he was the first to arrive. Do you want to speak to him?'

'No. Do you think he tripped me?'

'I don't think he did, no.'

'I thought he did. I was streets ahead of everyone. He got jealous, so he tripped me. That's what I thought at the time. But now I don't think he tripped me at all. I think you did.'

'I—'

'You were near.'

'This is one of the reasons—'

'You stuck out your leg and I went head over heels.'

'This is why I wanted you to come, to apologise, to try to make—'

'You admit it?'

'It wasn't entirely deliberate.'

'My God, you admit it.'

'Like I said—'

'I wasn't sure it was you, but here you are, holding your hands . . . holding your hand up to it.'

'I don't know what to say.'

'I was coming here to tell everyone I've moved on. I'm past it. I've found new challenges. I'm in great shape and I don't think badly of whoever tripped me at all. How about that?'

'Well, that's good.'

'It's crap. Now I know for sure it's you, I hate you. I could've gone to space.'

'I know.'

'It could've been me up there right now. Up in the stars.'

'Or me.'

'Yes, but mostly me. Everyone knew that.'

'I'm sorry.'

'I was the firm favourite.'

'Yes.'

'The Captain said so.'

'Yes.'

'I couldn't watch the launch. I felt too sick.'

'I got dizzy.'

'Good. I'm glad you got dizzy. You deserve to get dizzy.'

'I know.'

Pause.

'I'm going to a bar with this Triple Three driver. She knows a place where they bad mouth astronauts.'

'Come back.'

'I don't want to see anyone.'

'Please.'

'You shouldn't have tripped me up, you shit.'

Chip throws the Orbiter bottle against the wall. Glass covers the lobby floor. He waits to see if the hotel will slide into the Righteous Stream.

I name this party the *Titanic*.

From the lobby he sees that a couple of men from a company called Intense Tents are erecting a small marquee in the car park. They have the framework assembled and they are dragging a blue tarpaulin out of a truck. Chip can see bunting. He can see trestle tables. He can see plastic chairs.

They throw a canvas over the poles and work from inside. They lift the tent up onto its knees, then to its feet. Guy ropes are pulled and weighted. A banner is unfurled. Space Party. It has a picture of the shuttle on it. A black face waves from a porthole. Nine people wave back. In the picture he has two arms. The breeze makes it flutter.

The tent door is zipped shut and one of the men jogs over to the E Z and slips an invoice through the crack in the E Z doors.

The doors whimper.

He gets into the truck and the Intense Tents men drive away.

Chip picks up the fire extinguisher and hurls it at the doors.

It bounces back.

He sets off the fire extinguisher. A little dribble of foam emerges from the nozzle. He shakes it. It splutters and spits then spurts onto the doors.

The doors open an inch then close. Then open an inch then close.

Staff are armed.

Staff are armed.

Staff are armed.

ROOM 16. THE CHEF.

<Music>

'Thank you for—'

Bleep.

'You have chose—'

Bleep. Bleep.

'… 'ot girl—'

Bleep. Bleep. Bleep. Bleep.

'Hello?'

'What's so fucking special about the NASA sniffing guy?'

'Hey—'

'What is it? Has he got a foot-long cock or something?'

'You've elected Friendly Conversation. That's not very friendly.'

'You think he's Neil Armstrong 'cos he's got a NASA jumpsuit, right? He tells you he's been rigorously trained, he's had his nose tested out by top scientists. He tells you chemicals evaporate quicker in a capsule. He tells you that a bad smell can jeopardise whole missions and he's got the most important job in the space programme. He tells you astronauts need to wear nappies on space walks and that he has to sniff those too and that really turns you on.'

'Give me a break'

'What's his name?'

'This is none of your business.'

'It's something butch, isn't it? Something faux pioneering like Buzz Picard.'

'Don't be stupid.'

'Something made up and Russian, Vladimir Asimov.'

'No.'

'So, what's he called?'

'I'm not telling you.'

'Ha! I knew it, he doesn't exist.'

'He does so exist.'

'You're making him up.'

'I'm not, he's kind and funny and I'm cooking him *Coniglio Affogato Alla Ligure* tonight.'

Pause.

'Well?'

'This call has been <voice 2> three minutes long.'

'You still there?'

'I hope you damn well choke on it.'

Hey Jesus pumps from Lost Property. Modern rock hymns. The cleaner drowning out her door voice. The Jesus broadcaster blares out. The Lord loves the repentant. He hears them. He's there for them. The broadcaster is hoarse. All that shuttle shouting. But there's still passion in the cracked voice. He tells his listeners a shuttle won't help them reach the stars. Shuttles are just lumps of metal carrying bad hopes and bad dreams. Only the Lord could start a ministry on Mars. Only the Lord could tell aliens about the Heavenly Father. Only the Lord would put a cross on the moon. Being an astronaut doesn't make you a saint. The commander was a test pilot. Did he see God at twice the speed of sound? The commander was blind to Him but He was there.

The pilot flew over the Holy Land, did he see Jesus' smiling face in the clouds? The pilot was blind to Him but He was there. The crew were scientists. Did they find the Holy Spirit inside atoms and between molecules? They were blind to It but It was there. He saves the space tourist for last. He says she saw a black Madonna on top of a mountain in Italy and knew that she too had to get up high. And thought she could do it in a tin, he says. An unholy tin! His voice crackles. He breaks down. The signal buzzes. Perhaps too much spit has hit the microphone. He takes calls. He prophesies.

Someone rings to say they can see streaks of light in the sky.

Praise be, says the broadcaster. Don't put on dark glasses. Be blinded by the light. He is weeping. Sobs rack the E Z Sleep. Chip puts his fingers in his ears.

Now is the time to confess.

Now is the time to acknowledge your failings.

ROOM 11. MR MOULIN AND NANCY CARTER. OUTSIDE LINE.

'This is the E Z Slumber Hotel, part of the E Z chain, my name is Dennis, how—'

'I thought I told you to cut that down, Dennis.'

'So you did, sir, sorry.'

'Get me Jackoff Jackson.'

<laughter>

'Giggle all you want, Dennis, you can have that one for free. Jackoff Jackson. It's pretty good, isn't it? I'm on fire today.'

'Yes, sir.'

'I'm surprised you haven't heard it before.'

'We have another name, sir.'

'Good lad, what is it?'

'I probably shouldn't—'

'Come on, I'm the top of the E Z food chain here. What is it?'

'Jellyroll Jackson, sir.'

'That's not bad. It's not as good as Jackoff Jackson but then that's why I'm the head honcho.'

'Yes, sir.'

'OK, put him through.'

'Putting you through now.'

Click click.

'Hello?'

'Mr Jackoff Jellyroll Jackson?'

'What?'

'You know, I'm starting to warm to Dennis on the desk, he has a hitherto hidden sense of fun. You should probably fire him for insubordination, but he'll certainly bounce back.'

'What time is it?'

'Six? I don't know. What do I care? Listen, my mind is diamond sharp here, I've been bitten by this Le Dormier Facile concept and I can't shake it off. I'm thinking total refurbishment. I'm thinking we ditch all our existing food arrangements, in particular the club sandwiches. I'm thinking Orbiter in every room. I'm thinking we sever our arrangement with the Pancake Parlour.'

'Sever?'

'Right. Have you ever set foot in one of those places?'

'We have a Pancake Pantry here, sir. I was planning on dining there for breakfast this morning.'

'Dining? Not the word I'd use. I'm thinking continental breakfasts, Jackson. Croissants, real butter, linen napkins. That kind of thing, *what do you think, hot stuff?*'

'Well, sir, I—'

'Not you, I'm asking Nancy here. *Would you go for hot croissant first thing in the morning?...* She's nodding here, Jackson, I think this idea's a winner.'

'Nancy, sir?'

'Yeah, Nancy. You could bounce a tennis ball off her ass and it'd ping back and hit you in the nuts before you had time to blink.'

'Really.'

'We haven't tried that yet, but it's on the agenda. In the meantime, Le Dormier Facile, come on, give me ideas, let's brainstorm.'

'As I said before, sir, this may not be quite the right time. I think we have some rather important guests staying with us for the next couple of days.'

'Important guests? What the hell are you talking about? No one important stays at the E Z chain.'

'Dennis thought he saw some secret service men checking out the security arrangements yesterday.'

'Dennis said that?'

'Yes, sir.'

'Well, that's just his excitable imagination. Dennis is just a kid, he wouldn't know a secret service man if he got poked in the ass by one. I'll bet it was just a couple of guys in mirror sunglasses. Well-dressed truckers. Or homos.'

'He seemed pretty sure, sir. What's more, the entire hotel has been block booked, including the conference suite.'

'What?'

'Booked and paid for. The hotel's been emptied.'

'Emptied?'

'The guests who were already here have been put on a coach.'

'Well, who's coming then? Some Saudi? Why's a Saudi wanting to stay at the E Z?'

'It's not a Saudi, sir, we're thinking it might be something political.'

'Not some fucking neo-Nazi outfit, I'm hoping.'

'Something a little more significant, sir.'

'Well, what then? Who? Do we have any names?'

'The booking's been made under the name of the Global Security Council.'

'Who're they? What do we know about them?'

'Dennis is making some inquiries.'

'Dennis? For God's sake, Jackson, take this one on yourself. Why wasn't I told about this sooner?'

'Well…'

'This is bad management. I should come over.'

'I wouldn't have said that was necessary, sir—'

'Wait a minute, I've got another call.'

Click click.

'What is it?'

'Chip on Reception.'

'Quick, what?'

'The doors are jammed. No one can get in or out.'

'Did you press the panic button?'

'Yes.'

'You asshole. Don't press anything. Get someone out to fix it.'

'No one will come.'

'Don't bother me with this stuff. I'm dealing with a major situation here. I've got something called the Global Security Council coming to the Slumber and I don't need to think about jammed doors.'

'Sir, it's important that guests can—'

'Jammed doors are a low priority.'

'I appreciate that.'

'I don't even know what the Global Security Council is but it sounds more major than jammed doors.'

'Yes, but—'

'Ring any bells for you?'

'I don't have any idea, sir, perhaps it's the Bilderberg group. Either way, these doors—'

'You what?!'

'I think there must be a main fuse somewhere. If we can just—'

'You think it's the Bilderberg boys? Christ, Chip.'

'I don't know anything, sir, I'm just saying—'

'Like a kind of *nom de guerre*? It's possible. These guys are pretty secretive.'

'Well...'

'Fuck. The fucking Bilderberg.'

'I'm saying if we can find the fuse then perhaps—'

'OK, OK, let me think. Right, good. Chip? You've done well here. I... I've got to ring off. You stay put.'

'I can't get out.'

Click click.

'Jackson?'

'Yes, sir.'

'It's the Bilderberg group.'

'Sir, with respect, I hardly think that's likely.'

'Chip recognised the name straight off. It's a pseudonym.'

'One-armed Chip?'

'He's a smart kid. English. He probably went to school with some royal and got to know about this kind of thing. I'm coming over.'

'Sir, perhaps just give us a few hours to look into this. I'll make some inquiries and then you can decide. I honestly think it's something more straightforward.'

'When are they arriving?'

'The hotel had to be empty by nine, so perhaps that's when—'

'This morning?'

'Yes, sir.'

'For crying out loud. Why am I being told this so late?'

'I didn't think it was important, sir.'

'The course of world events is about to change in one of my hotels and you didn't think it was important?'

'We don't know for sure—'

'I'm packing now. Call me here if anything happens.'

'Sir—'

Click click.

'Reception.'

'Chip, I think you're right, I think you're on to something. I think we've got the Bilderbergs on our hands.'

'Here?'

'No, not here, God help them if they came here. I mean at the E Z Slumber in Alabama. I've got to get up there, order me a cab.'

'What about these doors, sir?'

'You know why they're called the Bilderberg group, Chip? Is it run by someone called Bilderberg?'

'It takes its name from the Bilderberg Hotel, in Holland, where the first meeting took place.'

'Jeez, you're kidding? Takes its name from a hotel?'

'Yes, sir.'

'We could have a splinter group calling itself the E Z Slumber Group.'

'Well…'

'That doesn't sound too good, does it, Chip?'

'Not too good.'

'Perhaps I should move hyper fast to get the name changed to Le Dormier Facile.'

'Are you sure it's the—'

'Anyway, these are details, I've got to get moving, I've got to make sure that Rockefeller, or the Spanish prime minister, doesn't get fucking microwaved club sandwiches. We need you there, Chip, to fry the bacon up specially.'

'Thank you, sir, but—'

'I'm not being serious, I need two-handed staff on this. Get me a cab. Get me a good one. I don't want the Dutch premier seeing me get out of a crapheap. In fact, get me a limo. I want to arrive in style.'

Chip makes a sign:

> Space Party. Doors broken. Wait in marquee. If you need a
> piss or shit then…

He crosses it out. His phantom arm slaps his side. It finds the stuck
doors hilarious. Should've anticipated mechanical failure, Chip mutters.
Should've…

He looks through the Yellow Pages. Lightning Conductors.
Lightweight Furniture. Lime Suppliers. Limestone Quarries. Linen –
Decorative. Linen – Household. No Limousines.

There used to be a Luxury Limo Company. It only ever took
people to the Club California but Club California got shut down
because it watered down its booze with Fresh and Clear. People
noticed that their cocktails tasted of mouthwash. So when Club
California went bust, Luxury Limo went bust too.

There are only cab companies now.

And Jim.

Jim was stashing cash away for the time when space tourism was
available for the likes of one-legged cab drivers. He advised Chip to
keep some back too. Then they could go together. Drink cocktails on
the Space Station. Perhaps get lucky with a couple of foxy cosmo-
nauts. These holiday romances were the sweetest.

Jim would need to spruce up the cab to achieve a limo standard.
Give it a wash. Put new cushions in the back. But Jim had a peaked cap,
left behind by a zoo keeper. That would give him the chauffeur feel.

OUTSIDE LINE.

'Where are you, Jim? I think I may have a fare for you.'

'Buying me off, huh? Party guilt.'

'Don't be like that.'

'I'm at the airport, and I tell you, the 747s look lumbering compared to the shuttle. When you've seen the vertical take-off these runways look mediaeval.'

'Are you coming here, then?'

'As it happens I am, Chip. I'm on my way. I'm driving with the window open, and the air is cooling the cigarette burns and defumigating the car.'

<laugh>

'Is there someone in the car with you, Jim?'

'I can't divulge that to you, Chip.'

'I thought I heard a laugh.'

'That's just the air bag.'

<laugh>

'Have you picked someone up, Jim?'

'I told you. The air bag's got a mouth on it… <Hey>… it looks like a woman now, like if you had a sister… <laugh>… I think it might be more sympathetic, it might lay off the dirty jokes and talk to me positively, stress my good points.

<laugh>

'Jim…'

'So I think your party might go with a swing. I'm thinking that I'm going to be gatecrashing because I've seen the quality of your guests.'

<laugh>

'The party's a non-starter.'

'It'll be starting soon, friend. Starting with a bang. I'll be there in twenty. I'll break some speed limits.'

A s Sally passes over South America she prods her stomach. Her insides turn over. Perhaps the increased land mass is pulling her organs off course.

She prods again above the Pacific Ocean. Same.

She puts it out of her mind.

She thinks Captain Cook might have written 'explorations are full of little tragedies' on the side of his ship. And if he didn't, someone did. Perhaps a philosophical crewman dying of scurvy. Carving it with a penknife after Cook tells him that now he's observed Venus crossing the sun he wants to go south to New Zealand. The crewman thinks Tahiti to New Zealand is two months and he hates Cook. He carves 'I hate Cook' and because he's got time on his hands he makes an ornate job of it. The Maoris hate Cook too. They chuck spears at him. Cook opens fire and kills a couple of them. Then he goes to Australia, New Holland on his map even though no Dutchman had set foot in the place. Cook names some capes and some bays. At Botany Bay a couple of Aborigines take offence at Cook. They want Cook to get the hell off their land. They throw darts at him. Cook thinks they might be poisoned so he shoots them too. A couple more little tragedies of exploration.

Sally thinks she may be having a little tragedy of her own. She asks the commander if anyone has performed surgery in space.

He tells her that astronauts have been living and working in space for over thirty years without the need for surgical procedures. He stresses the word astronauts.

She says studies of Polaris submarine statistics revealed 269 surgical cases in 7,650,000 man days, of which 70 were appendectomies. So although it was rare, these little anomalies did …

The commander asks if she still has her appendix.

She says no, sir.

Well, there are you then, he says.

Well, there you are then, says Houston.

She asks if anyone else has their appendix.

No one has.

She tells them that technically the appendix is an organ. An organ with no known function except that of being available for agonising removal.

They grunt at her.

She was terrified of this as a child. Her father told her that the appendix was much bigger in man's early history and he used it to digest rough, woody foods. Since man now ate soft, yielding food it had no purpose so, feeling neglected, it would spectacularly explode, spurting poison into the bloodstream. She ate bark to give it some utility. She had to have her stomach opened and the bark removed. That was her first hospital visit. She begged them to take out the appendix too. After she came out of the anaesthetic her father said they had done.

Though the twinges are still there and she's not feeling so sure any more.

The crew have stopped listening.

Houston butts in. Houston says they're checking her medical records. They say it's impossible to perform any kind of operation in space. They've only done it on the shuttle *Columbia*. But that was on rats.

Did they live? she asks.

They're checking that too.

They check it.

No. They died.

Houston says the best plan is to take antibiotics and kill any infection while it's at the early stages. It would, however, make her a little nauseous and she would experience a drop in energy.

She says she understands.

Houston says they'll monitor her readings and make a decision in an hour if her situation has in any way deteriorated.

Understood, she says.

The commander looks over at her.

Are you sweating? he asks.

It's good sweat, not bad sweat she says. And she smiles. And she tells them she'll stop interrupting now. She'll stop making a fuss.

She drifts away.

With the Probable Winner gone, the nine looked for a new front runner. No one wanted the lead. They were thinking of the pace-makers in middle distance races who took the pack to record time then got overtaken as the finish line approached.

The nine found a target in the garden. Twenty feet in diameter. Sprayed on the grass.

The Captain spoke with urgency and determination of purpose. He issued crucial instructions. They listened and their stomachs tied themselves in knots.

That afternoon she jumped out of an aeroplane.

Her cameraman jumped with her. He had a camera attached to his crash helmet and he filmed her face in close-up. Eyes and mouth wide open for both fear and delight.

She shouted, 'This is something else, isn't it?'

The cameraman didn't answer.

She shouted, 'I hope I miss the barbed wire.'

She shouted, 'Whooo-hoooo!'

The cameraman didn't crack a smile and landed like a ballet

dancer. She wondered why he wasn't chosen to go into space.

She hit the ground and rolled. She stood up. Breathing hard. Legs shaking. She looked up and remembered she was as high as a cloud.

Chip landed near her. He was laughing too. He said he was lost for words.

The Captain ran up to Chip. He knew that people said unsophisticated things after they'd jumped out of a plane. Relief and adrenalin gave them a child's vocabulary. He wanted Chip to squeal or cry or hug the Captain. The Captain had a good put down if he tried to hug him. He told the cameraman to film Chip from an unflattering angle.

Chip said that as he was drifting down he saw a house on fire on the horizon. Smoke and flames and sparks. He saw fire engines speed up approach roads. He saw a crowd of people trying to help, and on the breeze he heard wailing and crying and the shouts of desperate men. He smelt burning wood and burning tar. He said when he left the plane he was terrified of being in the air but when he saw the house on fire he was terrified of being on the ground.

The Captain was disappointed. He wanted Chip to whoop so that he could say, 'This is child's play to an astronaut.' He didn't want Chip to tell him about a burning house on the horizon.

The Captain said he landed like a sack of potatoes and missed the target by a mile. He told him to gather up his parachute and go to the house.

I didn't see a burning house, said Sally.

Chip said he didn't either, but he pointed one out to his cameraman so the cameraman would try to film that rather than film Chip's terrified face.

They watched the Holiday Rep descend. The Captain ran out to meet her. She was excitable, she'd give him his whoops and cries.

She landed in a heap and the parachute drifted down on top of her, covering her.

The Captain started pulling it off, laughing and joking and telling her she had landed like a shot pheasant.

She screamed and snatched the parachute away from him and pulled it back over her head.

He asked her if she was hurt.

She told him to leave her alone.

He said it's common to break an ankle.

She said she hadn't broken anything, she just wanted to stay under the material.

He said she had to fold up her parachute and go back to the house.

She said she was staying put. She wasn't going anywhere and anyone who tried to make her was going to get scratched and bitten.

The Captain turned to the camera and said, 'This sometimes happens,' though he'd never seen it before in his life. The Holiday Rep stayed under the parachute all night. She didn't let a cameraman under so it was filmed from a distance. Inside the house the rest of the nine glanced out of the window, saying how excitable people were subject to these wild ups and downs.

Chip brought her out an apple and some milk and stayed talking to her under the material by torchlight. In the darkness the parachute looked like an insect pupa.

Chip came back inside.

What's up? asked the others.

Chip said she had chronic vertigo. Space was the last place she should be.

Sally looked out of the window early next morning and the chute was flat. The Holiday Rep had gone.

The Captain said, 'Yep,' like he saw it coming.

OUTSIDE LINE.

'EZ Sleep.'

'Hi, Chip.'

'How great. Where…? Are you coming?'

'I'm in this big tent in your car park.'

'Really? I didn't see you go in.'

'It's nice. Is this where we've having the party?'

'Yes. I've got party poppers and some Orbiter.'

'Funny being under canvas again.'

'Canvas? Oh, I see…'

'I think what I'll do is unzip some of the window flaps to air the inside.'

'Good idea.'

'And while I'm here I could arrange the tables and chairs.'

'Don't feel you have to.'

'And perhaps use one of the tables as a platform.'

'A platform?'

'For speeches.'

'I wasn't thinking of having—'

'I've got mine written out. I wrote it on the plane, on a napkin.'

'Oh.'

'By the way. I don't know if you noticed, but I've got this marker pen and on the space party banner I've blacked out your eyes and your teeth and I've drawn devil's horns on your head.'

'Yes, I see that now.'

'Pretty funny, huh?'

'Look, I understand why you might be—'

'Do you want to hear this speech? You might want to vet it.'

'Well …'

'I'll tell you what I've got, just so you know where to place it in case there are other speeches.'

'It's—'

'"Ladies and gentlemen, I'm sure we'd all like to thank Chip for inviting us today and for hosting this event on this special day."'

'That sounds fine.'

'"Like you, I was hoping to write off this particular chapter in my life, but sometimes it's good to revisit painful times and so let's raise a glass to Chip for reopening this wound. To Chip." What do you think of it so far?'

'Like I said, I wasn't thinking of having—'

'After the toast, I was going to continue thus: "I wonder if any of you have heard of benign paroxysmal positional vertigo." Then I thought I'd ask for a show of hands. And I mean that in the nicest possible way, Chip.'

'Look, about that—'

'"Benign paroxysmal positional vertigo. This is a condition caused by crystals of calcium carbonate in the utricle. Its symptoms include nausea, imbalance, and altitude panic. Sounds serious, doesn't it, ladies and gentlemen? Well, it is. Under normal circumstances, the crystals would be dissolved and reabsorbed by the dark cells of the labyrinth. Did you realise there was a part of the ear called the labyrinth? Well, there is and its job is to dissolve crystals. But some circumstances aren't normal, some circumstances are stressful, an astronaut selection programme for example, and if you feel light-headed and disorientated it probably means the labyrinth is infected and that's very serious, that's a real kick in the guts because there's no known cure. It can hamper one's daily activities, it can cause unease and distress, it can prevent the sufferer from, off the top of my head, going into space." '

'Please...'

' "Yes, ladies and gentlemen, symptoms are precipitated by change of position with respect to gravity. How do I know this? Because a medical expert told me. A medical expert? you ask. Actually no, ladies and gentlemen, that was no medical expert, that was Chip. Chip thinks it's very dangerous for someone with vertigo to go into space. And here to tell you more about this condition is Chip. Chip, ladies and gentlemen." At which point I thought I'd invite you onto the stage to say a few words.'

'I know this is difficult...'

'Then I thought you'd take the microphone, we do have a microphone, don't we?'

'No.'

'We should get one, amplification is important. You take the microphone and say that it's true that someone with an infected labyrinth should probably avoid space, but symptoms of light-headedness and disorientation could be anything, could be stress, could be blood sugar, could be the rush of blood from a first parachute jump. In fact, the chances of it being benign paroxysmal positional vertigo were about a million to one and, on reflection, and you have had a number of years to reflect, on reflection it was silly of you to shine the torch in my ear and tut and say that you could see pus and inflammation, and that an infected ear should have been picked up at the medical. On reflection it was perhaps unkind to make me cry and say how humiliating it was to be eliminated by the Captain and how it was so much more dignified to slip away quietly and avoid the cameras. You think, on reflection, that you misjudged the situation, and that now you're very sorry for taking advantage of my trusting nature and you hope that my return to the holiday trade hasn't been too much of a let down.'

'I'm—'

'At which point I was going to grab the microphone and shout, "As it happens it has been a terrible, terrible fucking let down." '

'This is why I wanted—'

'Is it all right to swear? We're adults. I think we're probably OK with that.'

'This is why I wanted you to come. To apologise. To—'

'I went to the launch, Chip.'

'I know. I saw you on the TV.'

'In space, you're so high up you're beyond vertigo.'

'I know.'

'Far beyond. That's what you should have told me.'

'Yes.'

'You should have told me something kind and reassuring.'

'I know. I'm sorry.'

'Hire a microphone, Chip. I'll need to hear it loud and clear.'

Sensors have detected that there is enough daylight in the E Z lobby and the fluorescents flicker off. The Night Time Lavender air-freshener switches to Dewy Morning Pine. Chip drinks another cup of Orbiter. He pops a party popper. He sucks an E Z Mint. Should've anticipated bitterness, he mutters. Should've . . .

Soft Furnishings, Solar Energy, Spas & Whirlpools.

No Sound Equipment Hire.

He takes an E Z Map and rolls it into a cone. He speaks through the small end.

I'm sorry.

The sound bounces off the end wall of the lobby and returns to him sounding hollow. He screws up his E Z Megaphone. He would just have to shout if those at the back missed his apology.

Space Planners.

He wonders what the space planners do. He calls them up. A recorded message tells him he can organise his apartment, and thereby his life, in three easy steps. They will help him clear his room, his heart, his mind, but there is currently no one in the office to take his call.

ROOM 15, NANCY CARTER, TO ROOM 11, MR MOULIN.

'I've left my earring in there.'

'Nancy, sorry to kick you out.'

'Practically threw me out the door.'

'Things have moved on apace here, I've got to deal with a situation. I've got to get busy with the telephone. You understand.'

'Sure, sure.'

'You can have the room, I'm going to Alabama. Just give me a few minutes to pack. I'll leave the earring on the bedside table. Don't get cold on me, this is important.'

'Yeah, the Bilderbergs shmilderbergs are at your other hotel, la la la.'

'Now look, you shouldn't have been listening. I was having a private conversation. Technically that's spying.'

'Spying? You had your hands on my ass.'

'I'm not going to get into the ethics of this, Nancy. Suffice it to say I don't want you blabbing about this, OK?'

'It sounds like a pretty good story. I might tag along.'

'Don't you get any Pulitzer dreams about this one, Nancy. This is major league. If it's true, this is an organisation which is full of very, very serious men. You start wagging your tongue and someone in a big car with tinted windows will pay you a visit and shoot you in the face.'

'I don't think so.'

'I mean it, Nancy, they don't fuck around. You think the people who, I don't know, started the Gulf War or killed Kennedy would think twice about shooting some nobody journalist?'

'Even if they had a nice ass?'

'You better take this seriously, young lady. You better give yourself the cold shower of reality.'

'The what?'

'You want to spend your life looking over your shoulder? Puking with fear every time the doorbell rings? They'd make it look like suicide too. The police would find your prints all over the gun and a note in your handwriting saying how you couldn't stand it any more and your life's been a tissue of lies and make-believe.'

'It has.'

'Come on.'

'I mean it, it has.'

'Look, all right, I don't want to get into this right now. You're playing with fire, so let's just agree that you'll keep this Bilderberg thing to yourself.'

'What's it like at the E Z Slumber?'

'You're not coming with me, Nancy. Seriously, forget the whole thing.'

'Does it have a swimming pool? A casino? I like glamour.'

'It doesn't have any of that stuff, OK? It's faceless and functional. You'd hate it.'

'Champagne in every room?'

'Perhaps the odd bottle of Orbiter but nothing to write home about. Please, Nancy, let me get on with this.'

'Why is such an important group of people staying then?'

'Precisely because it's so anonymous. God, don't you see how clever it is? You've got a lot to learn, kid. But you're cute, you know? I had a great time. Perhaps when I've revamped this whole chain and there actually are swimming pools and casinos, then maybe we can get together again. Stay in the Moulin Room.'

'E Z Slumber has a Moulin Room?'

'No, but when it becomes Le Dormier Facile it'll be the premier suite.'

'You gonna torture people to death in there?'

'What?'

'Electrify the bed?'

'Moulin means mill in French. I'm going to have a windmill theme in there.'

'Windmills?'

'With old millstones in the restaurant and bags of flour.'

'People will think the room refers to Jean Moulin, leader of the French Resistance. He was tortured to death in a hotel room.'

'I didn't know that.'

'You could have the cleaner come in and break the guests' arms.'

'All right, perhaps the Moulin Room isn't such a good idea, look—'

'You should have a Sacha Distel Room instead, more romantic.'

'I'm not discussing this any more.'

'Or a Charles Trent Room. You could pipe in "La Mer" to get honeymooners in the mood.'

'Sure. Good idea. Bye then, Nancy. Chip'll give you a call when I'm out of this room.'

ROOM 11. MR MOULIN.

'Chip. Any way of disabling the room-to-room function on the telephone?'

'No.'

'Damn. Did you know Jean Moulin, leader of the French Resistance, died in a hotel room?'

'Yes, sir.'

'I find that kind of creepy.'

'Sir, the front door—'

'What the hell is that in the car park?'

'It's a marquee.'

'Who authorised that?'

'Well, I did, sir, I was meaning to—'

'There's nowhere to park any more. How the hell is my limo going to find a space?'

'I think we need to address the problem of the door, sir.'

'Smash them open. When this limo arrives I'll need to leave by the doors.'

'Sir…'

'I'm not climbing out the windows, boy. I don't want to shake the British prime minister's hand with broken fingers.'

7.00a.m.

C hip feels watched. The old man has been sitting in Pancake
Parlour all night. From his window seat he'd glance over at the
E Z every once in a while. Chip noticed him eating eggs when the
Chef arrived. He was drinking coffee when the Probable Winner
jumped off the roof. He was picking his teeth when the marquee was
being erected. Now Chip can see him standing at the payphone near
the Pancake Parlour toilets. He is dressed smartly. A suit. He has a
snazzy tie around his neck with a matching handkerchief in his breast
pocket. Chip wonders what…

OUTSIDE LINE

'E Z Sleep.'

'Your party looks a little crappy.'

'Who is this?'

'Where is everyone?'

'I don't know who you are, sir, but—'

'An invitation addressed to my daughter dropped through my
letterbox.'

'Oh…'

'I would've passed the invitation on but I don't know where she
is. I've been opening her mail for some time now, her polling company
want her to do surveys about shopping habits, her tax return is due,
she's won a holiday to Dundee. I forward them to addresses in Spain,
France, I can't remember. Your invitation was so decently written and
it sounded like such a lovely idea that I thought I'd come in the hope

HELLOLAND

189

of catching up with her. She's bad at keeping in touch, you see. Very bad. I thought she might be here, might fancy a little reunion. Anyway, I've been watching the doors and I haven't seen her arrive.'

'Hardly anyone has arrived.'

'She didn't come yesterday?'

'No.'

'I can't see her skulking in the corner, can I?'

'She isn't here.'

'Oh. Well that's disappointing.'

'Yes, it is.'

'Perhaps I could attend in her stead so that if she regretted missing it, I could give her a moment-by-moment description of the event. And take pictures. I've got my camera.'

'I was hoping it would be a private—'

'That's the sort of thing fathers should do for their children. Do you have children?'

'No.'

'You should try and rectify that as soon as possible. Children are made after one's own image. They might deny it but they're cut from the same cloth. They are a chip off the old block, if you'll pardon the expression.'

'Sir...'

'I'm very proud of my daughter. And I have reason to be. She was one of the favourites. She wasn't strictly speaking eliminated either. She just walked away. That takes a special kind of maturity. To know what you want, and know what you don't want.'

'She ran away.'

'Don't take that tone, sonny.'

'Sorry.'

'Don't take that tone about my daughter.'

'I didn't mean to.'

'You're not so perfect yourself.'

'I know.'

'There was talk of you sabotaging a couple of the other candidates. What do you think about that?'

'The purpose of today was to try to—'

'Sure, some of them, no doubt, needed sabotaging. Especially the one who won, the black… the black…'

'What?'

'I bet you sabotaged my daughter.'

'No, I didn't.'

'Saboteurs are capable of anything, particularly denials.'

'I admit that I may have, in a few cases—'

'There. There from your own mouth.'

'Listen—'

'Guilty! Guilty of ruining everything for her. For me. For our whole family. I knew it. I've been brooding above it all night.'

'No.'

'You shit. You little shit.'

The old man runs out of Pancake Parlour and grabs a big bin on wheels and he drags it over towards the E Z.

Chips tapes the panic button closed so there's no danger of it popping out.

The old man gets up a head of steam and sends the bin careering towards the doors.

The doors brace themselves.

The bin hits top speed and crashes through them.

Glass and rubbish burst into the lobby. The doors collapse.

Chip ducks flying splinters.

The doors' voice shrieks and slurs and then stutters out of breath.

Packets of Shuttle-Shake mix, old bacon, waffles, coffee filters, and napkins, spill out onto the floor.

The old man breathes hard. He uses what strength he has left to run away.

Chip's heart pounds in his chest. Should've specified no families. Should've...

ROOM 11. MR MOULIN.

'What's the problem?'

'We had a breakage in the lobby, sir, the doors have been smashed.'

'Not that. What's the problem with this fucking limo?'

'Sorry, sir, I haven't found a suitable company.'

'Come on damn it, get me out of here. I've got some half-wit called Dennis at the E Z Slumber about to offer the head of the World Bank E Z Krackers 'n' Kream.'

'I have a friend who is able to give you a ride.'

'A friend?'

'Jim, he doesn't have a limo but—'

'You want me to drive to the Bilderbergs in a car driven by someone called Jim?'

'Well, he's—'

'I need a limo. I need it bad. There are things going on at the E Z Slumber which could make your other arm fall off. A new war could be getting planned, or some coup against your own prime minister, and I'm stuck here like a tit in the breeze.'

'It's only me on the desk.'

'Don't burden me with domestic crap, Chip. I'm beyond this. I'm too high up. I don't need to know whether my wife is menopausal, or whether Room 8 has lost his shoes, or whether Room 6 has pissed his bed, or whether Nancy has ordered cream for ass warts, I just need you to get me a limo. Go. Move. Don't speak. Act. You can hold on to your job here, Chip, by prompt and efficient execution. Next time you call, it's to say there's a big stretch outside and the driver's got lead in his gas shoe and can make a whisky mac with one hand on the wheel.'

'Yes, sir.'

ROOM 12. MRS BAINS.

'I heard a smash.'

'We've had a breakage in the lobby, Mrs Bains.'

'What time is it?'

'Gone seven.'

'Can I hear music too?'

'*Hey Jesus* is playing.'

'How long would it take to get from here to the King's Bay Naval Base in Georgia?'

'I don't know, Mrs Bains.'

'Take a guess.'

'Well, it's a good distance. I imagine it would take about three hours.'

'That's what I think.'

'Do you need to go there?'

'No. I don't want to ever go anywhere near the place again.'

'Right.'

'I don't want my son going anywhere near it either.'

'Well ...'

'Selfish, selfish child. I wish I'd never had him.'

'You don't mean that.'

'I wish he'd never been born.'

'Mrs Bains—'

'I need comfort. I need a reassuring voice.'

'You could—'

'I want to hear some of that music. I tried to tune to *Hey Jesus* earlier but I just get static. I go straight from *The Early Bird* to *Wake Up With Wanda* with no *Hey Jesus* in between.'

'You probably need to tweak it.'

Pause.

<music>

'You're right, Chip. That's got it.'

'Mrs Bains.'

<music, loud>

'That's nice, Chip. Uplifting. That helps me.'

'Could you—'

'That makes my day better.'

'Mrs Bains—'

'That helps an old lady whose son hates her.'

'Would you turn it down a bit, Mrs Bains?'

Hey Jesus wafts over the hotel. Music becomes prophecies. Reports coming in of a sighting in Alabama and were there any pure hearted *Hey Jesus* listeners who could verify? Does the *Hey Jesus* signal reach that far? The lines are open, local rates applied.

Wee Willie Winkie struggles out of the E Z Clock. Ten minutes late. He's been trapped inside. The figurine has been buckling behind the jammed mechanism. He's had to force himself through. Now his nightcap is chipped and his nightdress has split apart revealing a wooden peg and a spring as a body. He opens his mouth to say 'Seven o'clock and all's well' but it patently isn't. His jaw falls off. No sound emerges. The mechanism rotates him back inside.

ROOM 12. MRS BAINS.

'I didn't mean to say I wished my son had never been born.'

'I know you didn't, Mrs Bains.'

'I say silly things sometimes. I'm a silly old woman.'

'I don't agree, Mrs Bains.'

'I'm glad he was born. I'm very proud of him.'

'So you should be.'

'Please forget I said the other thing. The silly thing.'

'It's gone from my mind.'

'Thank you. You're a comfort. Do you know how long a sailor has to be absent from duty before he's officially AWOL?'

'No, Mrs Bains.'

'A couple of hours?'

'Probably a bit longer.'

'A day? A night?'

'Maybe.'

'All right. I've bothered you enough.'

'Could you turn your radio down, Mrs Bains?'

Through the evangelism, through the hum of the switchboard, through the clink of dishes at Pancake Parlour, Chip listens for the sound of Jim's cab. A roar, a rattle, the crackle of radio frequencies, the squeal of tight cornering. He listens for the sound of laughing, a map rustling, a full tank sloshing, Orbiter fizzing. He listens for the sound of exits and escapes, the sound of Jim babbling: here's a trip for you, buddy, forget the damn party, we'll drive to the airport and fly to St Petersburg and in St Petersburg we'll get into a taxi which will take us to an address out of town and we'll go inside and into a lift and it'll ascend to the top floor and we'll emerge and go along a corridor and up to a door where we'll find a name and a bell and we'll ring it and it'll make a chime like *Close Encounters* and a man will answer and he'll have a strong jaw and a twinkle in his eye and we'll say SURPRISE and Mr Gagarin will look right at you, Chip, and tell you that it's like looking in a mirror, old friend, just like looking in a mirror.

The twinge becomes a little stab. Sally draws breath. It passes. It comes again. Harder.

She's two hours in. A reaction to the launch. A bit of tension, nothing more. This used to happen to her. Every exam she took. She plain sailed it, then when it was over her stomach tied itself in knots.

She tells Houston she thinks it's tension.

Stand by, says Houston.

She wishes she could apply sun cream to make her feel like a proper tourist. It might relax her.

How would others be in her position? Chip? The Chef? The Pollster? Would they have stomach ache?

The Pollster was considered a good bet because she could remain detached. Plus her parachute landed on the bullseye. She didn't want to be a favourite. She said the situation was a bit like that book by Agatha Christie, *Ten Little ...* She stopped herself.

'You can say it,' said Sally.

'*Ten Little ...*'

'You can say it if you want to,' said Sally.

'*Ten Little ...*' She didn't want to say it.

'It was called *Ten Little Indians* at my school,' said the Comedienne.

'That was the film,' said the Radar Operator, 'the book is actually called *And Then There Were None*.'

The Pollster apologised for bringing it up.

'You have to say it now,' she said, but the Pollster really didn't want to.

'Not on camera,' said someone under their breath, but everyone heard.

The eight were put in an altitude chamber. It was painted red and inside they sat with the Captain and another person who said he was the Instructor. They held clipboards. The eight had masks.

The chamber was decompressed and they were observed.

'Have we started?' said the Model.

'How high are we?' said the Chef.

'I like things in black and white,' said the Pollster.

Chip said his feet tingled and his arms were numb.

They were instructed to play the game pat-a-cake. The Chef and the Model tried it and got nowhere. He missed her hands and brushed her breast. He apologised. He said that hypoxia often caused these embarrassing little faux pas. He said a lot of men suffered from it and women should be more sympathetic. He touched her breast again to illustrate the point.

Sally paired up with the Comedienne and said, 'Pat-a-cake, pat-a-cake, baker's man, bake me a cake as fast as you can.'

The Comedienne said so far so good.

She said, 'Pat-a-cake, pat-a-cake, batter cake, bake, make a better cake, man, as fast as you can.'

The Comedienne said so good so far.

Sally said, 'Thank you.' She said the Comedienne should say something witty now because in the oxygen depleted environment it would be hilarious.

The Comedienne said she couldn't think of anything.

Sally laughed and laughed.

The Pollster just sat.

'Play the game,' said Chip.

The Pollster said she wouldn't play. She was feeling sick.

The Captain and the Instructor told the eight to untie then tie up their shoelaces.

The Pollster said she was wearing slip-ons. Ha!

The Instructor told them to touch their noses. He told them to take the pads of paper beside them and write their names down.

The Pollster flushed. She was dizzy. 'Stupid test,' she said.

The eight were told to draw a picture of a house.

The Pollster said be more specific.

The Captain said draw your own house.

The Pollster said she lived in a flat.

The Captain said draw that then.

The Pollster said her pen wasn't working.

The Captain told her it was working fine.

The Pollster said it damn well wasn't.

The Instructor made a note on his clipboard.

The Pollster said don't write anything about me, you fucker.

The Captain told everyone to put their oxygen masks on.

The Chef said masks were for Zorro and Zorro alone.

The Model said she couldn't move her fingers properly.

Sally gave a mask to the Comedienne and said be sure to assist your children before seeing to yourself.

The Comedienne said Sally was doing 'absomolutey exermently' and said that 'hypermopoxima' really suited her.

The eight breathed oxygen and their brains speeded up. The chamber was recompressed and they were led out.

On his clipboard Chip had written Chipolata. The Radar Operator had missed the page. The Model had drawn another house. The Chef had written on his hand.

The Pollster had written 'ten little niggers' five times. She tried to rip the paper up but it was taken off her before she could. She asked the Captain if that bit could be edited out. He said it was out of his hands. She said give me the damn paper. He told her to calm down.

She accused Chip. She said Chip had written those words.

Chip denied it.

'You fucking liar!' screamed the Pollster. 'Check his handwriting.'

The Captain told her to take it easy.

'I don't use words like that, Chip does. I've heard him.'

The Instructor led her away. The Pollster said she had the bends and asked to be taken to hospital. The Instructor told her she was fine.

She said these tests didn't tell anyone anything and she distrusted everyone involved. They weren't proper tests, they were... they were... she ran away. Sally ran after her to try to make light of the situation but the Pollster gave her the slip by climbing over the wall. Something she wouldn't've been able to do a few weeks ago, said Sally, so it hadn't all been wasted.

The seven missed the Holiday Rep. She was infectious. They missed the Probable Winner, she set standards. They didn't miss the Pollster so much; at least, they didn't admit it.

Chip told Sally she was probably favourite now.

'Oh, come on,' she said.

'Seriously, I think you're the favourite,' he said.

'Don't be silly.'

'I'm not being silly, we all think you'll win it.'

She said not many black people went into space. She said the first was a Cuban Air Force pilot, Colonel Arnaldo Tamayo-Mendez, who flew to the *Mir* space station aboard *Soyuz 38* in 1980. He was part of the Russian space programme and the fact that he was Cuban got under America's skin. After Tamayo-Mendez came America's own Colonel Bluford with his PhD in Aeronautical Engineering and his veteran's record of Phantom combat missions in Vietnam. Even with those credentials he wasn't made the shuttle pilot, he was the payload specialist.

'Baggage handler,' she said.

Chip said she stood a great chance.

She said, 'We'll see.'

The next day the seven took it in turns in a flight simulator. They tried to land a jumbo in a storm.

The Captain whispered in Sally's ear, she had to consider the lives of five hundred passengers behind her, she had to bring them all home safely, she had to avoid crashing into the hospital to the west and the orphanage to the east, she had to ignore the fatally food-poisoned co-pilot moaning for help, she had to concentrate on the job in hand.

She said it didn't seem like a very sophisticated simulator.

The Captain said it was the one real pilots use.

She said it was more like an arcade game.

The Captain set the weather to Tropical Storm and told her she shouldn't think of it as a game. He hissed in her ear something about how much he'd like to see her bugger this up.

She concentrated hard and landed with a bump but no casualties. 'Any kid could've done the same,' she said.

The Captain said the safe landing was more luck than design. He told the actor co-pilot he could stop moaning now.

Chip made a perfect landing, so did the Comedienne. The Radar Operator got lost, he flew around and around and then found a different airport. He took hours but no one died.

The Chef was blasé. He speculated about the cause of the co-pilot's food poisoning. He went on about how pre-packed food on aeroplanes was a breeding ground for bacteria. He was told to concentrate. He said that though chicken was the most dangerous, there were also hazards to be found in soft cheese, cooked meats, even peanuts.

He hit the hospital, he clipped the orphanage, he landed upside down on the runway and the plane careered into the terminus. There was digital carnage.

The Captain told him that if it had happened for real it would have been one of the worst aviation disasters in the history of the world.

The Chef went into the toilets and wept and wept. The camera in the airvent zoomed and got the tears in close-up. He got eliminated. He packed his bags and left without saying goodbye to anyone, not even the Model who had been telling him he looked like the young Harrison Ford.

ROOM 16. THE CHEF. OUTSIDE LINE.

'This call has been <voice 2> one hour long.'

'…I caught a train to Southend. It's a town on the south coast of England. I took out five hundred pounds from my bank, changed them into coins and took them to the end of the pier and started feeding the flight simulator and telling kids to piss off. I did hour after hour after hour and was still lying only ninth behind JAX, BEX, DAN, DAN, AAA, FIS, RON, and AAB. I got kicked out at the end of the night but slept under the pier to be the first next morning. I played so much my eyes started blurring and after a couple of days I'd slipped down to thirtieth, then fortieth, and then I was off the scale. I ripped off the joysticks and threw them into the sea. I got arrested. I think I was on the news.'

Pause.

'I sell pans now. The Enama-perm range. Durable oven/hob cooking for the professional or competent amateur. All sizes. Ten year guarantee. I have a catalogue with laminated pages. Before I flew here I had a demonstration. *Il Gamberini* said they'd buy the range if they saw it in action. I drank to loosen up. I started a complicated fish soup. I bought fancy ingredients. My hands shook. I covered everyone in squid ink. I got hold of a rare fish to impress them. I didn't know what to do with it. They asked me what it was. I said something about it being from the pollack family. They said I was way out, I'd got hold of a left-eye flounder, a *Platichthys albigutta*. They said it wasn't going to work at all, the left-eye flounder was going to make the dish taste disgusting so I threw it away. They said I could've fried it, frying it would have been fine, but now I'd wasted it. They watched me hack into a crab and cut my hand and dribble blood into the meat. They saw me cook bad mussels. They said I was going to kill them all. My fish stock developed a layer of scum. Shellfish beards floated to the top. The pan burnt the onions. It turned the butter black. I scraped at it and chipped off the enamel. I used the Enama-perm mortar and pestle and it crumbled. The langoustines oozed shit. The pan handles melted. They let me continue to the bitter end. I presented a foul smelling, messy dish. "What are you calling this?" they asked me, because they sure had a few names. I put everything in the back of the car and drove to the airport. The stinking mess is still in the back of my car for when I get back.'

Pause.

'Are you still there, Portia?'

'Yeah.'

'Sorry about before. Being rude. I got … I don't know.'

'Don't worry.'

'Are you really in Chicago, or are you local?'

'I'm local. I have a little apartment above a takeaway.'

'Nice.'

'Not really. I'm saving for something better.'

'Do you want to earn something on the side?'

'Sure.'

'Because we're having a little get-together here at the E Z Sleep and I wondered if you'd consider a singing telegram.'

'I don't know.'

'Nothing sleazy. Just a little song, a little dance.'

'I guess that would be possible.'

'In costume. Something spacey perhaps. An astronaut, or an alien.'

'I don't sing that well.'

'It doesn't matter. I'm sure you'll be a breath of fresh air. I'd like to see you.'

'I haven't got an alien costume.'

'Well, something else then.'

'I've got something that could work as a stewardess. And I could make a little NASA handbag, how about that? A shuttle stewardess.'

'That would work.'

'How much?'

'A hundred?'

'That sounds very generous.'

'How about if you strip too, how would that be?'

'Don't spoil it.'

'For a hundred. Or a hundred and twenty.'

'I'm not stripping.'

'Oh come on. There'll be women here too, it'll be fine.'

'I don't want you to see me naked. I don't want that.'

'I do.'

'Don't ask me.'

'A hundred and fifty.'

'No.'

'Two hundred.'

'Stop asking.'

'Two hundred and a ride in a sports car.'

'I'm hanging up.'

'You're not allowed to do that.'

Chip uprights the bin. He finds a shovel in the cleaner's store cupboard. He wonders why she needs something as major as a shovel. Then figures she needs it for occasions like this. He starts piling rubbish and broken glass into the bin.

A van drives up and parks outside.

Two men get out and open up the back. They lower a ramp and

gently wheel down a great big cake. Three tiers. Four feet high. On a little trolley with castors.

The two men push the cake up to the smashed E Z doors.

Is this the E Z Sleep? they ask.

Chip nods.

You had a ram raid?

Something like that.

You want this cake here or in that marquee?

Chip stands aside.

They push the cake through the broken doors. One of the men cuts his knuckle on the way through and curses. He gets a bit of blood on the cake. The trolley castors grind the glass.

Chip gets a broom and sweeps the way clear.

They leave the cake in the middle of the lobby.

Chip signs for it.

The injured man asks for a plaster for his cut. Chip gets him one from first aid. The man thanks him and tells him not to eat the bit of cake with blood on it. He's had hepatitis.

The men leave.

The cake is pink. It has red ribbons round the edge. Ten candles. It has Happy Launchday written in blue icing on the top.

Chip sticks his finger in the cake then licks it clean.

It tastes of fumes from the delivery van.

ROOM 11. MR MOULIN. OUTSIDE LINE.

'Thank you for calling the E Z Slumber Hotel and Conference Facility for the discerning...'

'Shut up, Dennis. Are there any secret service guys with you?'

'Sir, when I said they were—'

'Do they want us to install bulletproof glass in any of the rooms? The conference room maybe?'

'They didn't mention anything, that's why I think—'

'Get me Jackson.'

'I believe he's having breakfast, sir.'

'What? How can he eat at a time like this?'

'A time like what?'

'Dennis, have you any idea who's staying there today?'

'I don't think anyone is, the place is—'

'Didn't the secret service guys give you some inkling that something was up?'

'As I said, I don't know for sure if they were secret service guys.'

'Of course they were, we've got some high-powered guests arriving. Look sharp will you? This is a landmark day for the E Z, Dennis, the day that the Bilder— Actually, Dennis, you don't really need to know this.'

'We've got builders coming?'

'Forget I said anything. In fact, forget everything.'

'Why should the secret service bother themselves with builders?'

'Dennis, pretend I haven't said anything at all. This is out of your league.'

'Sure, sir.'

'If anyone asks, the hotel is empty this weekend.'

'It already is, sir.'

'Tell them – in fact, yes, tell them the hotel's closed because we do have builders coming, they're going to renovate the upstairs, they're putting in some ... swimming pools.'

'Swimming pools, cool.'

'And a casino.'

'Sounds great.'

'Yes, it is, it's very exciting. When does your shift finish?'

'Eight o'clock.'

'OK, good, you'll be gone by the time they arrive.'

'I might stick around, I'd like to see a swimming pool and a casino built. Will they be bringing wrecking balls? I love those. And big dozers?'

'Don't stick around, Dennis, it'll put them off. In fact, if you stick around you're fired.'

'Oh. OK then.'

'Just go home and don't think about who's coming to stay at the hotel.'

'I never do, sir.'

'That's . . . well that's bad, but in this case it's commendable.'

'Thank you, sir.'

'You can go home now, in fact.'

'Great.'

'Jackson's over at the Pancake Pantry, yes?'

'I expect he's lingering over his waffles.'

'Jesus Christ.'

Chip walks around the Launchday cake. It oozes. He finds a cigarette lighter and lights the ten candles. He watches them flicker and melt. Wax drips onto the icing and gives off the smell of burning sugar. Thin trails of black smoke drift up from the ten candles.

The lobby sprinkler detects the smoke and spurts water. It douses the cake. The candles fizz.

Chip lets the spray hit his face. He holds out his nothing arm and cups his nothing hand. The spray hits his nothing fingers. A tingle on his nothing skin.

It rains in the lobby.

The rain hits the E Z stationery. It fills his pockets. It smudges Chip's drawing of the Space Station. It blurs the cupola. The solar arrays expand. The habitation compartment leaks. The centrifuge unit blotches.

Rain lands on the registration cards. Names blur. Telephone numbers blur.

Rain hits the TV.

Rain hits the *E Z Manual for Effective Hoteliering*. It smudges Chapter 7: Emergencies <non-natural>. It blurs the information about how to turn off the sprinkler.

Rain hits the switchboard. Chip covers it with an E Z Map. Rain drowns the Oasis Shopping Emporium. Rain hits the Cactus Inn. The colours swim. Drops land on the Lucky Horseshoe Living Centre. New Homes for New Lives. The residents explode.

The map is pulped. Chip throws the sodden mess away and spreads out another. Rain lands in the ocean. Rain hits the reception bell and gives it a watery ring.

Rain hits the cake. The cake starts to mush.

ROOM 11. MR MOULIN. OUTSIDE LINE.

'Jackson?'

'Yes, sir.'

'How can you stuff your face with waffles at this time is beyond me.'

'Breakfast is the most important—'

'Don't finish that sentence, Jackson.'

'OK.'

'Now is not the time for the homespun.'

'No, sir.'

'Can you imagine informing Henry Kissinger that breakfast is the most important meal of the day?'

'I can't imagine that, no.'

'You've got to be thinking sharp. Thinking on a higher plane. I don't want the Bilderberg group all trouping into Pancake Parlour and getting told that breakfast is the most important meal of the day.'

'I think they'll request alternative breakfast arrangements.'

'I'm sure they will, and we've got to be ready for them. I'm going to get myself a natty bow tie, the kind that the British Chancellor of the Exchequer will probably admire. You should get one too.'

'Well . . .'

'We should put fresh flowers in each room, roses on the pillows, that's a nice touch I think, what do you think?'

'I—'

'I think the German Chancellor would be into a rose on his pillow. Or is that too homosexual? Should it be something more serious? A plant or something, a shrub, what about . . . or a cactus by the telephone . . . no, let's stick with roses.'

'I don't think the German Chancellor is coming, sir.'

'Germany out of favour, are they? That's a dangerous sign. I hope it doesn't get nasty. Perhaps we should fill up every bath with champagne. These heads of state will probably bring their wives and they like the high life. Might relax them. We don't want another cold war. Don't use expensive stuff, use Orbiter. Then hide the bottles. We've got to keep alert. Jeez, this isn't going to be easy, is it, Jackson? Are we up to it, do you think?'

'I think so, sir. The hotel is empty now and we're being told to be on standby. Someone will be here to update us shortly.'

'That's the spirit. Fighting talk. OK, I'm waiting for a limo to arrive, then I'll be straight over. I should get there just before they arrive.'

'A limo?'

'I need to make an impression. Plus they have fax machines in limos, you can fax me things en route.'

'What kind of things?'

'Memos and so forth. Plus I'll need a drink to help me unwind, limos have drinks cabinets. And TVs. I can watch the news so I'm up to date with current affairs. I don't want to get caught out on the Middle East crisis by some tricksy Nobel prizewinner.'

'Sir—'

'Perhaps I should ask that Nancy Carter chick to come after all. I think a couple of hours of ass-touching might help calm me down.'

'Um...'

'So in summary, don't panic, Jackson, I'm depending on you until I get there.'

'Right you are, sir.'

'Good. Excellent.'

It pours in the lobby. A thunderstorm. Rain bounces off the floor. The cake droops.

Chip thinks he should cut a slice for the Chef before it disintegrates; after all, he'd made the effort to—

The top of the cake flies off and out bursts a spacewoman.

'Happy Launchday!' she shouts.

Chip jumps out of his skin.

The spacewoman looks around the lobby. It is empty apart from Chip, the smell of rubbish, and the spurting sprinkler.

She has a white padded jumpsuit with a British flag sewn on each of the arms. She wears big gloves. She wears a homemade space helmet which has steamed up and has bits of cake stuck to the visor. She tries to wipe the cake off. It smears.

The spacewoman takes off her helmet.

The Model.

Not so pretty any more.

She stares at Chip.

Chip stares back.

She has the letters F and C scratched into her cheek. Little drops of blood ooze from the wounds and have dripped onto her spacesuit. She touches the scratches on her cheek.

Chip asks what happened to her face.

She smiles. She forces one out.

Chip forces one out too.

She says... she says... you look... how are you? How's your...

Chip nods.

She looks around. She was expecting a big crowd. She was expecting nine people. There aren't nine. There's only Chip. It's a little disappointing. It was to be a big moment. She'd planned it. She missed the launch for it. She's been in the cake for hours.

She sways and falls over. The cake breaks around her. It's a cardboard construction covered in a thin layer of sponge then iced. She and it collapse on the floor. The floor is a puddle. Water and broken candles fly.

Chip tries to help her up. She tells him to leave her where she is. She's flushed. The heat of the suit and the journey in the van have dehydrated her and the sprinkler feels good. She lets the rain splash her face.

Chip offers her Fresh and Clear.

She refuses. She can't touch another drop of that muck.

After getting kicked out of the programme she went to Fresh and Clear with her heart on her sleeve. Fresh and Clear put her on an exclusive contract. She has to be seen drinking it if there's ever a camera near. She has to drink it in bars and in restaurants and in clubs at parties, or on chat shows. Fresh and Clear are thinking of removing the clause because she's often filmed visibly grimacing at the taste.

Did they scratch their logo on your face? asks Chip.

She said she etched it herself. She'd be surprised if the Fresh and Clear make-up artist can cover the wound. She feels sure this is the end of her and the minty water company. Or any other company.

She starts to cry. Her tears taste of peppermint because of all the Fresh and Clear she's obliged to drink. Her piss is freezing. Her sweat is sticky. Her puke is minty.

Chip doesn't know what to do for her.

She wants to be left for a moment.

She lies back in the cake and the rain and she shuts her eyes.

OUTSIDE LINE.

'E Z Sleep.'

'Do you think I could speak to Nancy Carter now?'

'I'll try for you now, sir.'

'What's a big blue flower with tall stems?'

'Is this a joke, sir?'

'No, I just want to know.'

'Cornflowers?'

'Really? Is that what they are?'

'I don't know.'

'Cornflowers, that sounds about right to me. Is it illegal to pick them?'

'I don't think so.

'OK. Put me through.'

Click click.

'Moulin here.'

'Oh, sorry, I asked to be put through to Nancy Carter.'

'She's moved out. Get off the line, I need to keep it clear.'

'What do you mean she's moved out?'

'She's not here. What do you think it means?'

'If she's moved out it sort of implies—'

'I can't afford to have this conversation now, OK? Christ knows who could be calling me. The head of General Motors could be trying to call me. I'm putting the phone down.'

'Mister, I—'

'Unless you're the head of General Motors, or a limo company—'

'I'm not.'

'Then get off the phone, you prick.'

The sprinkler still sprinkles. It's washed away most of the sponge and icing and jam from her spacesuit. Cake is dissolving in the puddles.

She's soaking wet. She gets to her feet.

She's left her suitcase in the delivery van. She's only got the spacesuit for the whole weekend.

Chip says there are dressing gowns in the rooms.

She wants to know if the party is taking place in the marquee.

Chip guesses so. They look over. The Holiday Rep is throwing pebbles at a tin can.

She asks if there's a TV in her room.

Chip nods.

She wants to catch the launch on the news.

She gets into the lift. The lift doesn't move and doesn't speak. Perhaps it's too shocked at what's happened to the doors. Perhaps it doesn't work if it's raining inside. The Model goes up the stairs. She's tired and cramped and she walks as if she's on the moon.

Should've specified no fancy dress, mutters Chip. Should've...

OUTSIDE LINE.

'E Z Sleep.'

'I spoke to a guy who said Nancy had "moved out" of his room.'

'I'm sorry, sir, my mistake...'

'What did he mean by "moved out"? 'Cos those were his exact words.'

'Connecting you now.'

'Because "moved out" to me means—'

ROOM 15. NANCY CARTER.

'What?'

'Nancy?'

'Oh, hi.'

'Who was that guy? I just spoke to a guy who said you'd "moved out" of his room.'

'He's just a guy who's got a double bed.'

'What were you doing?'

'I was trying to get us his room.'

''Cos to me "moved out" implies that you'd previously "moved in".'

'He has a double bed, honey, I just went to ask him if he'd be willing to trade.'

'Asking him to trade is very different to "moving in".'

'I didn't move in.'

'So why did he say you'd "moved out"?'

'I don't know, perhaps he's nuts, perhaps he's a stupid French nutbag.'

'Is he French? He didn't sound French.'

'French blood. He gets his words mixed up.'

'He sounded pretty fluent, he called me a prick.'

'I'm sure it's just a language thing.'

'You don't start using words like "prick" until you have a solid grasp of English.'

'Since when were you such a language hotshot?'

'I think it's a big leap from "she's left the room" to "she's moved out".'

'What's the matter with you?'

'It's hard to get the two things confused.'

'This is ridiculous. *Partir*, that's the verb To Leave. It's also the word the French use for when they move house.'

'Really?'

'Sure.'

'Because I'll check up on that.'

'Don't be an asshole.'

'Seriously, Nancy, you think you can fob me off because you're smarter than I am but you never know if I'll follow these things up. It'll be something there between us. You'll think I've forgotten about it and then I'll turn up with a French dictionary in one hand and divorce papers in the other.'

'Honey, take it easy, will you? I just wanted us to have a double bed because you got so upset about the twin room. I asked the guy, he said yes. End of story.'

'I mean it. It's straight to the library.'

'Well, good. What will you give me when you find out I'm right?'

'Um, I don't know. Something.'

'I hope so because you'll owe me.'

'How about a big bunch of cornflowers?'

'That will be fine.'

'I'll fill up the car with them now, in case.'

'You're not still in the field, are you?'

'It's really beautiful.'

'Get in the damn car and drive here. What's the matter with you?'

'The smell. It's heavenly. And the sun's coming up.'

'Pick me the flowers and get over here. Come on, look at the time.'

'Reception guy seemed pretty subdued. Has the party started yet?'

'I think it's about to.'

'I'll take some pictures of the flowers, and be straight there, how about that?'

'Don't use up your film.'

The commander has opened up the cargo doors to cool the shuttle down. It got hot and bothered getting there, and this is nice for it. Like unbuttoning a few buttons, letting the sweat dry. The crew's thirsty too and so the shuttle has made them some water. It's mixing liquid oxygen and hydrogen in its fuel cells, its cocktail shakers, and it's serving it to them ice-cold. What a hostess.

The commander asks Sally how she is.

She says fine. The pills are doing their job.

She turns her back on everyone. She's sick. She catches it in a bag. A little globule of it floats over towards the commander. He grabs it in a bag too and asks Houston to advise.

Stand by, says Houston.

The local area network is set up. The OMS will burn again soon. Little adjustments.

She's told to go to pre-sleep.

She says her schedule tells her she's not scheduled for pre-sleep until—

The commander knows. She should get some rest.

She stops thinking.

She forgets her speed. She forgets her altitude. She loves being so well-trained. She doesn't want her body breaking rank.

She hasn't put a finger wrong yet. Why don't her guts stop hurting?

The system works.

She has to work.

She hopes the antibiotics work.

She tries to be optimistic.

Houston confirms that she still owns her appendix. Her father lied to her to stop her from worrying about it. He's still at the launch site with his head in his hands.

She floats around her room. She has a room which she's made to look a bit like home. She has a picture on the wall and a little light to read by. No bed, but a sleeping bag to stop her from drifting. She could sleep upright, horizontal, upside down. It makes no difference. What is up, anyway?

She has Whizz toothpaste and a Gleam Rite toothbrush. She brushes her hair. She floats around.

She has eight hours of sleep scheduled. She wonders how many of them will be spent sleeping, and how many will be spent monitoring her pain.

Her temperature has risen.

She closes her eyes.

In the house there were still six. They were woken at three in the morning and given thirty seconds to get into warm clothes. They were given a kitbag and then blindfolded and bundled into the back of a truck. The truck drove for an hour, perhaps two. A couple of the six fell back to sleep again.

The truck stopped. The Captain opened up the doors, pulled off their blindfolds and kicked them out. The truck drove away.

They were in the middle of a wood. Beyond that they couldn't see anything.

'I guess we find our way home,' said the Comedienne, who had stopped saying funny things on the whole and was just saying ordinary things.

The Stenographer suggested that the truck could've been driving round in a circle and they might only be a few metres from the house.

NICK WALKER

Clever, said everyone else, and her odds shortened.

Sally asked her what it was like working in the courtroom.

The Stenographer said she worked there because she believed it would be reassuring. The courtroom was a place where justice was done and seen to be done and this would have a calming effect on her. It would place actions into context and she would feel that life had a sense of order and purpose.

And does it? asked Sally.

The Stenographer said she transcribed forty murders, two hundred violent attacks, three hundred frauds, a dozen kidnappings, six hostage-takings, two tortures, and a war crime. She'd detailed humanity at its most depraved, its most abject, its most hopeless, and she had become numb. She hadn't felt a thing in years. She was hoping space would give her a new sense of perspective.

Everyone nodded.

The Stenographer told them she'd have a quick look over the horizon, if there was a horizon, and would be back in five minutes.

'Course there's a horizon, there's always a horizon,' someone said.

The Stenographer ran into the darkness.

The rest of them sat down. They opened their kitbags. There were plasters, biscuits, socks, and tin cans which heated up when you opened them.

They talked about orientation by the stars. They talked about constellations and auroras and how stenographers probably thought more laterally.

The cameramen had infrared. One of them said when you looked through the lens, everything was green. Then he shut up. He wasn't allowed to speak. He had to walk away because he could feel the floodgates opening.

'How long has she been away?' someone asked.

No one had a watch. No one could tell the time by the moon. No one knew if that was possible anyway. A cameraman said that ephemeris time was reckoned by the orbital periods of the moon and not subject to the irregularities of the earth's rotation. This uniform measure formed the basis of theories of celestial dynamics.

They again wondered why the cameramen weren't chosen to go into space.

They split up to look for her.

Sally paired off with Chip. They called out the Stenographer's name. They did this for a quarter of an hour and then sat on a log.

He asked her what God made of space travel.

She said just between herself and Chip and the cameraman's microphone, she didn't have a clue. She didn't really know if He existed. She thought the world might be between gods.

She was only a believer by virtue of Pascal's wager. Either God existed or He didn't. If she believed in God and He existed then heaven was the pay-off. If she believed in God and He didn't exist then there was no heaven to lose and all she'd have done is wasted a few Sundays at church. If she didn't believe in God and He also didn't exist then she'd never have bothered with heaven anyway and would've been right to spend her Sundays gardening. If she didn't believe in God and He did exist then she was screwed. She was in hell. She thought that any sensible gambler would put their money on the first option.

Chip asked her if she could really choose to believe in God like that.

She said that was why she didn't think she was a proper believer.

He asked her where she stood on premarital sex.

She said she stood around waiting for it to happen.

Chip laughed. So did she.

The cameraman's tapes ran out and so did his battery. He told Chip and Sally that his name was Alan and that making this programme had pretty much destroyed his marriage.

Chip said that when people came to watch the programme the

two of them would be referred to as the Quiet One and the Believer, for the sake of quick identification.

Alan said they were more likely to be known as the Orphaned One and the Black One.

Chip said he hadn't said anything about his family circumstances. Alan said that the narrator would probably mention it at the outset. He said it'd add poignancy to the Quiet Moments.

Sally hoped that people would remember actual names, for crying out loud.

After an hour they thought the wood was lightening. She guessed it might be four o'clock. At half past they could see each other's faces. At five they saw streaks of red in the sky and some gold.

They heard, drifting on the air, a male shout of 'Hello!' followed by a female shout of 'Hello!' The Radar Operator and the Model, hoarse and wanting company. They were answered by another shout and three voices converged on each other.

Chip and Sally shouted then. Shouts intersected. Shapes and bodies met. And soon all of them except the Stenographer were under an oak tree.

Nobody had found her. Nobody had really looked. In the woods, in the dark, they had split up and done almost nothing.

They thought the Captain would be disappointed with them but he wasn't. He was disappointed that the Stenographer had been handed to the police for stealing three hundred reams of stenographic paper. The production team grabbed her in the woods. One of the cases stuffed in her bag involved an action against Fresh and Clear which claimed that the town's reservoir water and Fresh and Clear were one and the same. Fresh and Clear had a drill high in the Redrock Hills which claimed to cut deep in the rock in order to siphon off 'the freshest spring water, purified through nature's own filters' but the siphon was for show. The Fresh and Clear company had a pipe direct to the reservoir and just filled its bottles with the same crap that came out of the taps. They added mint to disguise it. The case fell apart because some Fresh and Clear workers refused to testify. There was talk of intimidation.

She was tried for theft in a magistrate's court and given a suspended sentence. The others guessed that must be a strange experience. They wondered if she felt her fingers automatically twitch, transcribing her own trial.

Do we really want such an unreliable company sponsoring us? they thought.

Well, it hadn't been proved, they thought.

Wee Willie Winkie stumbles out of the E Z Clock. He tries to sing 'Morning Has Broken'. The sprinkler sprays him. Wee Willie stops singing and starts to spark. His hat frazzles. His platform short-circuits and he gets thrown to the soaking lobby floor.

There is only water and cake and broken Willie Winkie in the lobby.

There is no Jim in the lobby.

Chip calls him up.

Nothing. Dead line.

He hopes Jim hasn't gone off the rails. Stuck in his car hearing the air bag screaming at him. Telling him he knows shit, he has shit for brains for living like a stinking dog in his stinking car, a freak who's wasting his life behind the wheel, giving himself ugly sores on his ass, breaking his back, getting sick on gas station food, disgracing himself in multi-storey car parks, shouting out of the windows, breaking aerials, stealing oil, scratching expensive cars, wanking into ashtrays.

When the air bag starts talking this way Jim stabs it with his penknife. He pulls the car over and hacks the air bag to bits till it's empty of air and slashed to pieces.

ROOM 11. MR MOULIN. OUTSIDE LINE.

'Thank you for calling the E Z Slumber, my name is—'

'Shut up, Dennis, get me Jackson.'

'Mr Jackson has left, sir.'

'Left?'

'And I have to go too.'

'What?'

'I have to lock up and leave the building.'

'Dennis, what—'

'I'm not allowed to be on the phone any more. I'm being told to leave right now by a guy who's about eight feet tall.'

'You are not authorised to do this, Dennis.'

'The phone is being taken away from me, sir.'

'Stay at your post, Dennis.'

'...'

'Dennis?...Dennis?'

The cleaner opens the door of Lost Property. There's a sprinkler in there too and it's drenching her lost possessions and making the radio crackle and hum.

The *Hey Jesus* man wants to get out of the radio station and see for himself the visitor from the sky. He doesn't want to be late for the Lord, or whatever it is. He shouts through the rain.

Chip's shoes are full of water. He doesn't know how to stop the sprinkler. Nor does the cleaner. They both think they're drowning.

Chip tries Jim again. Nothing. The switchboard is shorting out. Water is getting onto the plugs.

Sportswear.

Spraying Equipment.

Spring Manufacturers.

Sprockets.

No Sprinkler Systems. The Yellow Pages is pulp.

His party is a washout.

ROOM 11. MR MOULIN.

'Cab, Chip. Cab! For crying out loud.'

'I don't know what's happened, sir.'

'Goddamn it!'

'I know.'

'The E Z Slumber has been shut down.'

'I'm sorry.'

'Christ alive. What the hell's going on?'

'I don't know, sir.'

'It's started to rain in my room.'

'I don't know how to stop it.'

'Get me out of here.'

OUTSIDE LINE.

'Get me Nancy, will you?'

'I'll try, Sir.'

ROOM 15. NANCY CARTER. OUTSIDE LINE.

'Hello?'

'I'm still in the field.'

'Just come, will you? Why... why are you still in the field?'

'There's a car here, Nancy.'

'What?'

'These flowers, or weeds, or whatever they are, they're knee high. But there's tracks where they've all been squashed down and cut away. And I followed them and it must have been half a mile, or it felt that way, and at the end of it is this car.'

'Did it come off the road?'

'I haven't looked inside it yet, I've just seen it. I think there's some smoke coming out of it.'

'Smoke?'

'Or steam.'

'Take a look.'

'I think it's steam, it disappears quickly. Smoke lingers.'

'Go carefully, I don't want it blowing up in your face.'

'Is that guy with you?'

'He's in his room, but by the time you get here—'

'He's "moved out"?'

'Let's not start with this, huh? Go and check out this car.'

'It's red, it catches the sun.'

Pause.

'Is it sunny where you are, Nancy?'

'Yes.'

'Does it shine through the window?'

'Not in this room, it will in the other one.'

'East-facing?'

'Yeah.'

'Sounds like a prime room.'

'You at the car yet?'

'Nearly. You had much sleep, Nancy?'

'Not much. Is there a smell in the air?'

'Aside from the flowers?'

'A fuel smell?'

'Maybe.'

'Perhaps you should hold back. Perhaps you should go back to the road and call the police.'

Pause.

'Honey?'

Pause.

'God.'

'What's the matter?'

'This is a car crash, Nancy. This is a car on its side all dented and smashed up.'

'Yeah?'

'This is a car that's spun off the road and ended up here, fucked up and tangled up.'

'An old wreck?'

'Brand new, Nancy, this is a fresh crash.'

'Is it definitely steam?'

'A man's gone through the windscreen and he's sprawled out over the bonnet.'

'Oh, honey.'

'He's all twisted up. His joints are wrong. He's dead, Nancy. He's not moving.'

'Oh…'

'He's got a jacket on. His tie's all crooked. Jeez, his leg's gone.'

'Are you sure he's—'

'There's a woman too.'

'Is she dead as well? Next to him?'

'She's twenty metres away. She's walking away from me.'

'Walking?'

'Walking across the field.'

'You're joking, right?'

'She's got a summer dress on. She's playing with her hair and picking the flowers and sniffing them.'

'This is just to get me back, right? About the guy in the room, this is you just—'

'No, Nancy. There's a wreck and a tangled man and a standing up woman.'

'Perhaps you should call out.'

'What?'

'Call out to the girl.'

'You think I should? I don't want the shock to kill her.'

'Do it in a friendly way.'

'How do you mean friendly? I'm standing next to a tangled-up man.'

'Try not to sound panicked.'

'I am a little panicked.'

'Try not to sound it.'

'I'm feeling sick.'

'Try not to sound either. Try to keep it light.'

'Light?'

'So you don't alarm her.'

Pause.

'*Hello.*'

'Did she turn?'

'She didn't hear me.'

'The call was too light then, honey. Call a bit louder.'

'*Hello!*'

'Anything?'

'She's not responding. What do you think I should do? Should I go over?'

'Try again.'

'*Hello!* ... Nothing.'

'Then perhaps you should go over. Say what you're doing first.'

'*I'm going to come over!*'

'Get nearer but don't startle her.'

Pause.

'I'm wading through these flowers, Nancy. I'm surprised she can't hear the rustling.'

'Go gently.'

'Do you think I should tell her about the tangled-up man?'

'I'd hold off on that for a bit, honey.'

Pause.

'Has she turned yet?'

'No.'

'Don't be too stealthy. Don't creep up.'

'What do you think happened, Nancy? Do you think the man fell asleep at the wheel?'

'I don't know.'

'Or perhaps they got hit by a hit and run.'

'I couldn't say. Are you near her?'

'Perhaps there's another car somewhere. Or more. The flowers are so high, the field could be full of wrecked-up cars.'

'Just concentrate on the girl for now.'

'It could have been a multi-vehicular incident.'

'Don't fret about what happened, just take care of the girl. Are you with her yet?'

'I'm there. She hasn't heard me. I'm an arm's distance away. I could touch her on the shoulder.'

'Don't do that yet.'

'What shall I do?'

'Say something.'

'Like what?'

'Ask her if she's all right.'

'*Are you all right?*'

'Did she hear you?'

'She might have blood in her ears.'

'Try blowing on her neck.'

Pause.

'I blew.'

'Has she turned round?'

'No.'

'Blow again.'

Pause.

'I blew quite hard then, Nancy. A bit of spit came out and hit her.'

'Did she turn?'

'No. Not even with the bit of spit hitting her.'

'Touch her on the shoulder then. Gently.'

'*If you can hear me I'm just going to touch your shoulder. Don't panic now. Don't lash out. I'm just…*'

Pause.

'Honey?'

Pause.

'Have you got her attention?'

Pause.

'She's turned round, Nancy.'

'Is she OK?'

'There's blood down her face but she's giving me a smile.'

'Lots of blood?'

'Quite a bit. There's quite a bit there.'

'But she's smiling?'

'Yes.'

'You better smile back.'

Pause.

'I'm smiling.'

Pause.

'Ask her name.'

'What's your name?'

Pause.

'What did she say?'

'She's scratching her head. I don't know what to do here.'

'Tell her everything's going to be OK.'

'That's not true though, her boyfriend or whatever is sticking out the windscreen.'

'Don't mention that, honey, she'll need to hear good things now.'

'Are you OK?... She's nodding at me.'

'Nod back.'

'She's laughing now.'

'That's a good sign. See if you can take her hand. I think you should try to get her back to your car.'

'Is that a good idea?'

'You need to sit her down.'

'She's a mess.'

'Even so.'

'*Do you want to come and sit in my car?*'

'Hold out your hand to her.'

Pause.

'Oh.'

'What? What's happened?'

'She's running away. I reached out and she giggled and now she's running away.'

'Go after her. I don't think you should let her run around.'

'*Hey! Wait! Wait a second!* ... She can run pretty fast.'

'Don't let her get away.'

'For someone with blood all over her she can really move.'

'Keep sight of her.'

Pause. Running.

'I don't think she can be that bad, Nancy, if she can run at this speed.'

'Stick with her.'

Pause.

'She's fallen over.'

'Go and pick her up.'

'*Are you hurt?*'

'I think you're going to have to carry her back to your car.'

Pause.

'*Do you want some help?*'

'Keep smiling. Smiling and nodding.'

'Damn.'

'What?'

'She's up. Up again and running.'

'Don't lose sight of her.'

'She's running so fast ... *I'm not going to hurt you!*'

Pause. Out of breath.

'OK. OK. She's stopped. She's come to a dead stop.'

'What's she doing?'

'She's feeling her head and looking at the blood on her fingers.'

'Ask her if she's in any pain.'

'*Are you hurt?*'

'Is she wounded? How bad?'

'I can only see blood, but she seems happy. I don't know what to do.'

'Can she speak?'

'*Can you speak, miss?...* She's holding out her hand for the phone.'

'Perhaps she wants to call for help.'

'What shall I do?'

'Give it to her.'

'You think? She's pretty bloody.'

'Don't worry about that now.'

'If she gets the buttons sticky, it might stop working.'

'Hand it over, honey.'

'I don't know if blood and electrics really mix.'

'Just give her the phone.'

'OK, but if she cuts out, it's because of the blood thing.'

Pause.

Air rustling through the phone. Breathing.

'Hello? My name's Nancy, what's yours? Can you hear me?'

Pause.

'Are you hurt? 'Cos it sounds like—'

'Is that you, Chip?'

'No, I'm Nancy.'

'I've got my dress shitty.'

'Well, don't worry about that now.'

''Scuse my French but there's shit on my dress... I think I did a poop which isn't like me as you well know. And I'm telling you this because when you see me wearing it with shit all over it you'll think

I'm making a point, but I'm not. You'll think this is a dirty protest against the launch. It isn't, honest.'

'I believe you...'

'I wanted you to see me wear it 'cos you'll see how much I like it and how... I don't know the word... what's the word, Chip? I'm not being funny, I'm not funny at all any more, I'm un-comic now, I really am. You'll see how much I like it and how... what's the fucking word?'

'I don't know.'

'Sorry for the blue language but I can't... hey, now you see what I've done, I've given away the surprise. God, I can be a klutz. It was supposed to be a surprise visit. So, well, SURPRISE! Anyway that's ruined now 'cos you know I'm coming, although now I think about it, it isn't a surprise at all is it? This was your idea. But I just wanted to explain about the dress and the shit, so, Happy Launchday, Chip. I hope it's a good day today but we're going to be a little bit late because we're having a picnic in the woods. Your pal Jim has driven us off the road and has commanded me to get some fat leaves that will serve as makeshift plates, he's very good like that, he's a survivor... you know, damn it, I shouldn't have said Jim was coming, that was a surprise too. So. Well. SURPRISE, CHIP! Jim heard me call for a cab and he picked me up from the airport. He says he's your best buddy... no, wait, he said only buddy, that's what he said. And though he's had a wasted, wasted life, he's a nice man, Chip. I'm glad to see you've made some friends out here. I see you've gone for a guy with one... you have something in common with... I wish I wouldn't... bad girl... I've got you a big present and I am simply not going to tell you what it is, you can push me and laugh at me and call me a weak shit but I am not letting this cat out of the bag. I've let other little secrets out but this one's staying behind locked keys. Is that OK to keep it a secret? For now? Chip?'

'That's fine but I'm not—'

'A moonrock. I've got you a moonrock. I bought it because you deserve it more than any of us, don't you, Chip?'

'I'm not—'

'I mean, between you and me it's not even that nice a moonrock. It may have cost me an arm and a leg but it looks like a prick with two balls. I mean it, Chip, a big prick with two big old balls, like one of the Captain's. Now that's not going to win you round, is it? I mean, who'd want that on their mantelpiece? Not me. Not you either, Chip, I guarantee it. I don't know why I got it for you. You'll hate it.'

'Chip's on the desk, I'm Nancy, would you like to speak—'

'Why don't you give it to Jim? I reckon he'd love this big old moonrock. He can have it on the dash of his car. What do you think? He's got this shitty car but he's made an effort with a tie, he's wearing these shitty clothes and he's looking kind of thin like he hasn't eaten for days. I think a big ball moonrock would give him a bit of class. A talking point. So let's work it that way. It isn't wrapped up, Chip. I'm sorry about that. Given how much it cost it should be in a little testicle box, in a little classy bag. But it isn't at all. It's just wrapped up in a hanky. That's not presentation, is it, Chip?'

'No, but—'

'But, Chip? You listening?'

'Yes.'

'Look pleased with it, will you? I don't want you to throw it back in my face. That'll humiliate me and I think I've humiliated myself enough. Especially in front of the others. I tell you what, here's an idea. I've ordered some Hot Nuts 'cos they make me laugh, you get a tape of the launch, you get some fizzy stuff in and we'll all sit down and watch it together, how about that? What do you say? You do that and I guarantee the day will go well. It'll go off like a dream. You know I'm almost looking forward to it now. I couldn't help feeling a little nervous about today but now I feel... has anyone else showed up yet? Or am I the first? Will it be a full house? Or just me and you? I... so OK, so OK, then in that case let's all dress up in spacesuits... let's...

be naked ... no, not that ... let's wear fake arms ... no ... hang on, that'll confuse matters. Be nice about the moonrock. Say "I got a bit of moon in the end". You tell the Captain not to fuck me. I'll wipe the shit off my dress and it'll all go off without a hitch, what about that as a plan? Will that ...? Now I think about it, the Captain isn't coming. For reasons I can't go into. So, there you go. Back to plan A. I think that's a good plan ... I think ... what's happened to your voice, Chip?'

'I'm not Chip.'

'Who am I talking to?'

'My name's Nancy.'

Pause.

'Hello?'

Pause.

'Are you there?'

'I'm running.'

<Hey!>

'I'm running away now.'

'Don't run ...'

'There's a guy shouting at me to stop ...'

<Hey!>

'... but I'm haring across this field. I'm so fast, Chip, so fast.'

'Just stop for a second, huh? The guy's not going to hurt you.'

'He won't catch me.'

'He'll help you get to a hospital if you—'

'I think only one of the ten could catch up with me. The fastest one. Not her now, but when she was in her prime. She wouldn't stand a chance now. Her knee's fucked 'cos you tripped her up. Don't tell me off for saying fucked 'cos those are her words. "My knee's fucked," she told me. But if you see her, don't mention how fucked she looks. Don't say, "Hi, you, I haven't seen you in years, we thought you'd win, what the fuck happened?" Don't say that to her. Tell her she looks great. Tell her she can still do it. That'll put her at her ease. It'll relax her.

And then when she's relaxed we can toast the one who made it. Are you timing me, Chip? Have I run a mile yet?'

'Slow down now. Why don't you give the phone back to the man.'

'No man anywhere, Chip. I'm still a single girl, no one matches up to the Captain. I had a guy called Cock once, that was his name, but we didn't have anything in common, he disliked the film *Flash Gordon*, so I ran away. Good thing too, he stank of piss. Have you seen *Flash Gordon*, Chip?'

'I'm not Chip, I'm called Nancy.'

'It's a cracker. You'd love it, let's go and see it. I'll take you there tomorrow afternoon when the shuttle's all safe and sound and I'll buy you an ice cream.'

'How about stopping and giving the phone back to the man?'

'Can't...'

'Just walk for a bit.'

'Feeling...'

'Walk and then stop.'

Pause.

'Hello?'

Pause.

'Are you there?'

Pause.

'I've sicked on the dress.'

'Don't worry.'

'I have simply wrecked this garment. There's not one square inch that hasn't got sweat, sick or shit on it. And blood. There's blood on it too. I must have got a period. On top of everything. Don't tell the Captain.'

'You've hurt yourself.'

'Have you got anything I can change into when I get there? A cleaner's apron? Or something from Lost Property? Why do you work in a hotel, Chip? You could do anything.'

'Can you see the man anywhere?'

'I can't see much at all, Chip.'

'Are you standing up?'

'You know what? I'm not. I'm lying down now. And you know another thing? I'm thinking that in order to be alert and refreshed I might take a little nap, what do you think? I think Jim may be taking a little nap so I think I will too, just here. Jim'll honk the horn when he wants to get going.'

'I think you ought to get up and—'

'Forty winks.'

'I don't think it's such a good idea, I think we should get your head seen to … hey … hello?'

Pause.

'Can you hear me?'

Pause.

'Wake up!'

Pause.

'I don't think you should sleep!'

'Who is this?'

'It's Nancy, you fell over and were sick and then—'

'Is that what's on my dress? Sick?'

'Yes.'

'Where's Jim? Jim's picking me up 'cos we're going to … we're going to drive to the E Z Sleep for a surprise.'

'Listen to me carefully now. I want you to stand up and look around.'

'Jim says you wouldn't think to look at him but he's a very careful driver.'

'I'm sure he is, but you need—'

'He has some pills to keep him alert and he stayed dead straight. It was probably some other car that was veering everywhere. I think the other driver should take a leaf out of Jim's book and take some pills. Luckily Jim has got lightning reactions, so Jim swerved, we didn't even get hit, I don't think.'

'Don't you want to stand?'

'I'm lying down.'

'Do you feel dizzy?'

'Who am I talking to, please?'

'I'm Nancy, what's your name?'

'I'm in a field, Nancy.'

'I know.'

'And there are hundreds of birds. They're, let's see, what's the word, flocking I would say. Are they migrating?'

'Tell me your name.'

'Do you know a picture by Van Gogh? It's of a field of wheat and then flying over it is a great flock of black birds. I can see it now in a room. Which room would that be, Nancy?'

'I don't know.'

'It's the last picture he painted. Some say it's OK but nothing special. It's not "Sunflowers". Or the doctor guy. I saw *Lust For Life* and Kirk Douglas is doing that painting and just after painting it he shoots himself. And after I saw that film I bought myself a little magnifying glass and I looked at the picture hanging up in this room. I looked really hard to see if I could pick out any specks of blood in the paint. Because it would've splattered, wouldn't it, Nancy? Well, the birds and field picture is what it looks like here. Just draw a little shuttle and it'd be spot on. Even the sky is as blue. Maybe even bluer. In fact as I look there's just blue. Blue up and down and all around. With a little glint in the sky. What a day.'

S he closes her eyes.
  Houston is concerned.

Don't be. I'll be fine. This isn't really happening. Tension. Nerves. First-time flyer. Shuttle virgin. Hardly surprising.

She deep breathes. A relaxation technique.

She thinks of other things.

The Captain told them that today they must hide. Hide and Seek was revealing and useful and no one should think that they were merely playing a game. They had the run of the house. The Captain would count. Go. One, two, three, four...

The five spread.

Sally went up a flight of stairs and found a bedroom. She opened a window. Crouched on a window ledge was the Model. Shivering in the wind.

'Bugger off,' she said. 'Or give me your coat.'

Sally found a fire escape. She ran down it. She reached ground level. She opened doors to a cellar. It stank. It was waterlogged. The Radar Operator was sitting on a barrel. She turned to leave.

'You can stay if you want,' said the Radar Operator. 'I don't mind company.'

She said it was a bad place for her lungs.

'Don't go,' said the Radar Operator.

She went outside again. She entered the house through a back entrance. She found a study. Inside were seven cameramen on a break. They didn't have to film the Hide and Seek game. They'd get in the way. They were eating biscuits and drinking tea. They turned to look at her.

'Excuse me,' she said. She shut the door. She thought she heard, 'I hope she doesn't win.'

She went into the kitchens. She found a dumb waiter. She opened it. Chip was inside.

'Sorry,' she said.

'Room for two,' he said.

She heard, 'Coming ready or not.' She heard the Captain's footsteps.

She got in. Chip squeezed up. It was pitch black. They waited.

They heard the Captain crashing around.

Chip said the last time he played this game was aged six or seven at a fancy dress party. He came as a cowboy. He climbed onto the roof. No one found him. He watched the others get caught one by one and taken into the garden. Pirates, gladiators, spidermen. They all stood around shouting Chip! Chip! They had his prize ready. A digger.

Chip!

He kept quiet. The kids got bored. They started playing something else. The grown-ups kept looking. They were anxious. Society might hate them for losing a child who'd already lost his parents.

Chip liked the view. No one ever looked up. He decided to be a spaceman. To be above them all. He played with the TV aerial.

Chip! Chip!

He stayed up there all afternoon. When he got hungry he threw a roof slate at someone. It nearly knocked their head off. Chip was found. They didn't tell him off for the roof slate. His folks had disappeared, poor lad.

They heard the Captain find the Radar Operator. Thank God, said the Radar Operator. What a terrible game.

They heard a crash. The Captain found the Comedienne. Trapped in a suit of armour. Good effort though, said the Captain.

The dumb waiter started to move. Chip and Sally cursed. They rose in the dark. Someone was tugging hard. The hatch opened. The Probable Winner tried to scramble inside.

They asked her what the hell she was doing sneaking back into the house. She told them to be quiet, they'd get heard. She tried to get in but she couldn't bend her leg because her knee was strapped up rigid. She cursed. She started to take the dressing off.

Chip told her to be sensible. She told him to shut up. The dressing was taking too long. She needed the hatch solo. She dragged Chip and Sally out.

The Captain heard the noise and made for the dining room.

The Probable Winner got in and closed the hatch.

'Lower me,' she shouted from inside.

Chip told her to forget it.

'Lower me!' she shouted.

Chip told her she was wasting her time. She wasn't allowed to play.

The Captain came into the room. He was disappointed with Chip and Sally. 'Sitting on the floor is an ineffective hiding place.'

Sally said that the Probable Winner came back and took their spot.

Chip opened the hatch.

It was empty.

The Captain told them to pull themselves together. He took them to the lounge. The Radar Operator and the Comedienne were sitting playing cards. Chip and Sally joined them. Chip said the Probable Winner stole their spot.

'She's back?' said the Comedienne.

The Captain returned with the Model. She didn't mind. She was getting cold on the balcony. She said it was as fresh outside as Whizz toothpaste. But there weren't any cameras to catch it.

The Captain said that was everyone. They all got found in fifteen minutes and it wasn't a good showing at all. It demonstrated their lack of imagination.

Chip said the Probable Winner was still in the house. The Radar Operator verified. He was relieved. He thought he was seeing ghosts.

The Captain mobilised everyone plus the cameramen to find her. It took four hours. She was in a wall recess. She was told to leave again, even though she was obviously the best.

Five of them sat in a room. What a mess, they all said. When I go, I'll go with dignity.

They were allowed to drink.

The Captain brought them wine and told them that they'd done very well to have got this far.

The Comedienne drank the lion's share and said it was the only thing that loosened her up. She said the house was full of great individuals. The Model was great. The Radar Operator was great. Sally was great. Chip was great. Van Gogh was great, look at the field of crows.

It's a fake, said the Captain.

It's not the only one, said the Comedienne looking at him.

The Captain took her glass away.

She said, 'Listen to this,' and took out a piece of paper. She read: 'Late on Friday afternoon, 7 March, divers from the Eastern Space and Missile Center LCU, working with the space shuttle recovery operations, while characterising a sonar contact at a depth of approximately one hundred feet, made a possible identification of the *Challenger* crew compartment. Family members of the *Challenger* crew were notified.' She said, 'That's a bona fide NASA press release.'

'Why do you keep it?' asked Chip.

'I keep it because sometimes you think you're going to space but you end up in the ocean.'

The Captain said, 'That's it for the booze.'

Chip told her that there was a camera in spaceship waste units to help astronauts determine if they were shitting accurately. It used to be less high-tech. On the *Apollo* missions they had a kind of top hat with an adhesive brim which you stuck to your ass and because there was no gravity you had to pull the crap out yourself.

The Comedienne went pale.

On *Apollo 8*, said Chip, Frank Borman got the shits and globules of diarrhoea floated around the capsule.

The Comedienne felt faint and went to the toilet. The Captain followed her, telling her that she was doing fine. Just a little bit of nerviness. He was sympathetic. He stroked her hair. He told her not to worry.

She said she did worry. Of course she worried.

They went into the toilet. There was no footage from the airvent camera. Perhaps it had run out of tape, or got steamed up. They were in there for an hour.

The Captain took her to hospital. The cameraman wanted to come too but the Captain forbade it.

He came back alone.

Chip asked him what had happened. He said that there was something badly wrong with the Comedienne's bowel and she hadn't made the cut.

Chip didn't buy it. He said he thought the Comedienne had gone to have something else seen to, as she had been complaining of being late with her period.

The Model said that was scandalous speculation.

ROOM 15. NANCY CARTER. OUTSIDE LINE.

'Don't sleep. Can you hear me? You haven't told me your name.'

<the sound of birds calling>

'How about if I give you a test? That's fun, isn't it? Something to keep you awake and take your mind off your injury. Here goes. Remember the following sequence of numbers: one, four, nine, two. You got that?'

<the sound of the wind>

'I'll ask you to repeat that sequence of numbers to me in a minute. It's my PIN number. See if you remember it. I'll—'

'You shouldn't give out your PIN number, Nancy.'

'I know. You'll hit the jackpot if you find my cash card anywhere. But I trust you. Do you trust me? Tell me your name.'

'Only you and the bank should know it and I'll tell you for why. A man with a little knife came up to me in the street and made me give him my handbag. He had a little knife so I handed it over. He was really dirty. He just tipped everything out onto the ground and out came a few pounds, some make-up, and my cash card. He asked me what the number was. I thought of a fake one – pretty smart, don't you think? The year seventeen ninety. One, seven, nine, zero, I said. But the guy knew I was lying and he waved his little knife around. I said it was true, seventeen ninety was my number and I chose it because it was the year the French Republic was proclaimed. He didn't buy it, he said the French Republic was proclaimed in seventeen ninety-two. I said he could try seventeen ninety-two in the cash machine if he wanted, but only seventeen ninety would get him any money. He told me I'd got my history fucked up. And I think I had, I'm not so good at history. He said in seventeen ninety, things were only just kicking off, there was much beheading to be done. He said there was much beheading to be done now too, and he put his little knife up to my neck. He asked if I wanted to lose my head like a French aristocrat. I said no. Who would? He said I better tell him the damn number then. I said eighteen fifty, the declaration of emancipation. He screamed, "That was eighteen sixty-two, you dumb shit." He drew blood and told me I should bone up on my fucking history. I passed out and he ran off. In future I should either get my facts straight, or stay inside. But that's no life, is it, Nancy?'

'No, it isn't.'

<the sound of a plane flying overhead>

'How are you doing with that number? You remember it?'

<the sound of grass in the breeze>

'A clue. It was the year Christopher Columbus sailed the ocean blue.'

'I'm bad with dates, Nancy, I told you. I can hear blood rushing through my ears.'

'Try not to worry.'

'I can hear my brain, how about that? The brain is a very sensitive organ. A teacher at school made me close my eyes and put my hands into a plastic bag full of egg white and jelly. Yuk, huh, Nancy? It was to teach me about the brain's consistency but I took a handful and threw it at a boy who kept pulling up my skirt.'

'Good for you.'

'The teacher drew diagrams on the blackboard. Brains like cauliflowers, surrounded by the dura mater, connected to the inside of the skull at suture points to suspend the brain within the skull. Like an inner tent. That's how I remember it. You see? I'm not a dumb shit, I should be in space.'

'Are there spots in front of your eyes?'

'Who is this?'

'It's Nancy.'

'A few, Nancy. What does that mean?'

'I don't know.'

'Chip would say that my axons and myelin are torn. He would say my brain is swelling and is being pushed through my foramen magnum and compressing my brain stem. He's so smart, I'm really proud of him.'

'Can you breathe?'

'Yes.'

'Can you swallow?'

'I'm trembling.'

'How about that number? You remember it?'

<birdsong>

'No.'

'Can you see the phone man anywhere?'

<Hello!>

'Is that him shouting, Nancy?'

'Yes. You could try shouting back, what do you say?'

'Is he your boyfriend?'

'He's my husband.'

'Is he cute?'

'Sure.'

<Hello!>

'He's got a nice voice. Does he hit you?'

'No.'

'You want to get rid of him, Nancy. Don't let him get away with it.'

'He doesn't hit me.'

'He might.'

'Call out to him…'

<Hello!>

'He sounds like he's a violent fucker, Nancy, you want to run away.'

'How about if I call out? How would that be? Hold the phone away from your ear. HELLO! HEY! OVER HERE!… Did he hear me? Hold the phone up in the air… HEY! HONEY! FOLLOW MY VOICE! Are you holding it in the air? THE BLEEDING GIRL IS RIGHT OVER HERE, HONEY…'

<Hello!>

'Did he hear me?'

'Perhaps he didn't recognise your voice, Nancy. Perhaps he's forgotten what you sound like.'

'Can you stand up and wave?'

<Hello. Fainter.>

'You know the Captain forgot what I sounded like? We got together after the programme and we found a place to live. He helped me move out but we couldn't get the filing cabinet down the stairs so we lowered it out of the window on a rope. We had a pulley. He drew me a diagram to show how it would work. He told me the physics. I let the rope slip. I had moisturiser on my hands, or sweat, and he didn't jump out of the way.'

<Hello. Fainter still.>

'He was laid out. Like me now. A little dent in his forehead. No blood though. It turned red then blue. Then he started twitching and gurgling. He had to have an operation to relieve the pressure on his brain. I sat with him all night.'

'Please call out.'

'A couple of the ten came to the hospital. They suspected I'd dropped the cabinet on him deliberately because he didn't let me win, but they didn't say so outright. They gave me a wink and said,

"Good girl." I don't think they'd forgiven him for enjoying kicking them out. We thought he was so smart. We thought he could've gone to space himself. But I'm not so sure he was such a whizz kid. The filing cabinet idea was just plain stupid.'

'I don't think you should just lie there.'

'The Captain came out of the coma. He started recovering but it soon became clear that he wasn't all there. His eyes glazed over now and then, he lost track of sentences, his mouth lolled open. Short term he forgot names or what he'd eaten. He got much better but he stopped recognising my voice. He had to carry a tape around with him to remind him how I sounded.'

<hello gone>

'Sometimes he stopped listening to the tape and made himself forget my voice. Then he liked to screw me with the lights out and I had to talk dirty to him. A stranger's voice. He really dug that. Don't mention it to anyone, though, will you, Nancy? The Captain's not coming. He doesn't want anyone to see him. He can't look Chip in the face. Don't tell the others. Don't tell Chip. Not now. Water under the bridge. Let's just keep this between ourselves, huh? A girl thing.'

'How are you feeling?'

'I feel good, Nancy. Am I dead now?'

'No.'

'I think I'm disappearing. Say hello to everyone for me. Or goodbye. Either.'

'You're not—'

'Vanishing into thin air. Until only my voice is left, like Echo. How do I know about Echo?'

'You're still loud and clear.'

'I think me and the phone are lying in the flowers. And I only have your voice, Nancy, and that means you're kind of lying in the flowers too.'

'Yes.'

'And so there's just us and the sound of the birds, and the sound of the wind.'

'I'll send someone to find you.'

'...'

'Hello?'

'...'

'Do you know where you are?... Did you pass any landmarks?'

'...'

'Did you see anything?'

'...'

'Are you there?'

'...'

'Please speak.'

'...'

'Please say something.'

'...'

'You're thinking of Echo and Narcissus... I don't know how you know it... were you taught it in school?... Echo longs to speak but can only repeat... Can you repeat me?... Hello?... Can you say hello?...'

A spotty kid stands at the broken doors of the E Z. He's got a heater type machine with a transparent drum which coats peanuts in a chilli type dust then warms them up.

Hot Nuts for the E Z, says the kid.

Chip tells him the electrics are wet. The plugs are getting sprayed. He's trying to find the fuses. Trying to kill the power.

The kid tells him that the Hot Nut machine doesn't need electricity. You put oil in a burner at the bottom, light it, and then just turn the barrel. He wheels it in. He puts it next to the Fresh and Clear machine. He goes out and fetches two sacks of peanuts and dumps them on the reception desk. He gives Chip a tin of chilli dust. Tells him that he shouldn't get it in his eyes, or if he does, wash it out immediately with … just stand underneath the sprinkler.

A very tall woman appears. Unusually tall. Perhaps six feet four, with a shaved head and a pierced lip. She's dressed as a NASA stewardess.

Jeez, says the kid.

She looks at the pissing rain in the lobby and shouts from the broken doors. She said a chef ordered a sing-o-gram.

Chip tells her the party hasn't really got going yet. He was still waiting for some people. She could go and wait in the marquee if she wanted to.

She doesn't really want to. She has to go and meet her boyfriend. She just wants to do her thing and get out of there.

Chip tells her she may as well go, there's nothing …

She hates to leave a job half done and she could do with the money. She sings:

> I bet you thought it was a blast,
> Spinning round the world so fast.
> Now you feel a big old loser,
> You got close but no cahoona.

Her voice is loud and strong. She does a little tap routine, her vast shoes splashing in the puddles on the lobby floor.

Chip slaps his leg in appreciation. The song was depressing but lively.

The boy with Hot Nuts said now he really did have hot nuts.

She bows. She said she made up the words herself. She hopes it was appropriate.

Chip asks what a cahoona is.

She doesn't know. It seemed to fit.

Chip said it was very nice. He was sorry the chef missed it.

She wonders if she is good enough to make a career out of it.

Chip doesn't see why not.

She is too large to be a real stewardess. Too large for many things. She has difficulty fitting in.

Chip knows what she means. He gives her a hundred wet dollars from petty cash.

She and the Hot Nuts boy leave.

Should've paid more for her to stay, mutters Chip. Should've...

Another spasm. She drinks some water. It comes up again. Little sacks of water drift around her room. Wobbling, rotating, separating, joining.

Her head spins. Memories crowd in.

The Model said, who's the favourite of us four?

Chip said she was. He thought Fresh and Clear would be putting pressure on the others to mess up. They didn't have the Model's cheekbones.

The Captain wanted someone to take the reins. He wanted it to be a man. He looked at the Radar Operator whose beard made him look most manly.

The four of them stood on the edge of a swimming pool and were told that there were bricks lying on the bottom. The bricks at the shallowest end were at a depth of six feet. There were other bricks too, deeper.

The Captain was using a time-to-toughen-up voice. He pushed hard.

The Radar Operator muttered to Sally. He said he was having nightmares, he was dreaming about dead dogs.

Chip overheard. He asked if the dogs had space helmets on.

They didn't.

He asked if he was dreaming about dead monkeys too.

Yes, he said.

Chip nodded wisely. He said despite the lack of a space helmet it was obvious he was dreaming of Laika, the first dog in space, who, contrary to the official line, probably died about thirteen hours into the flight.

That's crap, said the Radar Operator, and besides, he was speaking to Sally. What did Sally think?

She didn't get a chance to answer because the Captain pushed her into the water.

She swam around and found a brick and picked it up. She swam to the surface and put the brick at the Captain's feet. The Captain said, 'This is supposed to be a race.'

She swam down again but faster this time, and found another brick. Her lungs were more efficient now. Her body could store more oxygen and she was able to look around. She saw the others, flitting around her, paler in the water, faces both pinched and bloated by the pressure. When they dived in they cut through the water like fleshy torpedoes before becoming all arms and kicking legs. She thought they were an awkward shoal. Bodies struggling, no gills.

At the deepest end she saw a shape. She swam over to it and found the Radar Operator holding three bricks in his arms, standing upright, feet planted on the bottom, held there by the extra weight. There was distress in his face and neck. It was a man hitting three minutes and wondering how to play it. Around his face his beard floated like lichen on a rock.

She saw Chip swim to him and touch his shoulder. The Radar Operator looked at Chip as if to say Leave Me Be. But also Am I Doing This? His goggles were round his neck and his eyes were wide. His lips were squashed and pursed.

Chip took the bricks from him and dropped them to the floor. Ballast gone, the Radar Operator floated upwards. He struggled to swim down but Chip held his arms. The Radar Operator's breath broke before he reached the surface. His lungs filled with water.

The Captain dragged him onto the side and started pumping his chest and blowing air into his mouth.

'I was going to be going through this with you anyway,' said the Captain.

The Model said the situation was similar to a driving test in that if you're faced with a genuine emergency stop during the test you didn't have to perform a simulated one later.

The Captain told her to stop talking. She muttered that he'd started it.

The Radar Operator coughed out a pint of swimming pool and turned onto his side. Everyone clapped and the Captain nodded, taking his due. Chip saw his eyes flick towards a camera to check that his heroism had been recorded. He caught Chip catching the look and said, 'What were you two doing down there?'

Chip said brick wise the Radar Operator had bitten off more than he could chew.

Sally verified.

The Captain said he hoped they'd all learned an important lesson. He said that when you took risks you weren't just risking yourself but you were risking the entire operation, he said it wasn't just a question of … at which point the Radar Operator rolled himself back into the water and had to be rescued again. Not by the Captain though, he was wearing a clip-on microphone and didn't know if diving into the pool would electrocute himself.

The Radar Operator went. Unstable. Three left.

The E Z safe shorts out and the door springs open. It bleeps. A watery bleep.

The cleaner hears the bleep and wades out of Lost Property and scrabbles around inside. She finds papers. She shields them from the rain.

She locks herself back in Lost Property to read them in private. The *Hey Jesus* broadcaster shouts. It's happened. A hit. A landing. A coming. Pinpointed. Confirmed. Praise the Lord.

The cleaner turns off *Hey Jesus* in case the evangelist starts railing against mammon, or revenge, or the law, or any of the things the cleaner might wish to indulge in as a result of the documentation she's found.

Chip closes his eyes and hums the sing-o-gram song. *I bet you thought it was a blast ...*

ROOM 12. MRS BAINS.

'Chip, the news is showing shuttle repeats and everyone is saying these are exciting times.'

'Yes.'

'*Hey Jesus* is also saying these are exciting times.'

'Yes.'

'I guess in all the excitement the room service card just went out of your head.'

'It did. I apologise, it's wet down here, every bit of paper is—'

'I'm not sure I agree with either the news or *Hey Jesus*. I think these are very dangerous times, but then that's just an old woman speaking. It's you young people who think these are exciting times.'

'As it happens—'

'People like you and my son. *Do you agree, son? Aren't these just the most exciting times?*'

'Who are you talking to, Mrs Bains?'

'I'm talking to my boy here.'

'I didn't realise you had your son with you, I thought—'

'No reason why you should. You didn't see us check in.'

'No.'

'We came yesterday.'

'That would be the reason then.'

'I wouldn't have brought it up at all in fact, but I'm feeling bad about ruining this little reunion of yours.'

'I'm sorry?'

'No need to be sorry, Chip. I'm sure my son isn't. He's never sorry. You can't hear him, Chip, as he has some tape over his mouth, but he's shaking his head.'

'He's got tape on his mouth?'

'Which won't make him much fun at this little gathering, will it? Won't help his conversation one little bit. Are you all down there now in the lobby? Talking about him behind his back?'

'I'm a bit confused about—'

'We all get confused, Chip. My son gets confused from time to time, *don't you, son?* Oh, he's nodding now, he doesn't mind holding his hands up to a little confusion. In fact if his hands weren't tied to the radiators I'm sure he would actually hold them up. *You'd hold up your hands to a little confusion, wouldn't you, son?...* Yep, that's a yes from him. About time too. So don't feel alone in your confusion, Chip. I'm confused almost all the time. Confused about what I'm doing. Confused about why I married the man I did. Confused about why I brought a son into the world only to give me thirty-five years of almost constant, gut-wrenching worry.'

'Could we go back a bit?'

'But you know what helps to end confusion, Chip?'

'No.'

'Decisive action. I tell you, I can't recommend that too highly. Decisive action is the way forward. Yesterday I decided I'd had enough, and I acted decisively and I haven't looked back. My confusion has vanished into thin air. Along with my worry.'

'Your son is tied to the radiators?'

'Yes he is, Chip. Speaking of which, how do I turn them down? He's finding them a trifle scalding.'

'Um, there's a knob on the pipe at the floor.'

'You know you're a hundred per cent correct there, Chip. I see it. I guess I just give that a little twist and the heat lets up.'

'Yes, Mrs Bains. Can I—'

'*Things are looking up, son. Things are really looking up.* You know what I see, Chip?'

'No.'

'I see a hundred men standing on top of a submarine at a naval parade. And a crew loading boxes of food on board. And a sea. Grey. Rough. And stone-faced military men. Weeping mothers. Helicopters. Radar.'

'Is this on the news, Mrs Bains?'

'And a submersible being loaded into a fat plane. And a picture demonstrating the effect of strong currents on a rescue attempt. And a reporter talking of the sound of knocking on the stricken vessel's hull.'

'Mrs Bains...'

'And unavailable government officials. And someone describing the procedures for rescuing a submarine. Talking in shorthand. SUBLOOK, SUBMISS, SUBSUNK. And how a choppy sea is a treacherous sea. And oxygen disappearing. And divers wrenching the hatch open.'

'Are you all right, Mrs Bains?'

'No. Hardly ever. These are the thoughts I have. Day in, day out. But not now. Now I see him safely tied to my radiator and there's not a grey sea, or a stone-faced military man in sight. I won't have him getting on board, Chip. Not any more. He's staying here. He's staying put. His sub will leave, it will leave without him. And this mother is very happy about that.'

'I'm going to—'

'As soon as the hatch shuts, that is it for the outside world, Chip. Sixty days underwater. Anything can happen and you would never know it. Your house could be burning down, your mother could be dying, the stock market could be crashing, the world could be burning. My son was underwater when his daughter was born, when his brother was stabbed in a bar, when his father died. They all went and he didn't know a thing about it. I don't feel so good myself, Chip. I'm getting on. Each day is a struggle. I feel sure that I'll perish the moment he gets underwater. I won't have him below the surface a moment longer.'

'What do you want me to do?'

'I don't want you to do anything, Chip. You've done plenty. You pulled him out of the water once before. Your duty's done.'

'That's your son?'

'Yes. My little boy.'

'I . . . I didn't . . .'

'He's here for the party, the reunion. I don't think he had a proper chance to thank you for pulling him out of the water. He's very grateful for that.'

'He didn't seem it at the time.'

'Well then I'm grateful for it. And he is too, now. He's longing to see you.'

'I see.'

'It's all right, Chip.'

'Is it?'

'I'll send him down shortly. Once his submarine has left and he can't get on it. Once he's AWOL. Won't be long now. *Not long now, son.* The whole situation'll be wrapped up in no time. Done and dusted. I'll go. Leave you to your party. You don't want an old lady interfering. You can send a cleaner up here, she'll give the room a quick once over, though perhaps some extra work is needed near the radiator, and the place will be spick and span ready for the next lucky visitor to the E Z sleep.'

Chip can't see very well. There's mist in the lobby. Lights are flickering.

He doesn't know what to do. He's sinking.

He wonders how an old lady could... the Radar Operator was a big man. Trained. Strong as an ox. Perhaps she tied him up while he was asleep. Or put pills in his wine.

ROOM 11. MR MOULIN.

'Sir, Mrs Bains in Room 12 has tied her son to the radiators.'

'That's not what you're calling me about.'

'Yes it is, sir. And the sprinkler system is flooding the lobby.'

'You're telling me there's a limo outside.'

'No.'

'It's going to be making a stop at a liquor store to pick up some Orbiter. I'm expecting the driver to break the speed limit and if one speck of oil or grease gets on my suit I'm going to sue him. Tell him I don't want any conversation unless he happens to know of a tight-assed escort we can pick up on the way. Tell him my preferences, blonde hair, twenty-five or under. Tell him that if he breathes a word of the trip to anyone he's going to get a visit from guys in dark glasses who'll cut a new smile in his face before shooting him in the guts. Get him to start up the engine and wait underneath the trees. See to it that no one sees me leave the building. Tell anyone who sounds like a journalist or a TV reporter that I'm still in my room but unavailable. Say I've got a bad dose of the shits from a club sandwich. Hoover the carpet. Change the bed linen. There's an earring by the phone, slip it under Nancy's door. If any faxes come for me from the E Z Slumber, memorise them, then put them in the shredder. Or eat them. If war breaks out in the next twenty-four hours, you don't know me and we've never had this conversation. As far as you're concerned you had a mature, dapper French guest in Room 11 who kept himself to himself but was courteous and tipped well. All right, that's all. I'll be coming out the lift in three minutes, don't acknowledge me.'

'The limo isn't here, sir, and the lift isn't working.'

'Don't tell me this, Chip, tell me the limo's revving up.'

'No one's here.'

'What about your pal Jim?'

'He's not here either.'

'Goddamn it.'

'Yes.'

'God-fucking-dammit.'

'Yes, sir.'

'This is killing me.'

'I know.'

'I'm dying.'

'I'm sorry.'

'I'm dying here.'

'I don't know what's happened.'

'I'm dying and my hotel's dying. And it's raining.'

'I know.'

'You know where there's life?'

'No.'

'Alabama. There's life in Alabama and I can't get there. There are moves afoot. There are men with purpose. There are lives being lived and affected.'

'Yes sir.'

'Can you drive?'

'Not any more, sir.'

'What about automatics?'

'It's possible but—'

'Is there an automatic car in the car park?'

'I don't know.'

'I want you to requisition one of the guests' cars.'

'Sir—'

'Requisition it in the name of the Bilderberg group.'

'I can't do that, Mr Moulin.'

'Help me.'

'I don't know how, sir.'

'Help me!'

'Sir, Room 12 has tied her son to the radiators.'

'Leave it and help me.'

'It's—'

'Get me out of here!'

'Sir—'

'Damn you!'

Chip walks through the rain and up the stairs to the first floor. The sprinklers are on in the first-floor corridor. The carpets squelch under his feet.

Room 12 has a Do Not Disturb sign. He hammers on the door.

He shouts out for Mrs Bains.

He doesn't get an answer.

He hammers some more.

No answer.

He tries his master key. Something's jammed in the slot.

He hammers again.

Mrs Bains tells him that unless he's got her room service card...

He hasn't.

...then he should go away. Hasn't he seen the sign?

Do Not Disturb is smudging. He asks if it's raining inside her room.

She doesn't answer.

Chip looks around for a fire axe. There isn't one. He thumps the fire-alarm glass. It sets off more sprinklers.

Chip splashes and skids down the stairs.

Should've called in sick today, he mutters. Should've...

ROOM 15. NANCY CARTER.

'Uh-huh?'

'Are you all right, Chip?'

'No.'

'It's started to rain in my room.'

'I don't know how to make it stop, Miss Carter.'

'And I heard a terrible thing.'

'It's Room 12, Nancy, she's tied her son to the radiators.'

'No. It's not Room 12, it's something else, something terrible. I think you should sit down.'

'I am sitting down.'

'I think you should have a glass of water.'

'It's wet enough here.'

'I think your friends are dead.'

'Uh-huh.'

'I think two of your friends are dead in a car crash. My husband came across this wreck and they were coming to see you. I'm sorry, Chip.'

'Don't worry, Miss Carter. I'm sure it's someone else.'

'She kept saying Chip.'

'No. Don't worry.'

'I wish I wasn't telling you this, I feel...'

'It's nothing, Miss Carter.'

'Chip…'

'The roads are very safe. It's space travel that's dangerous. Space travel requires care and concentration.'

The shuttle trail drifts over the E Z. Data and information satellites fly high above that. One of them will contain information about Jim's whereabouts but minor disturbing forces can cause them to drift out of their orbital slot. The gravitational pull of the sun, or the moon, can pull them off course. Hydrazine gas from thruster nozzles compensates for these irregularities but once the propellant runs out, the satellite drifts into space, taking all the information with it. Lost forever.

Chip wills Jim into the lobby. The lobby stays empty. Chip stares into nothing. He keeps his eyes open and they fill with moisture. He blinks and a tear runs down his cheek and over his chin and onto the E Z reception desk.

He tastes it. Salty. Perhaps a little tangy.

OUTSIDE LINE.

'Jim? Can you hear me?'

'…'

'You don't have to speak.'

'…'

'The sun's catching the sprinkler mist and there's a rainbow here in the lobby.'

'…'

'You should come and see it.'

'…'

'You're there, I know. It's this switchboard that's faulty.'

'…'

'That's what's happened. Faulty switchboard.'

S he drifts into sleep. The pain wakes her out of it. Nasty pain. Scary pain.

The crew are talking about her. She can hear them talking to Houston.

Eyes close again.

Other things.

She's one of three now, herself. Chip. The Model. The Model said, 'I was wondering if you were sabotaging us, Chip, but I think perhaps we're sabotaging ourselves.'

Chip agreed.

'Why would we do that?'

Chip didn't know.

They were driven to a hangar.

'Ejection seats can rescue a pilot from a doomed aircraft,' said the Captain.

He pointed to the Ejection Seat Trainer. The three could see it fine.

It was a tall tower. At the bottom there was an ejection seat – 'An *actual* ejection seat,' said the Captain. Around it was a simulated cockpit made of fibreglass. 'You have the fire controls,' said the Captain, 'but I have control of ejection G-force, from one through nine Gs of simulation.' The three were taught ejection decision parameters, procedures and situation awareness.

Chip was up first.

The Model said, 'Go Chip.'

He was put in the restraint system. He asked if the equipment had been properly tested. The Captain told him that over the years live testing of ejection systems had been done on chimpanzees and even bears.

He didn't mean that, he meant—

The Captain said, 'The number one cause of ejection fatalities is the pilot delaying ejection initiation until they are outside the system's survivable performance envelope.'

Chip wondered who had told him to speak in this way.

'So on the green light,' said the Captain, 'quick as you can.'

Chip waited. Red. Red. Red. Green.

Chip fired. He shot up the tower. The Captain gave him the full nine Gs and hoped his eyeballs would pop.

Chip was lowered. 'I can't see,' said Chip.

'You'll be eating a hearty dinner in an hour,' said a medic. And he was.

Sally was strapped in. She told everyone that an ejection seat from an SR-71 was believed to be being used as a throne by the ruler of a small island in the Pacific. She said she felt like a queen.

Red. Red. Red. Green.

She took the nine and came down saying, 'Again, again.'

The Model said that the effectiveness of the human cannon depended on Newton's Second Law which stated that the acceleration of an object was directly proportional to the net external force acting on the object and inversely proportional to the mass of the object. She thought that her lighter weight would mean—

'It's all been calculated,' said the Captain.

Red. Red. Red. Green.

The Model had the fire controls but she was still concerned about the physics and didn't want to touch them yet.

'Slow reaction,' wrote the Captain.

A minute passed.

'Very slow.'

They gave her the sequence again.

Red. Red. Red. Green.

'Compressing the spine can cause excruciating pain and long term posture problems. I've spent my life sitting and walking with a straight back. A straight back is essential for healthy living.'

Red. Red. Red. Green.

'The typical injuries from such a contraption are in the lower thoracic and lumbar regions of the spine,' she said. 'Look at the people who get shot out of cannons. They shrink after each firing. If I were to join a circus, I would be a trapeze artist.'

Red. Red. Red. Green.

'If you've got no backbone, no backbone to speak of—' She waited five minutes. Ten. An hour. They disabled the fire controls.

'If you've got no backbone...'

She stayed there all night.

Chip and Sally went back to the house alone.

The cleaner bursts out of Lost Property, skids through the lobby and heads towards the stairs.

Chip shouts after her about a mop.

She doesn't answer. I'm si-i-i-i-ging in the rain. Her voice is strong and powerful.

Chip shouts after her about the Radar Operator in Room 12. She doesn't answer. What a glo-o-o-orious feeling.

Chip shouts after her about Jim.

She doesn't answer. I'm ha-a-a-a-appy again. She splashes up the stairs.

Chip shouts after her about the faulty switchboard.

He just hears rain.

ROOM 14. THE MODEL.

'My room is spraying me with water, Chip. Should we evacuate?'

'I don't know.'

'Has the water filled the lobby?'

'No.'

'Where has it all gone?'

'I should think it's soaked into the hotel.'

'Will it destroy the foundations?'

'I don't think it's that serious.'

'Do you know any Dutch, Chip?'

'No.'

'I don't know much myself but my mother speaks it. It's beautiful.'

'I'm sure.'

'In Dutch there is an expression *plaatsvervangende schaamte*. This means a shame in humanity. A shame in being human. You see someone acting foolishly or stupidly and you do not laugh at him, you do not feel Schadenfreude, instead you feel a sense of humiliation that this is how your species can behave.'

'Uh-huh.'

'It is terrible to be the cause of this shame.'

'You've got nothing to be ashamed of, we all—'

'I have great teeth.'

'I know.'

'I've flashed these teeth for just about everyone, toothpaste companies, dental companies, floss companies. I have full lips.'

'I know.'

'I've used my lips for lipstick commercials, gloss commercials, cold sore commercials. I have a taut abdomen. I've rented it for deodorant commercials, fitness equipment, fizzy drink advertisements. I've used my breasts for bra commercials and shower commercials. There's hardly an inch of me left that hasn't been bought by someone. I'm never off the screen.'

'I've noticed.'

'I sit with my family and we watch the television and suddenly in a break I appear in a gymnasium with sweat on my body and a bottle of Fresh and Clear and I take a great gulp and my family all wince like they're watching me drink someone's piss. And my sister says, that stuff tastes like shit. And my mother says, it kills my plants. And on screen I'm gulping and gulping like there's been a drought in the gym, and it's dripping down my chin and over my neck and the camera's following it down my cleavage. And they all look away. They ask me if I like Fresh and Clear and I say it makes me sick and dizzy and they all stare at me and tell me that it's *plaatsvervangende schaamte* that's making me sick and dizzy. And why didn't I become a spacewoman?'

'How do you answer that?'

'I say I choked on the ejector.'

'Yes.'

'I say I did better than most.'

'You did.'

'I say the other eight have disappeared from view, I watch out for them but they've gone. They're nowhere.'

'I'm in a hotel that's full of water…'

'Exactly. I say Chip's in a hotel.'

'The Radar Operator is tied to a radiator.'

'Is he?'

'You might be able to do something about that, he's just in the room next to you.'

'Sally gets to go sky high. She's in the stars. She has a letter from the President in her spacesuit.'

'I know.'

'You know she actually has taken Whizz toothpaste with her.'

'Really?'

'Whizz toothpaste called me and told me they'd just found out. They asked me if I could remember if she has good teeth.'

'She has.'

'She's got great teeth, Chip.'

'Yes.'

'But not as good as mine.'

'No.'

'I did better than most.'

'You did.'

'I did better than the Chef. Much, much better.'

'Yes.'

'And the others.'

'You did very well.'

'I didn't do as well as you, Chip.'

'No.'

'You got further.'

'Yes.'

'You got almost as far as her.'

'Not that far, though.'

'No. She's miles away.'

'Sky high.'

'Oh dear, Chip.'

'Don't worry.'

'I wish I felt better.'

'I understand.'

'Do you feel *plaatsvervangende schaamte*?'

'Probably.'

'I do, Chip.'

'Yes.'

'I scratched up my face.'

'I saw.'

'Do you think it will scar?'

'Perhaps.'

'I haven't had much enthusiasm ever since—'

'Me neither.'

'And it was just down to you two at the end.'

'Yes.'

'You and her.'

'Yes.'

'You made it to the last day.'

'Yes I did.'

The Radar Operator falls from the first-floor window and lands on the ground outside the E Z doors. He lands on broken glass.

He grunts.

Chip grabs the first aid and goes out to him. The bandages are wet. The plasters have lost their stickiness.

The Radar Operator is dressed in uniform but has a wet patch on his trousers where he's pissed himself, and he hasn't got much of a beard any more. The tape has ripped parts of it off.

He groans. He has cuts and abrasions.

Chip asks him if he's all right.

The Radar Operator looks at Chip. Chip is soaking wet. His hair is flat and his clothes stick to his body.

He holds out his hand. Chip shakes it.

No, says the Radar Operator, help me up.

Chip tries to pull him to his feet. He falls over again. He asks the time.

Chip doesn't know. The E Z Clock has broken. He guesses it's getting on for nine o'clock.

Not too late, says the Radar Operator. Not too late at all. He stays put. He looks up.

Chip asks him if his mother let him watch the launch on TV.

The Radar Operator nods. He says Sally did well. Very well.

Chip agrees.

The Radar Operator said he'd once been trapped in a submarine. The rescue operation had been successful, but it had almost killed his family with worry. He left the navy. He'd been looking for a new challenge so he applied for the space programme. He'd realised in the swimming pool that a tin is a tin, and if he was going to be in a tin, he wanted to be underwater in a tin where rescue was possible. Not in the stars in a tin. So he rejoined.

Why be in a tin at all? asks Chip.

All the best journeys happen in tins, he says.

He gets to his feet. He winces. He brushes himself down. He sees the Probable Winner's beat-up car. Dented. Keys in the ignition.

He asks if it works.

Chip doesn't know.

He hobbles towards it. His uniform is filthy. He opens the car door.

Chip wants to know if it's raining in Room 12.

The Radar Operator nods.

Chip thinks he should get everyone out. The ceilings might fall in.

The Radar Operator made a deal with his mother. If she let him go, he'd quit the navy for good. She locked the door and flushed the key down the toilet then untied him.

He pushed her on the bed and climbed out of the window. He didn't like pushing her. No one likes pushing their mother. But he had no choice…

Chip asks if she is all right.

The Radar Operator points out that she tied him to a radiator. Course she isn't all right.

He looks at Chip. He apologises. He has to go.

Chip says it was good to see him after all this time.

The Radar Operator gets in the car and starts it. He says that as he was hanging out of the window he heard a voice drift over the breeze. It said, 'Are you jumping? Are you trying to kill yourself?'

That was the Holiday Rep, says Chip. She's by the marquee.

The Radar Operator looks over. He sees the banner. She waves at him. He revs. He thinks perhaps she was right. Perhaps he was trying to kill himself. Perhaps he is doing that now.

Where are you going? asks Chip.

I'm going to the naval base, says the Radar Operator and he shuts the car door and looks at the petrol gauge.

The Holiday Rep shouts at him to stay as Chip is going to be making a big speech. One worth sticking around for.

The Radar Operator puts the car into gear and drives away. Steam comes out of the exhaust. He weaves across the car park, the burst tyre shredding rubber. He snags the marquee's guy rope. Bunting gets caught in the exhaust pipe. He trails it across Freedom Avenue. The marquee falls to its knees.

The Holiday Rep jumps clear. The marquee staggers and then topples over.

ROOM 16. THE CHEF.

'I came out of the shower and there's another shower in my bedroom.'

'Sorry.'

'Is there a fire?'

'No.'

'What's that outside? Is that our marquee?'

'Yes.'

'It's fucked.'

'Yes.'

'Has my sing-o-gram arrived?'

'She went.'

'Aw shit. What did she look like?'

'She was very tall.'

'Tall?'

'Over six foot. With a shaved head.'

'Really?'

'Kind of pretty.'

'I wasn't expecting her to look like that.'

'Well, that's what she did look like.'

'Did she look Wet and Wanting?'

'She looked kind of wet, but then the sprinklers are—'

'How about Wanting?'

'I think she wanted something, I mean we all want—'

'I knew it. You know there's a guy out there somewhere, a guy with a good nose, who's got a hell of a dinner coming his way tonight.'

'Really.'

'One tasty dish, that one.'

'I paid her for the song. I should put it on your bill.'

'I don't think I can afford it.'

'Never mind.'

'Do you have people who manhandle non-payers like me? E Z heavies?'

'No.'

'Would the law get called?'

'I think we seize your assets.'

'I haven't got anything.'

'Then you might have to work it off, I'm not sure.'

'Hoover the hallways? Shine shoes?'

'I don't know.'

'That's not such a bad life is it, Chip?'

'No.'

'Could be the life change I've been looking for. Things haven't really worked out for me.'

'I don't think it'll come to that. You probably won't be charged for extras, in the light of the sprinklers.'

Chip sits on the lobby floor. The water doesn't rise. It's draining somewhere. There isn't a dry patch on Chip.

A coach pulls up outside the E Z.

Forty people inside.

Refugees from the E Z Slumber.

The driver gets out and asks what the hell happened.

Chip shrugs. Emergency non-natural.

The driver wants to know if Chip had the fax about the forty guests.

Chip says all the paper in the E Z has become mulch.

Well, have you got any rooms? asks the driver.

Chip has but it's raining in each one.

The driver covers his head with a newspaper. He says the E Z

Slumber has been hit by a piece of space junk. A Chinese satellite in a decaying orbit. It had been tracked and its impact pinpointed. It hit the Slumber square on. Knocked out twenty rooms and reception. The driver hopes the place was properly evacuated. Sometimes Dennis on the desk liked to sneak around and tamper with the TV channels. Set them all to porn.

The driver asks Chip where the next E Z is.

The E Z Rest, says Chip. Across state.

The driver says he'll call ahead. He sends his passengers over to Pancake Parlour. He gets out of the spray.

E Z Slumber guests drift out of the coach. They've had a long drive. They stretch. One or two ask if there's been a fire. A couple ask if there are any refreshments in the collapsed marquee.

The Stenographer gets out. She walks through the broken door and tiptoes through the puddles in the lobby.

She got the wrong hotel. She feels like an idiot. She asked a kid called Dennis where the space party was being held. He didn't know. Space perhaps?

Chip tells her not to feel like an idiot.

His missing arm is a shock to her. She didn't know. She's been laying low. She gets threatening messages now and then, and sometimes she thinks she's being followed. She's convinced it's the Fresh and Clear people but the police can't find any proof. She had a garbled message about today from her sister.

She wants to know if Fresh and Clear are responsible for his arm.

Chip shakes his head.

She asks if he's sure, they're capable of anything.

He's sure.

She asks if anyone else has arrived.

Chip nods. A couple.

She hasn't seen the launch yet. There wasn't a TV in the E Z coach.

Chip tells her that the lobby TV is full of water and she's better off catching it at Pancake Parlour.

ROOM 12. MRS BAINS.

'Does my son hate me?'

'You tied him to a radiator.'

'But does he hate me?'

'No.'

'He lied to me. He pushed me over.'

'I know.'

'I wish you'd let him drown in the pool, Chip.'

'You don't mean that.'

'I do. Then I wouldn't be worrying about it now. You know what? I watched him drive away. He was rough with the car, Chip. He couldn't wait. I saw him spin it forwards and bounce it over speed humps and rumble strips, nearly killing that poor woman by the marquee. I saw him roar up Freedom Avenue and head towards the highway.'

'I'm sorry, Mrs Bains.'

'But you know what's happened?'

'No.'

'He's broken down. I can see him from here, from my window. He's blocking the fast lane and there's fire coming out of the bonnet. He tried to put it out but he's worried about it exploding in his face and he's standing back watching it. There's a big jam building up. He's trying to stop people from getting too close.'

'Uh-huh.'

'He's waving people away. Now he's rushing about. I guess he's trying to find a telephone. He's limping. He must have hurt himself as he fell. Poor boy.'

'Yes.'

'Poor boy. I should go out and help him but I'm feeling a bit tired.

I think I'll take a little nap and then go and help him later.'

'OK.'

'If you do get round to that room service card, just slip it under the door, I'll probably be asleep.'

'In the rain?'

'I don't mind it too much, Chip. I don't mind it at all.'

Chip finds a fuse box. He flicks the switches. The sprinklers keep sprinkling. The Fresh and Clear keeps gurgling. The switchboard keeps humming. They must all be on separate wires. Kept alive by a secret system.

He lies down on the floor and waits to be washed away somewhere.

S he has a sweat and a temperature of over a hundred and three. She's in pain. She's in terrible pain.

Not now. Not now, God.

God ignores her.

Please be better, she thinks.

Please improve. Please heal.

She worsens.

She feels faint.

Please be in a safe place.

According to insurance companies, she is in one of the most dangerous places.

She closes her eyes.

She goes back.

After the ejection seat, she and Chip were driven back to the house together.

'Night,' he said.

'Night,' she replied.

'Good luck,' he said.

'Good luck,' she said.

She reminded him how on their first night in the house they both puked into their pillowcases. She told him she might again but thought it was more to do with a day in an ejection seat.

He pretended he didn't care by pretending to snore.

In the morning the Captain looked at them. You two, eh? he said, as if he could hardly believe it. They could hardly believe it either.

They were taken to another hangar. A long drive away. They cracked gags but they were both thinking, you or me.

They were put into scuba diving equipment and thrown into a big tank which contained a replica of the forward section of an orbiter crew station. It could be tilted, pitched and rolled on hydraulics.

The Captain showed it off. State of the art, he said.

And it was, she thinks now as she drifts. It was spot on.

They swam into the machine. They airlocked themselves inside.

They had to perform various procedures. 'Today is about co-operation,' said the Captain. 'Today is about working together as a unit. Do not think of yourselves.'

In the scuba she could hear her breath.

Their progress was slow and dreamlike. They were as clumsy as crabs.

Weightlessness is nothing like water. She is light. She could pirouette if she wasn't so sore.

She is four hours into the mission, and she should be asleep. Her schedule tells her she should be dreaming.

She isn't though. She's wide awake. So is everyone else. Houston has decided that an appendectomy is required under normal gravity conditions.

They have to turn back.

She wishes Chip was with her.

OUTSIDE LINE.

'I'm lying on the floor, Jim, letting the water fill my ears and I remember looking into her mask. She was able to wink at me.

'On a space walk, impossibly high above the earth, looking at the planet the way I looked at the moon, listening to my own breath in my ears, dependent, childlike, I thought if anything was going to hold back the terror then a little wink from Sally would do it. I wondered if the camera had caught it. I thought winks could end up being the most important factor. Winks could be the clincher.'

'...'

'Inside the crew compartment trainer, the lighting turned from white to red. And for the two of us this was the start of the Emergency Pad Egress and Bailout Operation.'

'...'

'This was crunch time.'

'...'

'The trainer started to tilt as if slipping out of orbit and red light turned to no light. In the darkness we had to secure imitation equipment, find the imitation airlock, and make our imitation escape, making sure that our imitation space colleague made it out with us. It was about pressurisation procedures. It was about pressure generally.

'I swam around blindly, trying to feel for familiar handles. I found that I was bad at orientation in darkness. I had useless faith in my inner ear.

'The compartment tilted. Levers that were normally pulled upwards now had to be pulled down and to the left, or rather to the right and ... I tried to work this out but the compartment shifted and I didn't stay relative to it. I thought that positive action was required now, this second, and at the same time "this second" had passed and I was thinking I was being too slow and I wasn't thinking of the job in hand, I was only thinking of being too late. I was aware of a body moving around me. It might've been my own.'

'...'

'A catastrophic re-entry came into my mind. Bad angles came into my mind. Wrong maths. Failing parachutes. I thought of being knocked out of orbit and spun into space. I thought of burning up and freezing up and shrivelling up.

'Claustrophobia appeared like the enemy over the brow of a not too distant hill. I stared into the enemy's eyes. It hated me and wanted to kill me. I found a handle and pulled it. A door opened and I swam into a smaller room, an antechamber. I knew it was smaller because I was bumping into things more frequently. Above me was another handle to a door. I thought above that door was the surface of the water. Or the bottom of the tank. The tilting contraption had made up down, and down up. My duties were straightforward. My obligations were clear. I was to make sure that she was with me. I was to wait for her thumbs-up. I was to close the antechamber door. Only then was I to open the top hatch. This was the agreed procedure. It'd been drilled into me by the Captain who hated me for not putting a foot wrong.'

'...'

'But I put a foot wrong now. It was just a little thing. I closed the antechamber door and I was alone. I opened the top door and swam out into the tank. I escaped alone. I panicked alone.'

'...'

'That was all. There was some light in the water. Above me I could see the watery outline of the Captain. He had a clipboard. I saw him write, I felt him write, "Chip is a disorientated man. He is an incompetent man, he is a lonely man." I wasn't ready to be shown the clipboard and I swam to the bottom of the tank and sat amongst the hydraulics and asked myself if I could pull things round. At the same time I questioned my inner resources. I asked myself, how brave am I? How much stamina do I have? How much fight is there in me? Have I got a good heart? Is my selfishness monstrous? How much would I sacrifice for a cause? For a loved one? Do I have any value other than general capability?'

'…'

'I saw a shape emerge from the top door. She had followed. She looked around for me. I saw her swim to the surface. I asked myself, how good a liar am I? I wondered if I could claim to have been told the wrong procedure, that I had my role and hers mixed up. That she made the mistake. I could claim to have swum around disorientated in the dark. Claim a fault in the orbiter doors.'

'…'

'I didn't think I could claim that. There were cameras everywhere. There was one now, looking at me skulking at the bottom of the tank. Seeing me hiding like a little boy. Indecisive. Pathetic…'

They look for protocols. They run through systems checks. They start a new time line.

She cries. Her tears float.

They run through procedures. They inform the Space Station.

A crew member floats into her room.

'Do you know about the explorer Captain Cook?' she asks.

'A bit.'

'Do you know where he died?'

'Was it Hawaii?'

'Do you know how?'

'No.'

'No one knows. He was thought to be Lonoikamakahiki. The God of Harvest. He was given the daughter of the High Chief. She got pregnant and gave Cook a child. But then he was found dead on a beach. Someone might have realised he wasn't a god and attacked him. He might have got into a gunfight. Perhaps a crewman got sick of travelling and poisoned him. Perhaps his appendix burst. There are many accounts…'

He nods. 'You're not going to die,' he says.

She isn't so sure.

'Listen,' he says, 'this is still space. You're still in orbit. You still got here.'

OUTSIDE LINE.

' A nd I thought, I can blame oxygen. I can tap my tank and shake it and look alarmed. I can have panic in my eyes. I can feign illness. I can shake my head as if trying to diffuse a dizzy spell. So I tried this. I tapped my tank and looked concerned. I saw a camera zoom and I thought, this is the way to play it. I thought, why not make a scene of it? Why not claw at my mask as if I'm not getting enough air? Or look around, wildly, as if delusional. I can be in great distress. I can say equipment failure, save yourselves. I can wrestle with my wetsuit. Yank the zips. I can try and kick for the surface but pretend to be trapped in the tilting mechanism, I can struggle like a trapped animal. I can give the emergency sign. I can say afterwards that I saw flashes of light in front of my eyes and I felt a numbness in my limbs. I can say that I was having a delayed reaction to the altitude chamber. I can say I had tingling, loss of colour vision, flushing, agitation, lethargy, uncon- sciousness, forgetfulness, cognitive impairment, inability to respond to emergency situations. I can say it wasn't a flaw in my personality or a failure of loyalty, it was a lack of oxygen, it was seasickness. I thought this would do it fine. This would make them re-do the experiment. Someone would say, "Take two." '

'. . .'

'The camera focused. Look at me now, cameras, thrashing my legs in the water, look at me tearing off my mask, look at my face contort. Look at the panic and fear, see the bubbles pour out of my mouth and upwards, look how wild my eyes are, look how sick I am, look at the pain I am in, what distress, send in the divers, send in the medics. Don't stop the cameras. Think what you can do with this, Captain. Put Beethoven behind it. Put Wagner. Get someone from *Apollo 13* to say, "I know how he feels." Sweat in the water. Salt in the water. Thrash thrash, kick kick. Don't let it drag though. Feeling exhausted. Let's not overdo it. I'm feeling it should stop now. Timing is all. Feeling the moment is over. Feel I should go limp now, drift upwards now... feel... ah look, here she is coming down to me. Dived in. Rescue mission. That'll win you some friends. Me for one. And look, cameras, look at the concern on her face, there's loyalty for you. Commitment to your colleague. She won't win it, this won't clinch it for her, she won't thank me for this, we'll have to do it again and I'll be perfect, I won't need rescuing. They'll wipe this tape. This isn't happening. Bad take. Save your energy. Let's go up now. Let's hit the surface and do it again. Enjoy it if you like, though. I'll give you this moment. Try and turn your face to the camera, let them catch your eyes. Compassion, bravery. There you are, this is good for all of us. This might be on a highlights episode.'

'...'

'I winked at her. The magic wink...'

T PLUS 4HH 10MM

And then she feels it lift. Suddenly.

The pain. She feels it lift and float away. It floats away from her and out into space. She sees it go. It disappears into the black.

Her brow clears. The sweat cools.

Weightlessness is even lighter now.

A breath comes. A deep clearing breath.

She waits for a returning wave. But it doesn't come. She is alone on the beach and the pain is a distant tide.

Wait, she says.

The crew stops.

Wait a moment, she says.

She thinks perhaps the pain has become so great that she can't feel it any more. It's off the scale. It's beyond her body's experience. And her body is in a new and strange land. It forgets the old land and in this state of numbness it looks around.

She asks God if she will die.

God tells her she won't die.

Houston tells her her temperature is stabilising.

The crew ask for advice.

Pills kicking in, says Houston.

Wait a moment, she says.

Wait a moment, Houston says.

They all drift. They all wait for something to happen.

Nothing happens.

Sally floats.

Nothing happens again.

OUTSIDE LINE.

' I woke up in the hospital, Jim. My arm had got caught between two struts of the machine which closed as the module tilted and cut it off. As good as cut it off. The hospital finished the job as it was irreparable.'

'...'

'The cameras went away and the television programme never went out. They figured public taste wouldn't tolerate an amputation. They asked me if I'd sign a release form permitting them to air it at some point in the future. Times change, after all. I said I'd lost my writing hand.'

'...'

'Hold the line, will you, Jim? I've got another call.'

ROOM 15. NANCY CARTER.

'Has Jim arrived yet, Chip?'

'Not yet.'

'I think—'

'Give him time.'

Pause.

'Jim's dead I think, Chip.'

'Let's not write him off yet.'

'Well...'

'Let's give him the benefit of the doubt.'

'I feel terrible about this, Chip.'

'He'll be here.'

Pause.

'I should tell you that I was here to cover your party.'

'Uh-huh.'

'I didn't really want to. I don't like human interest. I prefer travel.'

'Really.'

'Do you travel much, Chip?'

'I don't drive. My friend Jim does all the driving.'

'Oh dear, Chip.'

'He'll be here.'

'Do you and Jim go on road trips?'

'Occasionally.'

'Where do you go?'

'Here and there.'

'Rockies?'

'No.'

'Alaska?'

'Not that far. Just around.'

'Have you been to Europe?'

'I was born in England.'

Pause.

'What do you want, Miss Carter?'

'I don't know. I was hoping I could write some good things in this hotel room. Eugene O'Neill wrote in hotel rooms. The Hotel Sheraton. Dashiell Hammett wrote *The Thin Man* at the Regent Beverly Wilshire. Elvis wrote songs at the Regent. And so did John Lennon.'

'Really.'

'Howard Hughes wrote at the Boulder Dam Hotel. So did Bette Davis, Harold Lloyd, and Boris Karloff. Only letters, though. At the Gramercy Park Hotel they had Joseph P. Kennedy, he wrote memos.

And Humphrey Bogart, he even got married there, so I guess he wrote wedding invitations.'

'Yes.'

'I haven't written a thing.'

Pause.

'Have you seen the film *Flash Gordon*?'

'No.'

'Do you know the work of Van Gogh?'

'Some of it.'

'Do you think it's possible to forget someone's voice?'

'I don't know. Jim would know.'

'Jim's dead, Chip. So is your friend.'

'I'll give him a few more minutes.'

Pause.

'I'm going to get my earring back from Mr Moulin, Chip. This sprinkler isn't letting up and I think I'm going to check out. I want to be wearing them when my husband appears.'

'He's still coming?'

'I hope so. I hope he'll leave the meadow and just come.'

'Yes.'

'I can wait for him outside.'

Alan the cameraman visited Chip in hospital. His wife had filed for divorce on the grounds of neglect. And his son ostracised him. He'd told all his classmates his dad was making television. Alan told his son he was helping astronauts, but the son thought that sucked, space was yesterday. Television was today.

Sally visited him. She told him that Fresh and Clear were putting her through the system. Paying her training costs. A deal's a deal.

The Fresh and Clear executives visited. They wanted to know if he would object to the programme being carefully edited without him in it. Chip didn't care.

They came back saying they'd tried it and it was impossible. Chip had managed to get in almost every shot. They'd tried blurring him out but it made the pictures look like there was a ghost lurking around.

No one else visited.

Chip's wound healed and he left the country.

Sally eventually left the world. She's up there now.

S he's up there now.

And she thinks the pain has gone.

She's spinning round the earth and she thinks she's perfect again.

The new time line holds and the old time line is picked up. The two are put side by side and Houston tells them that both are still possible but the signs for the old plan are looking good, they're looking better.

She drinks water.

She is told to stay where she is.

Don't move for now. Be still.

Her old schedule tells her to sleep so she follows her old schedule and closes her eyes.

The crew work around her. They readjust. They catch up. They work to the old plan.

The old plan is so much better, she thinks.

The old plan has a lot more going for it than the new plan, the new plan was terrible.

She thanks her body for seeing the sense in the old plan. For seeing its merits. Its beauty.

T he tanks run out of water and the sprinklers sputter. The spray
dies and they start to dribble. Chip watches the drops develop
on the nozzles. They swell, they ripen. The drips combine, merge and
become weak little streams. The streams thin. Then break up. They
become a series of drips. The drips slow. All nozzles bar one dry up. It
stays dripping above Chip's head. Drip, drip, drip. Then slower. Then
they stop. The last drop stays suspended. Too light to fall. The drop
waits for volume. It hangs.

ROOM 11. THE CLEANER.

'I'm calling down to say that my husband has had a heart attack.'

'Is he dead?'

'I wouldn't say dead. He's blue, but there's colour coming back.
The mini fridge has been kicked over. His skin is clammy and his eyes
are blinking.'

'Oh.'

'He's daubed the walls here. "Born in a hotel room and,
godammit, died in a hotel room." That's a quote. That's Eugene O'Neill.
The sprinklers can't wash it off. How does he know stuff like that?'

'I'm sorry that he's—'

'I'm not. He worked me into the ground. There's an earring on
the table too. It's certainly not mine.'

'No.'

'If he dies, the place goes to me, you know that? I've got his will.'

'I see.'

'If he dies I'm thinking of changing a few things.'

'Uh-huh.'

'I'm thinking of shaking the place up, modernising. A digital, computer-operated, state-of-the-art switchboard system that works on voice recognition alone. Something like that.'

'Good idea.'

'Contract out the cleaning. Have a gourmet menu.'

'Yes.'

'I can't see you staying, Chip.'

'No?'

'My daughter's after work, I've got to look out for my family.'

'I see.'

'I'm sure you'll find something else though, you seem like an adaptable guy.'

'Well, let's not write him off yet.'

'No.'

'He might pull through.'

'Well, anyway, could you call the doctor for me?'

OUTSIDE LINE.

'E Z Medical.'

'We've got a sick person at the E Z Sleep, the owner.'

'The doctor's at the E Z Rest. They've got a food poisoning problem.'

'Right.'

'You need him quick?'

'Yes.'

'He's going to be a while, I'm afraid.'

'I see.'

'You need the room?'

'Not particularly.'

'I'll try and page him. I think he'll be wanting to get away. There's something wrong with the club sandwiches, bad batch, it's pretty messy.'

'I can't wait. I'll get an ambulance.'

The Chef walks into the lobby, showered, shaved. He has a little party popper in his pocket. He takes it out but drops it on the wet floor. He picks it up and pulls it. The string comes off in his hand and it doesn't pop. Wet streamers flop over his shoes. He tuts.

The Model comes down the stairs wearing an E Z dressing gown. She's put foundation over the scratches in her face but they're still visible. The Chef tries to kiss her on the cheek but she turns away. She lets him kiss her hand.

The Stenographer walks over from Pancake Parlour carrying a Shuttle Shake. She offers the Model a sip. Banana, she says. Pretty tasty. The Model doesn't want any. The Chef takes a big glug. Not bad. Needs more sugar.

The Holiday Rep has been trying to resurrect the broken marquee. She's been tying guy ropes to bins but the bins have wheels and don't keep the ropes taut. She gives up and enters the lobby through the smashed doors. The floor's slippery and she walks extra carefully. She tells everyone that she's back selling holidays. Did they realise that E Z hotels also offered E Z car hire?

No one did realise. Especially not the Chef who wishes he'd been told that before breaking the bank on the sports car.

That yours? says the Holiday Rep.

Want a ride? says the Chef.

I get travel sick, she says.

The Radar Operator gives up on the burning car on Freedom Avenue. He pushes it to the hard shoulder and leaves it for the fire service to take care of. He has grime on his face and his navy uniform is charred and smoke-damaged. He walks into the lobby. He looks around for his mother. No sign.

Hello, everyone.

Great… great to see you.

They stand around. They stand around in the wet.

Terrific party, Chip.

Sorry.

Pause.

Let's hear it for Sally, someone says.

Yes. Sally.

They clap.

The best person won.

Yes indeed.

Good for her.

Well done.

Let's watch it on TV.

The TV is sparking.

We should get out of this water.

Yes.

They stay where they are.

Someone coughs.

The Chef tells them that if you've got a good nose, you can smell things for NASA.

They murmur.

Arguably it's one of the most important jobs in the space programme.

Someone wonders if there's an application procedure to get that kind of job.

I'm sure there is.

And a selection process.

Probably.

No one is sure if they can go through something like that again.

No.

No. Everyone shakes their heads.

OUTSIDE LINE.

'This is the fire service. Have you got a fire?'

'No.'

'We've got a little light flashing above a sign which says E Z. Is that you?'

'There's no fire here.'

'Is it a fault?'

'Probably.'

'You want to get that sorted out, we nearly scrambled.'

'You didn't though.'

'No, but we very nearly did.'

'People very nearly do lots of things.'

'What?'

'Very, very nearly.'

Nancy Carter enters the lobby carrying her suitcases. Chip tells her it's all right. She doesn't have to go.

She thinks she will anyway. It's a bit wet.

This is Nancy, everyone.

Hi Nancy.

Hi. I was going to do a story about you all.

Oh.

They all stand around awkwardly. She takes a little notepad and pencil out of her pocket. She wants to ask them what they've been doing with themselves since the programme.

Selling pans, says the Chef.

Selling holidays, says the Holiday Rep.

Selling myself, says the Model.

Working radar, says the Radar Operator.

Working things out, says the Stenographer.

Working the switchboard, says Chip.

She has a disposable camera. She asks the group to stand in a line.

We're not all here yet, says Chip.

The Probable Winner went away in a cab.

The Pollster didn't appear. Her father might be around some-where.

The Comedienne, don't know where she is.

She's dead, says Nancy.

Really? says everyone. That's terrible.

Car crash, says Nancy. Awful.

Let's keep optimistic, says Chip.

Nancy Carter takes their picture. Everyone looks downcast with the news. The flash bounces off the wet walls.

Nancy Carter thinks it would be better if they went somewhere else. Outside, or the Pancake Parlour.

No one moves.

Has anyone got anything to say?

The switchboard's circuits crackle. Moisture is creating flowing con-nections. It whispers. They are aware of the steel bands, wires, receivers, transmitters, turning words into signals, signals into words.

Pull me out.

What?

Pull me out of this rubble.

Who is this?

Get someone.

We can hardly hear you.

I'm trapped.

Dennis?

The *Hey Jesus* evangelist tells his listeners in a hoarse and disappointed whisper that the satellite that crashed into the hotel in Alabama was partly made of teak. How about that? A wooden satellite. It was apparently still transmitting signals. Soaking up information about its surroundings and sending it back to China. China now knows about our disappointments, the evangelist says. It now knows about our dashed hopes and our desire to live better lives. I hope China doesn't use the information against us. The radio crackles and pops and fades out.

There was a rumour that Sally became sick last night. Puking. Terrible pain. Sweats. She was seen by the launch team who told her that it was probably nerves, but they couldn't be sure.

Everyone looks at Nancy.

Is that true?

They flew with her anyway. They took the risk. Nancy said there was a news embargo but the story leaked out.

Did NASA ring for a replacement? they ask.

Everyone looks at each other. Would they have tried to get a replacement?

Nancy doesn't think you can just step into something like that.

There's always a replacement, they say. Always back-up.

For a space tourist? asks Nancy. They don't have a job to do.

I wouldn't say that, says everyone.

They're not even operational, says Nancy.

That's a little unfair, says everyone.

Did anyone get a call last night?

I was on a plane, says the Chef.

Me too, says everyone.

Chip wonders if perhaps he had a call but they couldn't get through because the E Z switchboard is always buzzing.

Perhaps they called him because he was the nearest. He was only an hour away and could jump in at short notice. Jim could get him there in forty minutes if pushed. Chip is Sally's size too and would fit her spacesuit.

I don't think they'd have called, someone says. I mean look at us.

PMC OCA. All complete. We lost a few minutes.

Roger.

Pretty tired here.

Don't blame you. We'll call you in eight hours.

Eight hours, that sounds good, Houston.

Good job.

Thank you.

You sleep well now.

They will. And Sally will. And in three days the shuttle and the Space Station will meet and dock above the southern Pacific Ocean. A hatch will be opened in the Mating Adapter. The two crews will smile at each other and wave and everyone will sleep. When they wake again they will put on spacesuits and walk into space. And one of them will strap his feet to the fingertips of the shuttle's arm and it will stretch out and grab the new arm and it will attach the new arm to the body of the Space Station. The operation will be done gently and carefully and lovingly and the arm will stay in a sling until it's fully fitted, until the Space Station shoulder accepts it, and seven hours later, above the Atlantic Ocean, they will give it a new limb, its first limb. And then cables will be connected to give the arm power. Tendons. Muscles. Computers will fire up and nerve endings will be activated and the new arm will twitch into life. And above the Indian Ocean the Space Station will unfold its arm and make its fingers wiggle.

Then they will sleep again.

The waitress enters the E Z lobby.

She sees wet people standing around.

She's changed out of her waitress uniform. Her hair is clean, and her body no longer smells of hot fat.

'Hello, Chip,' she says.

'Hello.'

Chip gestures. These are some people I know.

Hello.

There's glass and rubbish and cake and water all over the lobby.

'What happened here?'

Chip tells her there's a river running under the E Z Sleep, a vanished river. No one really knows it's there. Sometimes it seeps through. The hotel is sinking.

'Really?' she says.

'No,' says Chip. 'Not really. Just the sprinklers.'

'You all right?'

'Hard to say.'

'Pancake Parlour is full to bursting.'

'I see.'

'Shuttle Shakes are going like hot cakes.'

The Stenographer says they're pretty damn good. The Chef verifies.

Everyone's thirsty. They all fancy a Shuttle Shake. They troop outside. They tell Chip they'll see him in there. But they don't go in. They drift away. The Chef gets in his car and drives off. The Model walks towards High Fashion to buy herself some clothes. The Stenographer walks to Freedom Avenue but refuses offers of lifts from strangers. The Holiday Rep heads towards the town. The Radar Operator flags down a police car. Everyone disappears.

Chip expects his phantom arm to wave them goodbye, but it's silent. Chip waits for it to twitch or ache, but nothing happens.

And when she wakes the new arm will have strength, it will flex itself, it will be able to make a fist, and it will slip off its sling and it will hand the sling to the shuttle. And the shuttle will reach out its own arm and accept it. And it will fold it up and tuck it into its payload bay for its return to earth.

Two hundred and forty miles above the earth there will be a handshake in space.

It will be such a complete moment, such a perfect moment, that she won't mind if the pain returns. Because even if it does, she'll have the memory of that moment. And even if she dies, she will die a happy woman.

Blip. Spark.

The switchboard shorts out.

The waitress walks to the desk and flicks the bell with her finger. She listens to the ting and speaks when it has died out.

'We have a TV in the Pancake Parlour,' she says. 'We were watching the launch and the sound distorted. The picture pixelated and crackled and disappeared. The manager went out onto the roof and found a shit inside the satellite dish. The shit looked pretty fat too. Human.'

'I did it.'

'Really? Why?'

'I wasn't sure if I wanted you to watch the launch.'

'Why not?'

'I thought the TV might show pictures of how Sally came to be there.'

'How did she come to be there?'

'I'll tell you. After I've found Jim.'

The waitress looks around the lobby. The Fresh and Clear barrel needs a refill. The leaves of the fake plants float in an inch of water.

She notices something in the E Z Lost Property. She goes in and comes out with a shop dummy's arm.

'Someone left this?' she asks.

Chip nodded.

She brushes it down.

'It's nice. A woman's, I think.'

'Yes,' says Chip.

She looks at him.

'You know,' she says, 'even though the Space Station is getting a new arm, it'll still only have one.'

'Yes.'

'The NASA guys decided that one is enough for it. They had a million PhDs on the case and they decided that one arm could do everything. One was better, in fact.'

Chip nods.

The waitress walks behind the desk and asks about the line that's still connected. And Chip says it's connected to Jim but he isn't answering. And the waitress says watch this, and she jumps in the air and in the air she twirls and then bends at the waist and then she dives into the switchboard too and they swim through a mile of cable carried by a swift electric current and they emerge in Helloland, and as they stand in the airy nowhere they hear half sentences and unfinished conversations and ghosts and intimate words and complaints and inquiries and perverts and speaking clocks and whispers, and the waitress says, do you know what my name is? And Chip says he thinks it might be Louise and she says you've guessed correctly and she says perhaps Jim is down here and they dive again and swim through thin wires, old wires and they find Alexander Graham Bell's connection and he is saying, 'Watson, come here I want to speak to you,' and these are the first words that are spoken on the telephone, and the waitress takes Chip by the hand and says, 'This way,' and they are pulled through a broken wire and a dusty wire and they emerge outside in a place which is just open and has no connection and Louise says you don't know anything any more and Chip says he is a chip, he is a little chip, and she kisses him and he likes it, he likes it, he loves it.

The waitress plays with the fingers on the dummy's arm.

'My shift is finished,' says Chip.

'Yes.'

And Chip, the waitress and the dummy's arm go out in the world.